FROM HELL

The Final Days of Jack The Ripper

Rob R. Thompson

Summer Wind Press
Attica, New York
—

From Hell

ISBN 978-0-615-30256-0

FORWARD

From Hell-The Final Days of Jack the Ripper is truly a period piece. A reflection of a London long since lost. Possibly for those that still live in London, it's a recollection best left to float through nightmares like the mists that rise from marshlands.

In the early days, not even Jack the Ripper would have supposed that his crimes would have made him one of the most famous serial killers of all time. Even though his identity has been debated for over 100 years this account will allow the reader the ability to step back into this dark time in London's history and truly experience the mindset of a man capable of such brutal crimes, crimes in which he took perverse pleasure. Rob Thompson paints a picture for the reader of just such a man in Francis Tumblety.

Jack was no general Londoner. He was knowledgeable with an obviously high IQ. Jack was a criminal ahead of his time, in every sense of the phrase.

One thing we know for sure is that Jack is dead. It is his memory and deeds that are still very much alive. Those early days of London's development, in the midst of the industrial revolution, are also gone. But this book captures that atmosphere and the lives of the characters involved, their dreams, their aspirations and ultimately their deaths.

Barry FitzGerald
Ghost Hunters International (GHI)
Sci-Fi Channel, USA

Acknowledgments

This work could not have been possible if not for the kind support and endless encouragement of Stewart Evans co-author of Jack the Ripper-First American Serial Killer. Stewart is the world's foremost student of the Whitechapel crimes and it is to him the credit for the use of many of the following photos is given. I'd also like to thank the Rochester New York Public Library and Sue Conklin Historian for Genesee County.

Fill for me a brimming bowl
And let me in it drown my soul:
But put therein some drug, designed
To Banish Women from my mind:

-John Keats-

CHAPTER ONE

"Fuck Keats!" I said clicking the cobblestone.

"Gross indecency!" That's what the authorities said of me.

"Their words, spoken so freely painted a mental course few could imagine."

"Fuck the authorities too!"

I sucked my lips waiting for rebuttal.

"Indeed, how dare they call me indecent!"

I swayed to unheard tunes.

"There are always plenty of spiked tongues. They are the proud, the boastful, the lunatics and the whores."

I brushed my right knee clean of invisible dust.

"I was called indecent by those who insist that their own ass never produces an offensive odor."

The voices in my head fell silent.

I walked over cobblestone, cursing those who made such judgment.

I listened for their replies and argued back yet again.

The sprinkles of rain that always peppered London increased gradually throughout the evening. Water hit me in sizable drops. I saw a dying raven, left so by a careless hansom cab.

I lined up my boot with its head and stomped in mercy.

The rain swept across the raven's wings.

"What did I do to deserve this?" The crushed bird seemed to question.

"What did any of us do?" I returned.

"Do all the dead ask such questions?"

"Who'd listen to a raven?"

"Who'd listen to a whore?"

In tapered cuffs I continued over the grounds of monarch crowns.

The oily grit from unmanned fires and the stench from corners of unwanted women made these streets the envy of Satan's vixens. As bad as their odors were, the whores were never too offensive to ward off the frequent visits of customers with well-guarded noses.

"Any prince, possessed of animal lust could shun the stink," I mumbled.

All of London, not just the East End, had seemingly grown accustomed to the stench. So this and every other foul wind was just status quo. I scraped the raven off my boot and turned to absorb the final twitches of my most recent guest. Bird or whore they died alike. They were all the alumni of life. If one is born on the bricks under the steeple's shadow, odds are they will die within that same shadow.

My perch was not a steeple but Mitre Square.

I brushed my frazzled left eyebrow.

"Not a hair out of place," my dear mother always said.

There have been countless poorly written memoirs about those who can dislodge themselves from this ditch, but always return, luckless, limbless and virtue free.

Charles Dickens wrote those kinds of stories, though his skills were better than the average. I heard him read once and thanks to him I learned the grace of nouns and verbs.

"They're all alumni," I said holding my chin to my vest protectively.

Those who by foot or nailed crossbeam seek riches from other lands will often die free of morals before finding their first shaft of gold.

I nodded a greeting to the leg of my guest thrown forward in a final spasm.

She too was a raven.

I was clever, as I often used words few knew and fewer could define. I learned to decorate my sentences, which so impressed the ignorant. I could think aloud at such an accelerated rate, that no horse could match the speed of my wit.

I was proud, some would say grandiose and I could outthink the grandest of maniacal men.

I was a gifted man. I was well mannered, and wished others within this royal ditch emulated me.

"This happy England could be content, if all souls were more like me," I told my guest.

"Pure souls tend to harvest gardens of flowers," I added.

"A garden, even the East End, piss from one side to the next, even it could prosper if properly tended."

My guest was smug in her silence.

I'd done my best to show them what was right and what was wrong. I should be emulated, not called indecent.

The voices of the authorities returned.

I swung my legs while sitting on the end of the bed. I had segued from what was to what is. I had wavered between then and now, before settling uneasily in the present. A tickling interrupted me.

I had an itch. With a well-aimed finger I entered my left ear. Like an unfound flea, the itch nibbled here and there within my ear. I took aim and with a firm twist I removed the darkened mound.

It was a waxy mixture of hair and dirt. I studied it with my puckered brows. Despite an occasional lump, it was round. I sniffed it. It seemed edible.

Clip-clop, clip-clop, clip-clop.

I tilted my head like a mutt at that sound.

I heard it regularly, hooves on cobblestone. When the hooves were this close, so was the morning.

Clip-clop was the centerpiece of all other noises. Rain on scuttled rooftops, or a monger on the street calling attention to his crate of unwanted wares.

"Fuck the rooftops, the mongers and the rain!" I swallowed what my ear provided thanking its creator.

"Ashes to ashes, dust to dust. From all beginnings an end is a must," I offered my novena.

The clip-clop, clip-clop, clip-clop echoed the little side street of a hidden alley.

The hansom cab and rain were impatient.

I had to create a distraction. I dragged my eyes across the room's baseboard. I loved London. I loved what the architects had made. After all, architecture is the flesh of society, man's creation. I watched the bugs and the dripping morning dew slither through a broken window.

I sat, nearly upright, on the end of the bed waiting for the sounds of dawn to end. That incessant clip-clop, clip-clop could drive anyone possessing the gift of hearing insane.

I had a mission in life. I was to rebuild the crumbling souls of mankind. I was the master builder.

I am Hiram Abiff!

The bed wobbled as I brushed the folds of my cloak.

Clip-clop, clip-clop, clip-clop.

The sound attacked from every angle.

"Never to tarry," I said to my guest. My departure would be perfectly timed.

"Be polite when you come and when you go," mother would say. To my right were scattered pieces of soiled garments. To my left would be more of the same. Layers of human drippings stuck to the wall. Drip and spray from men of all ages and abilities I imagined.

I raised my eyes to meet the almond face in the clouded, cracked mirror before me.

"Watching me are you?" I said to the face looking back.

I smiled shyly.

"Perhaps I don't deserve me."

I blushed.

"How do you do?" I asked the curious mirror.

The face reminded me that I was met to be. Long before man ever left God's garden I was destined. After some admiring moments I returned to the streets.

Clip-clop, clip-clop, clip-clop.

The horses too were sad victims of man's greed. Yet the world's success would pale without these four-legged silent partners. Day and night, the beasts served their hosts without question. The time would always come when some mare or gelding would snap and rush through the ashen streets.

At the base of the Thames stood the lunatic. He held a sentry's post. He'd skirt the horse's onrush. He'd skirt man. He'd skirt sanity just for insanities sake.

The face in the mirror watched as I delved further.

The sewage covered Thames trickled through London but regardless of its putrid taste, mare or gelding always drank.

The days never ended for those who wandered the cobblestone seeking pennies. The sound of horses, lunatics and whores could drown out the most reflective of minds, but mine was too strong for such drowning.

The hansom cabs clamor on the cobblestone was a constant reminder to the poor that they were just too common to ride. They would have to walk in the seasonal downpours, and watch those with money pass them by.

Lately, each night had come to a close with the tormenting sound of the hansom cab and the wale of the underfed mare. I fought to concentrate on my work but my mind fell victim to the incessant clip-clop, clip-clop. But as a doctor of reputation, I'd learned to deal with both men and nature.

Water was everywhere. The rain sizzled like it was hitting a stove. The crashing hooves would splash as I waited for morning.

The hooves would soon stop as I finished another well-done job. It was time for my night to end, and shortly the hag that rented out such shit as this four-walled hole, would come seeking that day's coin.

This soul was simple.

They were becoming easier.

Experience and increased confidence allowed me reflective moments. I could take more time to appreciate my ability, or expand my mastery.

I adjusted my ascot, which had become askew as dampness weighed it down. I hated looking out of place. Before I left, I had to make sure I was well kept. I had a reputation to keep, so nothing could be left uncombed or unchecked, or even under licked. Mother insisted that I be at my best in public. I couldn't let her down; she always watched me and always spoke to me. I'd listen closely for she could be behind every clip-clop, clip-clop with a message for me.

Bashfully, I asked my prone guest, "Did I lose a glove my love?"

I grew anxious while looking for it. Forgetfulness was a sin, so learning how to be fastidious saved me from much penance. I must admit though that at the end of most nights I was more angry than anxious. Tonight I sensed a growing anger.

The mirror confirmed it.

This mirror, all mirrors reflect only honesty.

"Has any mirror ever been anything else but honest?"

I thanked this mirror and despite its aged frame it did reflect me in a kind light. I slowly licked my mustache. It showed me as a noble fixture, walking history's roads and dreaming upon its waters. I had to appear as a noble seed.

Whether in dream, in cab or by boot I often found myself in the East End. Working by choice or demand often brought me down these trickling cobblestones of a once fair city.

"A once fair city," I said out loud.

"Happy is England, *sweet* her artless daughters."

"Fuck John Keats!"

At this stage of decay London's history was only in the books on little visited shelves. Few here ever flipped the pages of their own nation's past.

Many allowed others to tell their tale.

...Many have told or are telling my tale.

I looked closer at my reflection. It insisted I reform my current appearance. I crossed my legs, right over left, and my wrists, left over right. I was a good and decent man. I was a true public servant. I was neither ego dependent, nor penny driven and generations would admire me.

I came from noble seed. I was told in no uncertain terms that I came from the stock whose hands delivered to Rome a betrayer to the peace of man.

I'd come from the blood of Judas.

I looked again at the reflection that revealed only my shoulders up.

"Was there more to me then this?" I asked quietly.

My mind went to places no hansom cab ever took that rumored diseased Prince Albert.

My hands were moist from the night's labor.

I licked my hands clean, palms first, working my way up slowly to the fingertips.

"It was Cornish Pastry," I smiled at the salty taste.

My eyes never left the mirror.

I readied for my white gloves.

I had to keep them white. I was a true British gentleman. Lady Astor expected this gentleman to be well trimmed with pure white gloves. I was her homes ornament, the centerpiece for all her boasting.

With my knees crossed and mustache ends rolled tight I watched the talent of this aged mirror diminish as the muted voices returned.

Mother was watching me again.

Colors surrounded my face. They swayed, moving from corner to corner, dancing around my crown. Laughing hellhounds nipped at my ears, so real, so close that I could feel their hot, putrid breath on my neck.

I turned to catch their eyes, but missed them as I always had. As my eyes returned to the mirror, I saw faces from generations ago surrounding the colors. The faces laughed. One in particular always laughed.

That one voice always sang.

"I am forty generations deep, the seventh daughter of the seventh son of the seventh daughter of the seventh son am I."

Mother's words were always near.

This mirror brought back my life's critics.

When we look into a mirror, do we see ourselves for what we have been, are or, will be?

A mirror will always tell the truth, though our egos may seek to convince the reflection otherwise. This mirror had nothing to say to me. It knew who I was.

I swayed with increased fervor. I leaned forward then back, eyes on the mirror the entire time.

"Fuck everything!"

Whatever mirror I used, it always said more than what I saw. It would look deeper than just my surface. But I didn't want to know more then what was revealed, and I certainly didn't want to reveal more then what showed. I looked straight ahead into the reflective bastard's center, determined as ever to prove the world and all its mirrors wrong. My teeth clenched and my ass began to sing as I rocked.

Clip-clop, clip-clop.

The animal and his hansom cab taunted me.

My face grew red and my teeth were grinding like the wheels of the Red Sea chariots.

My face changed right before me. The play of life was well underway. I was baring witness to how life could slip out right from underneath me.

The mirror of man, the handmade tormentor of the disheveled and weak of mind spoke to me as no crucifix ever could. The mirror of man was painting the landscape I had become.

I focused on the horse outside.

My drool pooled.

The sound of the hansom cab delivered me back to the here and now. Birds pecked for crumbs in the horseshit left behind. They did know more than man for first come was first served.

I waited. The sun crept through the black air of industry, and half finished rain to peak gracefully through the unprotected cracks of this room.

The trickle of light blinded me. I looked away from the mirror towards the bed.

"It's morning, dear Mary," I said to my guest.

The House of Astor was anxious.

Breakfast would be refused if I returned later than Lady Astor demanded. Without hesitation I stood to loosen my tucked garments.

I was grateful to Lady Astor, for she had been affable, I dare say even motherly towards me. In her way, she cared for me and for only a couple shillings a day. The price made her glorious but I was tardy by more than four days now. She'd be angry in a way only the condemned knew if I returned without money.

I had no silver or gold, penny or farthing, but I had to return to her with an attempt of payment, a gift for her tolerance. However she wouldn't accept just anything. It had to be special if it wasn't the coins she wished for. The emptier my pockets the more anxious she became. The cab returned closer to the room this time. I could feel the vibrations of the hooves hitting cobblestone.

"I'm coming!" I shouted to the hansom cab.

In the shadow I heard the mare whinny impatiently.

"I'm coming!" I shouted back to the mirror.

"I'm coming!"

My rage was directed at impatience. It was a devil of a human trait. I jumped to straddle 'Ginger', my guest. I slammed the silk blade above her throbbing eviscerated entrails. I cut low and smooth, as if her body were simply warm, wet cheese.

Without rehearsal, I dashed the blade until I came upon my desire. It was easy to find, fat and brown in all the bubbling gore. I plucked it like a robin would a worm and dismounted her. I reached for my bag left by the peephole door.

I reached into the inner most pouches of my vest, pulling out a second tool. My reward smiled back at me. The red dew encircled my palm. My throat eased its throbbing. I smiled lightly for I had learned to retrieve from a carcass the healthiest of its meat.

Lispenard had taught me how.

He had taught me about cows and hogs. This cow was no different. There is nothing like fresh liver from any size, wide-eyed heifer to warm a hungry tongue.

The Civil War too had been a good teacher. It taught me how to kill when death was imminent, but slow in arriving. A slice here and a slice there wouldn't matter for either the fallen or the frying pan. The frying pan will only do what it's told, and the dead can only accomplish what they've been training to do all along.

I gently wrapped the graft.

I returned to the bed.

With each slice of the blade, anger was discharged into the intestinal steam of this animal, and I laughed.

With every flip of the blade I pissed just a little. My piss relieved me of tension in a way that even the plumpest of Scottish whores couldn't manage.

I laughed as I fingered my cock.

I was cutting rabbits again for the blind nun.

I was hacking a bloated buck for the widowed neighbor, and dicing runt puppies for mother and me.

I felt like a young boy again at meaningful labor with a slice here and a flap there, all for the house of that Astor hag.

Labor such as this is a gift from God; for it can without warning, take away the cares of the day. Such meaningful labor can hush the voices that'll sneak up on you. It'll hide you from the eyes of the ill-mannered and ill-sheltered neighbors. I slashed and diced in rhythm to the spattering of the red dew. My laughter, no hansom cab could cover.

Outside, a lonely raven in wait for its mate left its perch at my sound. With each move of the blade, I performed a master's task.

I wrapped the Queen's ransom.

On this evening I was a little more unkempt, due to my speed, but I made myself professional at this hour none-the-less.

I held the graft like a father would a newborn.

The cab slowed at the door.

Some might say Miter Square was sloppy.

"Perhaps it's true," I whispered.

I'd been careful with each guest as I had a reputation to maintain, though now I needed only a change of gloves. As quickly as the nights began, they'd be over, and with a quick departure end my spontaneous missions.

I grabbed my bag, and retrieved a second pair of handmade gloves. I left the old ones tucked at the base of that mirror.

The cab was close.

I looked at Mary.

She stared at me.

With a quick step I knelt across her and looked at her eyes.

"Fuck it," I said.

The eyes had to go; they are the mirrors of the night. I insisted that I be the last vision they had.

Did these know that death had come to claim them when they asked for three pennies a suck?

Did these eyes know that stale bread would be their last meal and this the last bed? Like a spoon my fingers plucked her eyes.

The sun was more than a trickle now, and the voices of the fruit and flesh vendors were beginning to bid for the copper of Buck's Row. The time for my leave had arrived for breakfast would be denied if I were not prompt. I looked around the room in mild panic. Sticking from one of the holes were some dated papers and old rags serving as wind block.

The graft still dripped so I reached for one of the rags. With the attention of a butcher I wrapped the meat. Lady Astor would celebrate such a fine offering of rental reconciliation.

Dampness was spread throughout the room in a way that would sicken many. As a final offering, I took my tool and speared the lifeless heart, plucking it like a pear and placing it on the nightstand.

I wiped my palms on the wall, and tipped my billycock to the mirror. The cab positioned itself skillfully to block the view of my departure.

I tucked the graft inside my pocket.

In the slight space available, I opened the peephole door and stepped outside onto the wet cobblestone. Within grasp with a second step, I pulled the cab door open, sliding in quickly before shutting it tightly behind me. The driver started without a word from me.

The beast whinnied.

The cold whinny made even me nervous each time it came.

"Good day sir," the driver's voice, either shy of sobriety or just overtired, greeted me as I took to the hansom cab musty velvet.

I nodded, "Yes it is, House of Astor please."

"Yes sir," came the curt reply.

I settled on the seat, unwashed since I last walked away from a petticoat vendor.

With a whip crack we came to a full saunter. The breeze rushed over my collar, cooling my face, and making its way up to my oily, dew filled brown hair.

I hid my eyes. I took no chance at being seen. The horse was well handled by my hand-me-down driver. He was a flap eared drunkard who'd narrowly escaped the debtor's warden. He was outwardly frail, and persistently unwashed. The beast that he managed knew this route with his eyes shut.

The rain splashed with each trot. The spin of the wheels sprayed the water up to my cheeks. I shifted away from the spray.

I pulled my arms against my chest. My eyes closed. My hands were as much my tools as the hooves were for the horse, we'd both be useless without them.

"Where would man be without hands?" I whispered.

I was snug.

I was secure.

I welcomed a nap.

I had no sooner begun to dream than I heard the whip cracking, debtor driver shouting, he was apparently informing a few unfortunates that they had best move their pirate whore of a woman or the horse would.

"Such language," I gasped.

I'd warn him at some point that manners were what would be remembered when our tombs are blessed.

The driver and I found each other back when I had been less then what I wanted to be, and he had been more then he could afford.

He would find, and I would fetch.

We were hunter and hound, so to speak.

The cab rolled on.

The wheels of the cab began to spin at full, they appeared to be above ground, and it was a buzz like no other.

Time was moving at an unfathomable pace.

Its hum was hypnotic to the exhausted.

Rested or not, it's when the humming stops that trouble begins, for instance, when morality is overthrown immorality will then rule.

But the hum was constant, and was delivered in such a manner that it allowed me to grasp a few more precious moments of sleep.

My head bobbed.

A sudden stop woke me. There was a commotion I could not define as anything more than my driver's string of vulgarities.

The air of the East Side was excited. The morning fruit market was a stir. On my walks I've often found that rotten apples received higher bids than the cleanest whores.

I looked out the corner of my eye through the cab's window. Several busy bodies ran both ways. The noise was a murmur of scattered dialects.

The banter was higher pitched than normal. "Perhaps the East End had fresh meat after all," I said to the voices in my head.

A young boys head popped up. "Grapes sir? Some grapes sir...?" I stared through the coal covered little shit to the murmuring masses behind him.

"He's back!"

"..again...did you...?" Came other words.

Echoes trailed off on each side of the cab.

They were unintelligible, scattered words. The boys face came back again, "Mister, some grapes? Buy some grapes, please!" I continued to ignore the half dressed little cock directing my ears to the voices instead.

"...Down here...over...he's back...one more..."

The boy selling of stolen grapes remained persistent.

I made no sense of their words but with a cockeyed smile I handed the boy three pennies for his grapes. "Thank ya' sa," he smiled, disappearing into the growing crowd of confused words.

I pulled the curtain completely closed.

After some pause I sucked one grape dry, then another waiting for the scene to discover the mystery and for us to be on our way.

"Be just a moment sir'...a moment more is all sir," the driver said.

With a gentleman's wave out the window I let him know that I'd heard his words.

The hansom cab swayed as careless walkers brushed it. The crowd was hurried. "They found, sa', one more...a whore....again..."

The words were too scattered and confused for me to fully comprehend. I had a sense though. The air was schizophrenic. I finished the last of the grapes as the cab thrust forward. The driver managed the cab quite well through the frightened crowd.

We were on our way through narrow streets packed with dozens of others in cabs. A stink wafted across my lips. In protection I sunk my chin and eyes below the rim of the collar. In only a few moments we would arrive at The House of Astor.

That's what the sign on the barbed gate declared.

"House of Astor. By night, week or month!"

I had come across the sea with great hidden accomplishments behind me when I first heard its name from a fellow traveler.

I was a trained man of herbs and natural medicine.

I was well trained at the trade I practiced. I studied it daily. I called myself a master as I boarded the La Bretagne in New York City. I knew London was the place to continue my study as a doctor of reputable note.

America had been my test and London would be my grade.

The La Bretagne trekked trade between New York and Le Havre, France. Beside the handmade baubles and poorly picked wheat commoners could catch a ride for fare or exchanged skill. I had a needed skill.

A week's journey such as that was a grand adventure for a young man. It was my first time on high water. In that trip I had held my stomach and ass in unison until familiarity overwhelmed me and I was able to engage in small talk. During those first stable hours, I learned of The House of Astor as fellow traders of skills painted a grand vision of it for me.

After days of listening to stories and being near swallowed by channel waters, I'd arrived from France on a chilled summer's evening. That night I was introduced to the portly, toothless, hair-lipped hag who'd soon bark breakfast for all. She was unwashed then, and even more so now.

On this morning we had arrived at the homes gate.

The debtor driver was so well practiced that he could open the door without looking. A twist of a chord was enough to allow my departure. I left the usual payment and stepped down, grabbing hold of the half opened gate. "I'll send the boy for you when the time comes," I said. He snapped the chord and the door swung shut.

My head lowered at the crack of the whip. The cab was gone before I finished my third step.

The House of Astor, how great that name had sounded to a sea faring young man.

It was that majestic vision that had kept me from jumping ship after my virtue had been seized. As the sea licked the belly of the La Bretagne, I'd begun to trade ass-hole for food. I dreamt of its grand vision, its Gothic frame and its striking gardens as man after man bent me over.

Such a striking picture I had painted. Imagining how the house would be for guests like me. It was made just for me. It knew I was coming, and the madam prepared her home just for me. The sea would bark, and the wind claimed my borrowed hats, but I continued to think of The House of Astor. "I'm coming," I sang into the sea spray. "I'm coming you no good rotten sons of bitches. I'm coming!"

The sea was left behind.

On this morning I walked slowly over a moss-covered walkway toward the front door.

During all those years the sea sang and the La Bretagne rocked. I'd shouted into the sea spray words with no meaning. Then, one night after countless shouts, with a sudden blast of excitement I reached for the man who wanted what only women possessed. Into the spray I shoved him.

A righteous kill my memory declared.

I neared the homes single rail.

A step or two more, my stride shortened as I moved closer.

"Lost at sea," the Captain said of the man I shoved overboard. Still, regardless of the shame or revenge, I was excited to be ashore and to soon be a tenant of The House of Astor.

For hours I walked the docks through London's heavy rain, until I found a ride, not that I could pay the fare.

"The House of Astor," I said with pride.

"Yes sir!" the cabman said with what could have been a grimace or comical grin, I couldn't tell which.

He took me to the house I had spent many hours imagining in my dreams. I had always dreamt. Always dreamt of other places, and of other times but that first night my dreams became reality.

That first night, just steps ahead of the demons forming in my head I had to face reality. I walked up and down Danville Boulevard. There was no grandeur, no Gothic trim or Baroque opulence, nothing from my dreams.

I was searching for a palace. The palace only dreams create. I walked up and down one street then two others. I walked an alley and a cove. There was no castles, no crown, no welcoming band of fife and drums waiting for me. There was nothing except a sad low hanging gate and a worn mossy garden path.

I have yet to experience such heartbreak as I had that first night in front of the majestic House of Astor. What color the house once had been long gone, replaced with green covered stone, and soon-to-be dead vines. The sign, made decades, if not centuries ago had been allowed to grow weak. It hung slightly askew alongside the home, which was falling victim to similar abandonment. Chips of gray and glass flaked along untended rooms and the porch, which at one time must have stood majestically across the entrance way, was now filled with unused coal and unclaimed luggage.

I stood shocked at what I saw that night.

Now, on this night, approaching that same portico, with the roof that looked liable to cave in on the unsuspecting, I didn't want to be seen.

My ego was, from time to time, my only defense. Standing near the door, I knew I was blessing this ravaged ground with just my presence yet I was always nervous entering while owing money for by gone days. Lady Astor was a fat greasy whore, unwanted for years for her sullied reputation and vileness towards her debtors. She could fight like a satanic horse, and drink like a gypsy moving through wine country. She wasn't patient, nor was she tolerant and would always state there were fifty others in line to use my sheets.

I adjusted my collar and held my head at just enough of a proper tilt to create interest in me. I gently curled the ends of my mustache, and stopped in front of the rod iron door. I leisurely reached for the knob, turning it slowly in an attempt to enter without being noticed.

"Breakfast you putrid lazy bastards," Lady Astor shouted, "Eggs and coffee too!"

Her cockney tone doesn't shine as bright in repetition as it did in person.

"Get it now or fight the rats for it," she continued.

The shuffling of boots on the hard wood floors echoed throughout the house.

I pulled sharply back from the knob at her bellow and waited for the rustling to end. I'd barely begun to turn the knob again, when the innermost door swung open. Staring at me, just inches away, was Lady Charlotte Astor. We stood across from each other silently for a long moment, and let the awkwardness clear my path. Her black, sharp eyes, said more than her tongue could.

"Good morning, dear woman. Seems like more rain is coming our way."

With obvious doubts to my sincerity, she opened the door never removing her eyes from my collar. "Almost late, Mr. Frank. Have you any money today?"

I walked inside, removed my billycock and black cloak, both damp from the dew and horse. Lady Astor slammed the door.

I entered the front room feeling her eyes studying me.

In my world, Charlotte Astor was a disguised Madame Defarge. She was a stout woman with her brows poised in a constant crook, whether of doubt or revenge.

"Have you any money Dr. Tumblety?" Lady Astor repeated.

"Dear Madam, my work is infrequent. I'll do what I can to see that my skills are more appreciated." I hung my cloak. "The times are difficult. People who need my work seldom come, or return with payment of any kind. I will catch up on what I owe you and will, as promised, pay you handsome bonuses."

She marched past me with feet falling as heavily as would a black-smiths' anvil. I placed my hat atop a stool, which stood over several overly ripe boots. The dining area, like everything else about this place, was not what I had envisioned. There were no arched doorways or, petals from fallen lilies covering hand-woven imported carpets. The table was only set for five, though it could have easily sat eight, maybe more.

I entered the room and subtly grinned at the man with his own bedeviling voices. His eyes grew wide in caution. I looked away and smiled at the wake of human shit that sat before me. They were various shades and shapes, all with odors successfully defending their owner's titles. There were only three of them, but what an audience it was. I nodded a thank you, or perhaps it was good morning, and took my chair next to a seaman with a lazy eye. He wasn't one for conversation, but his flatulence was greater than any stale corn fed four-legged nag could produce.

I offered a polite hello, but he kept his head down, shoveling food from his bowl to his small, cracked mouth. My slow, deliberate pace made the man with the voices quite nervous. I smiled at my place setting, and saw I had no bowl. To my left sat a boring looking man. He was neither ancient nor young, black nor albino for he was so dirty that his age and color remained a mystery. He ate with fingers, dipping them fully into cold gruel. No doubt the same fingers which had recently completed privy duty.

Across the table sat a quiet, nightly guest who had apparently also thought The House of Astor was a palace waiting just for him. His eyes dodged back and forth quickly, taking in the scum around me.

We'd not see him again after this meal.

Next to him on his left were the most unusual beings, the one with the voices, Lester James Gilchrest. I chose not to nod again in his direction for he'd interpret that as a confrontation. I did stare briefly as he talked to the potato he'd taken from the bin, and not the plate meant for him.

He whispered secrets only he understood, and sang aloud when the cream was late in arriving. My bowl sloshed in front of me without being announced.

I sat and folded my hands, still covered with my labor's dew. I thanked my maker for all he'd given me, and settled in as the choir of voices headed by Lester James Gilchrest consumed the room.

"T'ain't no God but the sack of coal beneath the wooden ship sending candle works east, you bastard..." Lester's words bounced across the table.

As he jabbered I took yesterday's unwashed wooden spoon, and dipped it in the bowl. There was more water then meal. I raised it to my mouth while Lester eyed me. He became agitated at my blink less slurping face.

Lester swayed, holding the potato in one hand and picking his nose, ear and ass with the other, "Better to borrow from the devil when man can only sing through a valley's sunken soul. Be devil to all, who claimed gold for a purpose that's left unsold," Lester sang.

His voices laughed.

"Poor thing!" Lady Astor said.

My eyes never left Lester.

I have to confess; Lester didn't care much for me, even when I was the only one who'd even paid him any mind. But as I slurped and watched him, Lester jabbered verses only he and I could understand.

The men at the table barked for more and more of what Lady Astor had. They cried like abandoned sheep when their meal was late. Nothing was recognizable as table talk, so Lester filled us all in on his views.

"Silent we all stood as the king of skewered souls labeled us, eyes unwavering." Lester threw the potato toward the one-eyed seaman who grabbed it without concern, buttering it in the same motion.

I was attentive, my eyes not once leaving Lester's performance. He stood and pointed mostly my way as if I was an annoyance. He sang, "Beckon I say, beckon he with a hat of discipline to reveal before man and the voice of Sinai, the land of stain and the one with the aim." Lester tossed a gesture at the man of flatulence as Lady Astor touched his shoulder gently, silencing his shrieks. Lightly she directed him back to his chair.

"The one with the aim," Lester looked at me, "The one with the aim shall meet me as the hours grow old."

The performance paused.

The one night visitor bolted from the table.

"The odd creature speaks from somethin' we don't know," the one-eyed seaman said.

I agreed. Lester wiped the gruel from his facial hair, and then licked what he'd found there.

"The crazed know more than many books, Mr. Frank," the seaman said.

His words made my face go pale.

I glared at Lester. Ignorance towards manners angered me in a way no bottle of perfumed beads could. His voices were strong, and had crossed the table to inflame me.

How could man, even in his worst state, allow that being to stroll the stones? Lester was growing uneasy at my changing hue.

"Eyes as sharp as a serpents tongue are this tables witness's," Lester said as he swayed. Drool began to run in a steady stream from the left corner of his mouth. A puddle gathered on the table. Lester stood again, delivering his sermon as Dickens may have read. "Distance is a great land when one is afraid of what the day and night holds. Be still the dogs that yip a message only their masters hear."

Lady Astor comforted him to no avail.

"Be still sea wenches, as the night has just begun, if virtue is soiled, a red dew will run 'cross fair England's throbbing stones.

"Hands and eyes aside..." Lester dodged the table and protruding belly of Lady Astor, laying a string of drool across bowls full of tomorrow's meal. Lester pointed wildly, grabbing the remaining spud. With unintelligible mumbles, he was out the door, his sermon unfinished.

"Poor creature, he needs a visit from the almighty," said Lady Astor. I sat straight back in the chair with a half-a-smile, my hands folded on the tables edge.

The seaman studied me. "Lester may be a fool destined for the butcher, but he understands what some are too shocked think."

I let the words flow as my anxiety was released with Lester's rapid exit stage right.

Picking at his ear, the seaman continued. "Never known the lunatics to lie. They're too insane to lie on purpose," he said. "The lunatics are good workers and story tellers, but they can't lie worth a shit."

I listened to his drawn out social evaluation half-heartedly, and slid my hand into the pockets of my vest. Lady Astor busied herself, trying not to seem obviously nosey, "Got your rent?" she asked again.

My right palm wrapped around Lady Astor's graft. I'd near forgotten it, thanks to Lester's chants.

"Never says much does he 'ay Ms. Astor," the seaman declared. She slammed the bowls and cups, broadcasting her irritation.

Lady Astor smiled at the seaman.

His rent was being paid in other ways.

She gathered in utensils and left the room with her hands filled.

I pulled the package, the blood dripping through, from my pocket and set it in my nearly empty bowl. Lady Astor was gone from the room, but when she returned she'd find it.

"Holy shit man!"

"What, in the name of St. Peter, is that?" The seaman asked. I looked at my neighbor and with a hearty grin said; "It's breakfast for the Ms."

CHAPTER TWO

Silently I rose, and dabbed my chin a final time before leaving behind the damp, loosely wrapped liver.

It smelled wet.

This scene was not the first, but just maintenance of the status quo. I stared at my breakfast bowl waiting for Lady Astor to return. The slamming from the adjoining room continued unabated.

Over her slamming and shuffling, I heard the hacking cough of the one-eyed seaman. Lady Astor's behavior was as much a routine as was Lester's ramblings. The changing bangs meant she'd soon return to the dining room.

I pushed the chair in.

I had socialized with these sows long enough.

"Good day," I nodded to my neighbor.

He nodded eyeing my graft.

"Bugger me," I heard him say. I slowed to his words wanting to send a shiver down his spine. It worked.

I walked through the front room and toward the winding staircase my spine was straight and hands clasped. My room was up the staircase, far to the back of the hall.

It had been my room over frequent years.

I was always cautious though, making sure as I entered to look for any disturbance. Nothing seemed out of place on this morning, but my paranoia looked for the smallest unfamiliar crumbs.

There were none.

I closed and locked the door behind me.

Removing my vest, I sat at the foot of the bed. A face in the better-kept mirror on my bureau instantly greeted me. It was a noble, handsome face.

"Was I the teacher or the student?" I asked.

"Can one exist without the other?" I wondered.

"Had I learned and taught satisfactorily?"

I crossed my knees, right over left, and wrists, left over right.

It wasn't too many nights ago, late August or early September when the teacher asked, "Who'll work today?"

I said I would.

I always raised my hand.

I've listened to the mirror and always done what they had asked. I swept the ash of man, their words and deeds all spread like ash and all sat at my feet.

"Words, what can they do?" I wondered.

Mother had words.

"Mere words such as eat worms you shit!"

"Just simple words, such as: fuck your mother boy!"

"Simply spoken words such as spread your ass for the man son!"

Words mean nothing to some, but much to others.

I swayed to unheard tunes.

"What did words mean to John Keats and Charles Dickens?" I asked. "They are just simple words but what fires they burned. What ash those flames laid upon the flowers of the world."

I was made into what I was by words, and others deeds.

I've learned from history's needs. For the world to be made right, the streets must be made clean.

History had called me to be the world's laborer, to be the world's architect, to rebuild it. History will call me Hiram Abiff.

It was on a summer's night when I began to sweep.

I did wonder if the world would take note?

I had to make the wrongs right. If the present is made clean, history cannot help but be free of filth. Whitechapel was therefore inevitable.

It began when I had come from Liverpool by train after suspicions grew about my relationship with a boy. I could not comprehend why authorities showed unwavering interest in my sexual desires, but they had. Words such as demented, grotesque, and animalistic fell on me they even called me indecent.

"They were words painted by others regarding my character, my nature," I hissed to the mirror.

"Truth did not matter as long as the liars were propelled to loftier perches because of the lie."

Since that that Liverpool boy, I was being prepared for something far greater than my daily monotony. I'd accomplished so much before that Liverpool lad, and before that Buck's Row whore.

When man's words forced me out into the night, I was drawn to the ash lying at the feet of the Queen. Victoria and her steeds that paraded atop it had turned the kingdom into chaos.

My eyes never left the mirror.

My words painted the pictures my eyes were seeing.

I swayed with fervor on the end of the Astor bed.

That late August night I was on a nearby Batty Street bench. The voices in my head beckoned me. They called for me to cleanse the fallen and build anew.

"You are Hiram Abiff!" I was told.

I walked the Queen's cobble.

It was past dark, closer to 11pm than 10. My hands were wrapped tightly around each other. I knew how to begin. I just had to wait for the proper moment.

It wouldn't be long they came like the wind.

I had met an unfortunate that night. An excessively homely whore had bumped into me unapologetically as she was tossed for from the Frying Pan Public House.

The Frying Pan was one of many such houses where the dregs of East London could claim a bed for a handful of pennies.

"You can sleep if you can fuck," it was practice as usual.

"My new bonnet will bring the extra pennies," I heard her say to the doorman.

"Suck for three?" he asked in return.

This one named Mary twirled away from the offer.

I stood watching in the shadows, and then walked toward the Frying Pan.

"Three pence, I'll be back you ol' cock," she spit back.

Her words trailed off as we bumped shoulders.

"I beg your pardon, dear lady," I tipped my billycock.

"Fuck off," she said tersely.

Her words found their mark.

I watched her petticoats drag along the stone as she moved away. She possessed certain charms, yet I'm sure, but like a rat, she scurried through the faces of Spitalfields.

I followed.

Something about her words struck me.

I smelled her salt.

"My bonnet will bring the needed pennies," her words echoed.

Her stench was enticing. Her bonnet was not.

The East End chime stated it was midnight proper.

My walk was austere at a gentlemen's pace.

I never lost view as she offered her bonnet for less and less. She huffed away when a lesser price was tabled but did exchange her warm, speedy grip for two pennies here and there.

"My bonnet will bring the pennies," her words echoed.

I grew warm repeating her words and watching her deeds.

They were just words, but what a fire they fueled. This woman, 'Polly' everyone called her, traded her virtue, her flesh, and her soul for pennies.

At a gentlemen's distance, through masses of filth, I saw her enter a small public kitchen. There she bartered for bread by pulling her petticoat high.

'Polly' was drunk and dripped of the cook's seed. I watched from a closer distance as she went up Thrawl Street.

Men shouted, "suck for a penny!"

"Stroke for two!" 'Polly' would shout back.

She'd stand on any number of unlit corners, scoffing at the drunks while offering her cunt for the highest bid.

I drew closer as she counted her coins. She counted them a couple of times then after pausing she chose whiskey over bed.

I hid my chin within my collar.

She tied, untied, and then removed her bonnet.

It's wearing didn't seem to be helping her at all.

She spit, and then reached for the back of her tongue to clear what the cook left behind.

The street was empty, which wasn't good for the vendors of flesh. She gave the look of desperation, and then crossed the cobbles, heading my way.

I stepped as she did with the purpose of bumping shoulders once again. A casual, accidental greeting was sometimes the best.

She hurried by, casting a momentary squint of recognition before continuing down Thrawl Street.

I bumped her but she said nothing.

I didn't speak either.

I kept my hands warm under my cloak. She neared Osborn Street. "Four pennies a fuck?" she asked a better-dressed man.

The better-dressed man looked at the body she offered.

He grabbed her breast determining if four was a fair price. 'Polly' was awarded her pennies as she was bent over a stone at the Jews' Cemetery. When the better-dressed man was wiped clean, 'Polly' straightened her petticoat, and began her walk again, smoothing her bonnet in thanks.

She stood near Osborne Street, and through dark I made my intentions known.

As I approached, she used her fingers to wipe what was left over from the four-penny better-dressed man. She licked her fingers.

My mind brought itself back to the Astor bed.

My hands and ankles were still crossed.

I still swayed.

I talked to the man in the mirror and he confirmed she was a good guest for a warm summer's evening in Buck's Row.

The area was safe for me. A hospital designed for the poor was only blocks away. I had offered my services there on many occasions.

I approached her.

"Good evening, dear woman," I said still hidden by shadows.

'Polly' didn't recognize me. Instead she looked at me, nose curled into a snout as if I weren't worth her time. Her look only fanned the flames within me. I was angered, not lustful.

"Pennies?" I asked.

'Polly' turned away.

I grabbed her wrist and offered a shilling for a fuck.

'Polly' pulled her wrist away. She doubted my offer, but was easily swayed as I showed her the coin.

"We're near the stables," I insisted, "Follow me."

"For a shilling I'll fuck anywhere," she nodded.

'Polly' had a soft looking neck. I admired it as she passed in front of me.

I smelled her salt too.

"Fancy my hole, do you love?" she asked.

"I do," I shut the gate behind us.

With little delay, 'Polly' reached for the hem of her dress and slowly bent over.

I held my hand up.

"First, please remove the bonnet, I don't like it."

She removed her bonnet.

She smiled drunkenly, and bent over again.

I smelled her ass as it split wide.

I reached under my cloak.

'Polly' was methodical in her business. Before I'd completely stopped, she backed her ass onto my trousers. She laughed when my cock remained soft. Her laugh was fuel.

I shoved it closer to her but the result was the same and she laughed even harder. The laugh, God damn it, that laugh of hers. 'Polly' was a penny whore and she was laughing at me, a reputable doctor.

I remembered all the laughs that night.

I fingered in vain my pointless cock.

I could smell all her unwashed holes.

That night a whore laughed at me. Her laugh clutched my throat as I gripped hers. I had had enough, rage blinded me, and with a quick swipe I introduced her to the voices that had so long followed me. She fell with a wet thud and we got acquainted under my terms.

'Polly' laid spread eagle, while I began a tale just for her.

I felt her sticky thighs.

"Your laughter is unkind. If you only knew who I was,' I said.

I rolled her onto her back.

"It began upon straw much like this. I was only a boy."

"Laughter, just like yours, changed me."

My eyes darkened and 'Polly' moaned as I shot a fist between her legs.

I sniffed my knuckles upon retrieval.

She lay oblivious to my words as I returned to my boyhood days aside the muck of Lake Ontario.

"I hid from my mother's screams. Neighbors said I was a dirty, ignorant boy, dug deep into our barns loft on straw just like this.

"There was one particular day that rings louder than all others."

I fingered a blade.

"Francis! Mother always shouted. Francis! She'd screech."

"Mother's voice was like hungry hogs at a fresh trough."

I lifted 'Polly's' hem, it'd be much easier for me from this position. I pushed her knees up and I scooted, kneeling, forward.

"I don't need your hands now, dear lady."

"My mother's name was Margaret," I said, "Many called her Mary, my father was James."

I pulled my cock out and pissed in 'Polly's mouth.

The smell was pungent.

"I was the last of nine," I said casually, "I recall only an older brother and sister though.

"Mother's words were incoming arrows, and each one found its mark. After time, I could dodge them. Hiding from my mother's words became a game, difficult at first but a game I'd master."

'Polly' feigned interest as I could only dry fuck her.

"Fuck mother!" I bellowed through clenched teeth.

I screamed my history as I tore from 'Polly' the one skill she had.

"Francis! Francis! The calling had begun one night. Her bellowing could be heard through all of Sophia Street. Mother's screams were piercing. I'd cover my ears, but her shrieks from the porch never went away. They have never gone away.

I fingered my cock, bringing my hand up to taste my seed and 'Polly's' blood.

"I'd lay in our barn's damp straw, from sunrise to sunset. I'd dream of other lands and I'd wait for my dreams to be answered. But, they never were."

I looked at the whore I straddled in the straw of Buck's Row.

"This is the new land," I said.

'Polly' had a blank look. I put a finger to her mouth as a call from outside sought her name.

"Hush my sweet one, hush," I whispered.

"'Polly' I have a bed!" A dry crackling voice, choking back its own labor, echoed up and down the Spitalfields stones.

I removed my finger from 'Polly's' mouth. The voice from outside vanished when a reply was not given.

'Polly's' lips were sticky.

The stalls straw was pissed soaked and the stink had long since settled in. I reached for 'Polly's' throat. As my fingers clenched the soft skin, I became a young boy again in the loft of Sophia Street.

"Francis...God damn it boy...Francis Tumblety get in here!" Mother paused before finishing her whale-like bellow. She could be heard from end to end along the Genesee trail. And like the whores of East End, my mother was often filled with mill men's seed.

"Francis, get your sorry ass in here!"

Every day, I was a sorry ass. I was never son. I was just a sorry ass needed for picking, scrubbing, and waiting outside till the men of the current payday finished with her. I covered my ears and ground my teeth as I begged to be taken to a far away land.

Those dreams came true, though not soon enough. I became what I wished, and I was taken to lands where greatness was in easy grasp.

Father worked the canals and left me to the care of his bride. He left me in our barn's loft, waiting for the men who laid seed for the nursery to finish fucking his beloved wife.

One-day father never returned.

"I was a boy tossed to the will of the wind and the desires of man," I continued, "I was a boy bent over for men who desired both woman and man."

I pushed 'Polly's' thighs further apart.

My lip quivered at the scent.

"Fuck the voices!"

I straddled 'Polly', tossing her bonnet further to the side. I clenched her thighs with mine. I sat on her as if I was taking a shit. I continued my story hidden within the shadows of slats and dew.

"You need to listen, then you'll better understand your fate." I wiped my hands on her hem, and watched as she bubbled, recalling so many others just like her.

My thighs tightened.

"I overcame those years of calloused youth. I even wore the badges of the Yankee blue." The voices bragged in my ear.

"I had danced with actors and generals! I loved the taste of men and they loved me!"

"It was that one night though that led me to this stall and to your lap. That one night that drives me more than any other."

'Polly' was silent.

My tone sharpened. "It was early spring in Rochester, and the water was high. What remained of winter had filled our ponds and creeks. The mud around our shack was thick.

"That one day smelled of late winter. The odor of old water and overused women."

I squirmed within the stall.

The bells of Whitechapel told me the hour was nearing three.

I started to cut above her ribs and delicately peeled back her skin to expose her organs. They radiated warmth.

Her eyes showed little interest.

I slid my fingers inside her organs. I thrust my fingers in and out then licking them clean.

My lips quivered.

"'Polly' my mother, howled just for me. Francis...God damn it boy I know you hear me! God damn it boy! God damn it boy! God damn it boy!"

I drooled as I rubbed 'Polly's' belly. It was depressingly scarred and covered with stink. She appeared overcome by the moment. Perhaps she was thankful that death had finally come for her.

My mind danced from year to year.

Memories were an evil trick that followed one after another.

My spittle dribbled.

Mother's face came back to me often.

I pushed my palms against my ears and clenched my teeth.

"Stop!" I begged the voices.

But the voices continued unabated.

The voices had brought me to Buck's Row.

'Polly' lay silent.

I spoke only to myself.

I let loose the whispers that had been fermenting since Rochester. I couldn't keep mother's words silent. They had teeth as sharp as any of the Queens' swords.

I couldn't rid mother's words completely.

I paused to listen for the morning vendors of Buck's Row.

There were none.

I continued my tale.

"That night I walked from the barn carrying a stick. I chose a spot where I could see mother bellowing from the door."

I squeezed 'Polly's' bruises.

I was well armed. I had to be armed for mother would begin swinging before I was within spitting distance.

I circled the shack.

I shrunk from her echo. If I came up behind her, it would perhaps be possible to make it to the door before she spotted me. I peaked around the corner. Mother was looking off to the right side of our Sophia Street home the street was small. Not many neighbors were near us William Post was the closest.

"The mill men fuck well but pay poorly," she'd laugh.

"That's information a son never needs," I admitted.

Father wanted to be close to the city so he built the shack. He had a chance to work the canal of the flour city, but he had no horse for travel. He built the home far from city center to hide his wife but once a whore, always a whore.

"More cocks in your mother than in any hen house," many would say as I begged for apples.

I looked at 'Polly's' silent body, "I dare say the same is true of you."

In a gust of history, I turned to 'Polly' and shoved my hand deep between her legs with a grinding twist.

"Good as gold when a penny is rare," I said scraping what she sold without care.

I grew red from memory.

I busied myself with more twists and turns.

'Polly's' belly was still warm. I smeared her blood as if I were wiping her clean. I painted her belly red and continued my story just for her.

"That night I edged closer to the scattered uncut firewood near our shack."

I fingered my cock to those memories.

"I took one step, than another and another closer to our porch."

I waited for 'Polly' to reply but none came. I waited for a smile, a laugh or snicker, but there was nothing.

I struck her lower jaw but just a puff of air came out.

"Fuck you bitch!" I said.

"Are you judging me?" the voices laughed.

I continued my story as if I was the only audience.

"As a boy I smiled frequently. It didn't matter if it was at something real or imaginary. I would smile especially if I tricked Mother. Some thought I was insane. Some say I am insane. I say I am uniquely profound."

I shoved my hand deeper into her cunt.

In a final grasp I pulled.

I studied it, tilting my head, admiring what I had done.

I licked her eggs from my fingers.

" 'Polly' that night as I tricked my mother, I thought of my father and how, when the opportunity presented itself, he had left the mud and whore behind. Or so I was told."

I licked my wrists free of 'Polly's' salt.

My lips quivered.

"Father had told others that he built the shack near trout less waters so he could walk the banks to work. Mother said frequently he had left because of me. One night she said otherwise.

"I'd walked gingerly around the firewood as mother rounded our shanties corner. However as I touched the first step on the crooked dock, the creaking board got her attention. She whirled around. "Never sneak up on me you piece of cock dribble!"

"I ran for the door, but her fat blocked my path. Grabbing me by the neck and ear, Mother followed through with words and blows, but not one of the far-flung neighbors screamed stop. I was left alone to bare the brunt."

'Polly's' shit was spreading like butter.

"The smacks were daily prizes mother delivered. I could mark days by the scabs and scars. That night, when I escaped my mother's grip, I returned to the barn's loft. Thunder grew in the distance as darkness settled."

I dismounted 'Polly' and sat adjacent to her bonnet.

I squeezed my testicles.

I continued my story.

"I was only ten when the last of my siblings left. They were much older than I. I had no one to teach me, so I had taught myself to stay strong to mother's blows. I could face the fiercest of oceanic gales now, because I stood so strong."

I leaned over to sniff what 'Polly' sold for pennies.

"I stayed strong by eating worms I dug from beneath the dampened boards. I stayed strong by lodging in rag packed hidden corners when she failed to return from her fucking on Mount Hope Avenue."

"That night as mother kicked, scratched and pulled all she could, I smiled for another life was only a dream away. I had survived by taking what nature put on the table for me. The only consoling voices came from the hellhounds on my shoulders.

"I stayed strong by just being a dream and escaping to that wished for other land. That night when Mother lost her grip, I returned to the barns loft filled with her words and hunger pains."

I fingered 'Polly's' shit.

Her eyes were fixated.

I grinned.

"That night from the loft of our barn I watched Mother as this night I've watched you."

The hour neared half-past three. The straw within the stable was rose petal red. 'Polly' was pale. "Don't be a pest by feigning interest, you slopped fuck."

'Polly' remained silent.

I sliced her clean from left to right. Her soul was now mine. Her loins, which were her prize, spewed forth my way. I licked what spilled on my hand. I cut deeper splitting 'Polly's' cord and much-sullied cunt. Just one cut made it meaningless to any sailor's penny.

My eyes could be as black as a widow's veil when I thought of fallen women. I took what she offered from between her legs digging deeper for what wasn't three pennies in price.

I licked my fingers.

I tasted her scent.

I pulled her stink out with more force than necessary.

"This will help us get to know one-another more then the pitiful, simple exchange of her majesty's coin," I said.

I studied her torso.

I furrowed my brows, picking what I could from her overused, unwashed flesh while regaining a strangle hold on my yesterday. I licked my fingers clean from the palm up. 'Polly' was silent. I let the straw soak her blood dry. I listened, straddling his chest, for any movement outside, anything rising with the early hours. After a few ear wrenching moments, I found a level of silence that was required. I reached over and closed her knees.

'Polly' lay with eyes half opened, her final question left unanswered. Would her earthly sins be forgiven or would she face the burn only unrepentant souls feel? 'Polly' had determined her destiny long before I had. I simply gave her one last chance to ask forgiveness before the tombs of Whitechapel sealed her.

I looked at 'Polly' as a dog would look at raw meat. And like the dog would drag raw scraps from a carcass, I dragged 'Polly' to just outside the gate nearest the wharf entrance.

The 4am chimes called the hour. The commoners would soon be shuffling about their business. They'd find her in their own clumsy way. I would assure that. With care I moved 'Polly' so I could see east and west simultaneously from the corner of my eyes. Many men would think 'Polly' just another bed less drunken hole.

A fallen unfortunate is how the police would see her too. They'd see her lying in a way many expected women of Whitechapel to lay. The police would be fools too. They would need some help, so I let her hand touch the gate of the stable. It'd be a sign to where they could find her soul before the hogs fed on the bloodied straw. Still it was likely they'd miss the sign anyway.

The blood that might work its way out of the straw would be confused with that of the nearby slaughterhouse. It would be a miracle if the scattered talent of a constable's lantern would find the blood, the whore or me. I dropped her black bonnet near the hand touching the gate.

"A fool could figure the clues," I whispered to the stones.

"But a fool would be a genius on these stones though."

I crossed quickly to the opposite side of the street as I heard scattered dialects approaching. I'd watch the scene from a distance, but close enough to allow for thorough observation. I'd be a character waiting for a train at Whitechapel Station.

The nights in the East End and in Rochester were so similar.

I neared the rail station. I'd choose a bench and watch as men came, one after another, followed by the lanterns I'd promised.

The night unfurled just as I knew it would. One would call out, while another knocked him over. Others would bump into walls and mules alike.

The voices that followed me teasingly rolled and chased their tails as I created history.

That warm night was one of many.

I'd watched history closely from my Astor bed. The mirror wouldn't let me go. I'd swept the streets of at least one that had spread their fallen soul to others. I was a servant of man; I was rebuilding his world one soul at a time.

I am their master builder.

I wished that I would have finished my story uninterrupted, but 'Polly', the morning vendors were determined to begin their days. My mind slowed its dance with the voices. Both of us settled upon the rail station bench.

I watched the light rain die as the soot overtook the water that was attempting to rinse the city.

I swayed anew on the bench.

I was a boy again.

I was a boy in Rochester. A city founded as a port on a great lake. The land was stolen for a handful of rusted coin from Indians too smart to warn the thieves of the evil in the soil.

The weather was punishment for taking by deceit what had belonged to others first. My thoughts drifted between these times.

Had I taught 'Polly' well?

I wanted the conclusion, so I'd watch from a bench that had been badly abused by the cities many winged peasants.

My feet swayed.

"Father taught me of good and evil, of partner and betrayer," I told the voices.

"Son, your mother furthers the blood of the betrayer. Remember that before she claims you too," he'd say.

My eyes darted, and mind drifted everywhere. It walked recent history, drifting back to The House of Astor. It saw young boys and seafaring old men; it drifted to nights such as this, and it leapt into the dark eyes of a mustachioed noble man named John.

I watched the story of Buck's Row unfold with a casual interest. The voices of the morning vendors were joined by more serious pencil wielding eyes. Eyes that no doubt wished they were still asleep.

"Rochester was a city of flour," I told the voices.

It was the promise of more than rotten potatoes that brought my parents to its labor ready soil. I always wondered though what father knew that the others did not.

"Was father warned not to leave the Land of Éire with the blood that he knew was from an evil tree?" I asked the voices. "Did mother and father breed just for me? If so, then for whom shall I breed?"

The voices laughed.

I rolled my ankle clockwise then back again.

Father had come to Rochester in hopes of a change that never came. Then, I woke one day and he was gone.

"Food!" she shrieked.

"He left for the sea. He was sick of you, you fuckin' shitty ass boy!"

Mother continued wailing as I shunned her arrows. She looked at me as if I were feathered fowl meant for dinner.

Would I fall to her axe?

"You're making me live without a man," mother shouted as I returned back to the loft's moist straw. My scars grew and the voices cried like newborns.

I ran.

Mother sang.

I swayed to unheard tunes.

"Condemned is the lonely woman cast aside by a man, who without ware must betray virtue for hidden opossum gruel."

Her words were a plague.

Mother muttered tunes like those when any man, still dripping from her cunt, left a dime less than what was bargained for. That one night though, she was like no time before, telling tales that few could ever possibly think of painting.

That day mother sat alongside a fire.

"I am forty generations deep, the seventh daughter of the seventh son of the seventh daughter of the seventh son, am I," she preached.

She was etching maniacal words.

The moon was near full.

Her haunting ramblings transitioned the hours into history.

"He was the betrayer, and so too has been my lot. I've been shunned and cast away, I've been betrayed in our time 'til time has no meaning," mother sang towards the loft.

I covered my ears.

I'd hide, always covering my ears and wishing the world away. It didn't matter if the audience was a handyman or a crew of five, she sold them her fishy crop nonetheless. For three pennies, at times a nickel, or for two fucks, perhaps even a dime.

I watched it all.

I learned the service of ridding the Land of Éire of that seventh daughter was why father had crossed the Atlantic. That land and its history had tainted mother's blood. Father believed it. Father believed in the tree of the betrayer and he believed in all its roots. Mother's tree was the tree of Judas, cursed and now rooted in America. I'd come from her tree.

That one night I recalled his instructions to be cautious and escape when possible.

Mother's face was more than an outline however.

My ankle drew circles in the air.

I pelted the voices with a practiced sermon.

"Cast aside the vipers of God for Christ is the rock the master builders shun. Let in the light from the swollen sea of man."

My words too had grown maniacal.

It was mother's voice that followed me. I loved her as a boy, and fucked her as a man. I did as she wished.

"Father couldn't bare it," I said aloud.

"He couldn't bare her," laughed the voices.

"Father had a sister who was sent away before all was cast down upon her limbs. Those fears are what brought father to America's shores."

My ankle stopped.

Judas took root in Rochester. It was a new land for old sin and old betrayers. Unleavened soil was plentiful. It was convenient for tramps and run away thieves to land in Rochester by trading fare for labor. My father was just such a tramp.

In Ireland, father's land of birth, sourness overwhelmed crops and man. That sour taint caused many families to seek America's shore. The potato was said to be the spoiled seed in Ireland, but it was in fact blood, my mother's blood.

Condemnation of faith was everywhere, and that too brought many to the land of wheat and feathered warriors. My father was the oldest son, orphaned early on in the smallish block of Protestant Belfast, Ireland. He'd struggled to feed his younger siblings. His sister, Anne Marie at thirteen was taken by buggy men for what she could offer to the regiment of her majesty's guardsmen. She'd been saved father said.

Father's words and shoulders were both broad. He wore the same clothes winter or summer. His arms were covered with hair. He had a tattoo or two, and a large onyx ring was the centerpiece of his crooked left hand. Now father was gone.

Beneath more then one seasonal quarter moon, she howled and sang words few could declare knowledge of.

Mother called it lamenting.

It was just mother and I from that day forward.

But that one night is as fresh as 'Polly's' scent.

That one night, she seemed more artistic than on others.

I held watch over her as she performed in the rain, under moonlit clouds and abundantly underdressed. That night, she entertained the crew from The Ellwanger Nursery. As thunder rolled she split wide her legs for a workhouse crew, from the northern end of State Street.

That night men drank and laughed as she performed acts better unseen by any son. As she stepped up on a wagon gate, the thunder rolled and as the lightening struck she preached to the worms and moon alike.

I now swayed on the Whitechapel bench.

The lanterns approached Buck's Row having discovered 'Polly' as I knew they would.

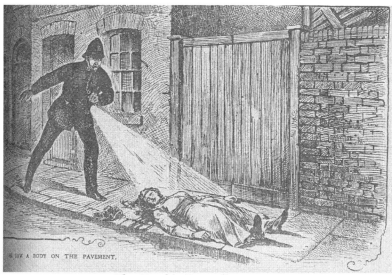

The Buck's Row discovery.

Mother's voice forced my drool.

"I am forty generations deep, the seventh daughter of the seventh son of the seventh daughter of the seventh son am I," she'd bellow.

Mother straddled buckboard and fat Germans that night while sharing stories told generations ago. "I am betrayed no more by the silence of raised eyes and ripping laughter!"

Mother posed squatting in mid-piss.

The drunkards laughed at her drips.

"Those who service me join me. Join me for this day old stew as tribute. My boy's stew, to sweet for him but good enough nonetheless."

I watched her while I was immersed in straw and rain. The men fucked her one after another eating her as well as the stew. Both were meaty, broth filled tributes, served in honor of the betrayer. The thunder rolled as men scooped bowls of homemade stew from a pot with thick clinging strings of meat meeting their mouths. I hated the look of it, though the smell tempted me for the worms that night was few.

A lonely wind appeared.

Steadily the rain disappeared.

Some sought second servings of mother and stew, but few were given second drips. "It's the boy's and he too must pay tribute!"

I watched, hidden among boards, as she became the naked gypsy serving up flesh, wine and carrots to the syphilis-crazed mill men.

"The shock of all has been passed from more than one mother's son and I," she sang. "I swear to the light from the moon, and I swear to Golgotha's crooked tree that my root, that my seed will be remembered as much as the first betrayer ever was."

She cracked her ass for any onlooker.

Mother prayed aloud that I'd be remembered as much as the first betrayer was.

"Betrayer?" I asked the moon. "What does she mean?"

"Watch as I do," the moon replied.

Lightning flashed without rain, and the light danced as much as my naked mother did. Her words were confusing to the most learned gentlemen, but to the stupid they seemed brilliant.

That night my roots took to the soil.

I looked deeper into all of life's mirrors from then on.

"I was mother's seed. All you traders of puss pouches and its juice, I am the seed," I declared.

I watched mother dance.

As I lay beneath worm filled wood, I was fearful of her words. I heard them in a different light that night. She'd sing similar things on different days, but the tunes on that night were new. I'd grown accustomed to her dance and to the strange men of all shapes, colors and pay, but her words were new.

"What did she mean by crooked tree? Her seed will be remembered as much as the first seed? Nothing seemed to make sense. Would I be remembered?"

I had so many questions, and no one to answer them.

The world stood still while that young man dwelled on words meant just for him on that night. That night changed what I was.

Mother continued her wail as I retreated into dreams.

I dreamed of other lands.

I dreamed I sailed the seas.

I dreamed my mouth welcomed older men.

"It was then...it was then, listen to this you sons of bitches! This will make you understand what is to be!" Mother sang.

That night was clearing.

From the Whitechapel bench I revisited Sophia Street, The House of Astor, and the stalls of Buck's Row all as one.

I was in three places at once.

I walked in three histories.

I heard mother's words, fresh as always. "All will see that these days were destined to be," she'd say.

It was that night that I knew I was meant to be. I was the seed of the betrayer.

I've said to all the mirror's faces, "You were meant to be. Before the raven ever sang, and before his neck ever popped, these moments were meant to be."

While mother stood atop the wagon gate screaming to the moon, I dreamt of escaping to this very bench.

I dreamt of standing above others and screaming at their faded flowers.

I watched the hustle and bustle of Buck's Row.

"'Polly', you were meant to be," I whispered.

On the rail station bench, I saw that my dreams had come true. "Faded flour and faded flowers, by woman and rose. Both have thorns and both have failing beauty," I said through pooled drool.

"Faded flour, or faded flowers, does your yeast rise for a pennies prize?"

I knew who I was and felt the twinge of pride at mother's words. "Faded flower, will the bee still make the journey from daisy to daisy?" With each verse I'd always slam a blade into my guests, and with each word the voices howled their approval.

That night as the men from the alleys finished their final thrusts into my mother the moon shifted, the campfires embers died and the last bowl of stew was served up.

"Save one bowl, you no good slaves of my ass. My boy must pay tribute too when the morning comes," she said.

"Paying tribute?" I wondered.

What could she mean?

The alley men were leaving bragging about their thrusts.

As mother grabbed at invisible mice she wiped her cunt dry and scurried for our backdoor.

I watched knowing she'd sit in our unlit shack, waiting for my return. Mother knew, she always knew, that from the loft I had witnessed her acts.

The laughter of the sex fed mill men carried the walls of the canal. Their laughs bounced across the river to the shocked sensitivities of the huddled nuns. I listened until I could no longer define their words.

Our yard was empty and the moon was exiting its stage. I was hungry and the stews salty odor had tempted me since the flames first licked the pot. I stood in a crooked, ancient form, hopping from stacks of straw.

"Escape, before her ashes fall upon you boy," my father's voice echoed.

"Ashes?"

"What ashes were meant just for me?" I asked.

I heard his warnings often. I slipped to the door of the barn, half hung from lack of care.

The air smelled of man.

A nearby Mockingbird sang loudly at the creeping sun.

I wondered what he thought of the scene.

The air was difficult to describe. It was just unwashed. I lingered, waiting for her bellowing to begin.

Mother was watching me waiting for her.

I believed I'd won the moment as I walked gingerly over well-trodden ground toward the fading fire and her stage.

I smelled what had been boiled meat.

The more I walked the worse the air smelled of old men and their muddied cocks.

I approached from a fair distance with mother's fallen virtue playing in my mind. I saw man after man filling her holes on the buckboard now stained with stew and man.

I saw a bowl shoved arms length within the buckboard.

I was hungry enough that I'd easily eat what the mother birds offered their young, so the undercooked stew was a king's banquet.

I grabbed the bowl and heard a howl from behind the slat board walls of the shack. Mother was watching her seed take to the soil.

I hovered over the kettle. There were some nice pieces of meat still floating at the bottom. I dipped the bowl into the cold broth, and scooped at the chunks.

Hungrily I sipped.

It was salty.

The shack laughed as I choked back the taste.

The broth only fed my appetite. I turned to the kettle, which sat upon the soon to be gone embers. I wanted more.

I leaned back over the pot, and noticed heavier pieces of the concoction at the bottom.

"Just for my boy," she whispered.

She was watching. I dipped the bowl three times feeling it gain in weight with each dip.

"Meat!" I called out.

I drank the broth like it was ambrosia.

A howl came from the shack.

It was so good.

A piece of meat went down without chewing.

Another howl came from the shack.

I ate is if it were my first meal.

I chewed strings of meat, some under and some over cooked. But it was a warm meal.

It was boiled, but I cared less about its presentation than its taste. It warmed things in me that hadn't been touched in years.

"So good," I declared.

Drops of broth dripped from my chin and I scooped a final piece or two of meat that was fair sized, one fatter than the other.

I slurped the broth.

I sucked the meat free from the larger of the two bones and as I moved the second piece to my mouth a large onyx ring fell to the ground.

CHAPTER THREE

A howl came from behind the shacks walls.

An invisible hand gripped my neck.

Hungry voices replaced dreams for other lands.

I could no longer escape by foot or fantasy.

I couldn't run or even speak. As the spit pooled upon the back of my tongue I had no choice but to swallow the last of my father's thumb.

Mother laughed.

Dawn had come as if it too were hidden behind the shack's walls.

The sun cracked wide with a fury only morning could bring.

Light peaked over the shack; one ray at a time until it hit the ground under my feet.

Night was over.

The weather-tested city had survived another storm, scurrying away like a mouse from a cat.

I was my Mother's mouse.

Another howl bounced from the shack into the mud. It was the last one, rising with the morning sun.

"That night was only the beginning of many to come," I whispered from the rail station bench of Buck's Row.

I swayed, as the scene was unearthed.

Slowly, once my anger, foot, and swaying abated, I returned to that Rochester drool.

"That night created me," I said to the voices.

Mother slung the door of the shack open. She was naked. With a step outside, she slipped in the mud, landing on all fours. She pissed where she was.

Then her shadow was gone.

I sat on the wagon's gate, my mouth full of father's flesh. Mother scurried up to the banks of the Genesee. That'd be the last I'd see her until I my toe closed the door. Mother would feed on bread alongside alley dogs, fucking them too from what I was told.

From that moment on, I was a young man left to my own talents, either actual or dreamt up. At times wondered how she survived, but that night was the start of the journey to this Whitechapel bench.

That night a seed was planted, and I've nurtured it since.

A blood soaked shack would be mine, just a skeleton of wood and full of holes. It was suiting. I too was full of holes. But I would build myself around moral scaffolding. My body was being patched as my costumes changed.

I walked three histories at once and returned to The House of Astor.

Lady Astor was murmuring from outside my door. Her voice seemed pleasant.

I heard her heavy feet coming toward me.

Had she discovered her morning graft?

Lady Astor knocked. "Doctor! Doctor!" I answered the door.

"Ma'am?" I asked.

"Doctor, your package, what you left for me this morning, fresh meat is greatly appreciated," she said.

"You're welcome, dear lady," I nodded. "Money is scarce, but I was provided meat in place of payment last night."

"I am on my way out," I said.

"Fry it if you must, but if I'm late you may serve it without me."

"I'll save you the finest cut!" she said, stomping away.

I shut the door, and paced like a caged animal. My face reddened. I could feel the heat reach my lower neck. The flush of my skin returned me to the watered cobblestone and to the night filled with clock chimes and sour straw.

I was everywhere all at once.

I had knelt in 'Polly's' shit and whispered poems of love.

I paced my room.

'Polly' didn't care.

I told 'Polly' that I carried mother's seed. It may have been her impulsive desires or an ugly curse, but regardless, I carried mother with me.

Though I taught people with my stories, few ever learned.

I swayed to unheard tunes.

I had tried to teach by deed and flowered words, but more often than not I was told to fuck off.

Had anyone learned?

Even the authorities acted as if they were spoiled children, always wanting more without deserving it.

Each hint I left was a release, but for God's sake, when is enough, enough?

I rolled my ankle.

Who is it that always stands proudly before the newspaperman preaching their prowess at solving crimes? Is it the police or the witness who gave them the clue?

Not long ago I'd hit them where it would hurt the most. Their pride, for those in authority it is always their ego that's the most frail.

They are nothing without me.

One day, not so long ago, I swiped at their pride with a simple scribble.

"I am the witness, am I not?" I asked the mirror.

"I am the background," it replied.

"Abberline, Littlechild, even Lusk all want the lead line, all want to be boss."

One night with paper in hand I nipped at them.

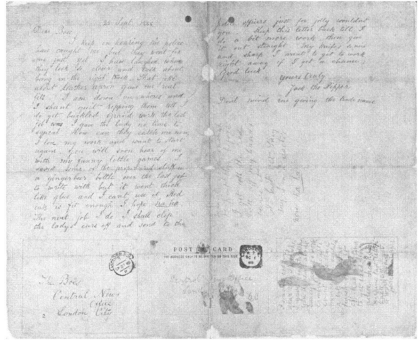

The Dear Boss letter.

I blew on the paper, before finding an envelope.

I'd left plenty of signs for all to study. I had wanted them to learn about me but they hadn't.

I gave a boy a shilling to deliver the letter to the desk of the Central News. The boy smiled at his reward.

Days passed.

I was pensive.

Pacing.

Panting.

I wrapped my cloak around my shoulders and gave a nod through the window to the seaman, who was rubbing Lady Astor's upper thigh. The night air was damp. I'd have to leave London. Perhaps the clues had been too much after all. Perhaps the stupid had learned. Perhaps I had confused them long enough and now they may have at last come to the correct conclusion.

I packed what few things I had in my room.

I left a Ginger Beer bottle behind.

On my walk I would leave behind some trinkets, which were better hidden then carried.

I walked toward the docks. I was proud. I'd done well and would carry little with me. Steamer trunks were sent ahead.

I strolled as if I were an actor on a stage, folding one hand gently into the small of my back.

Even those who stared downward would admire me.

As I walked I relived the taste of her, neck, lips and ear.

I walked with prideful remembrance of outwitting those boasting swine that missed the simplest of clues. They were trying to fish for marlins, but netting only minnows.

I strolled along the East End Streets, one after another carefully. Rounding a corner I saw an unfortunate. I knew him well. This time I stopped to listen to his nonsensical limericks. He wailed into the wind, and sang to birds that only existed generations ago. He painted pictures of the colorful battle that exists on the border between sanity and genius.

I listened with a cocked smile and in thanks presented him a gift, my bloodied tools. He was the lunatic of the bridge, whom all had come to know, and now regularly ignore. His name was Aaron. Everyone called him Aaron the Jew, the Slavic Jew.

In his way he thanked me.

"Nothing but an unfortunate," ladies had called him, "A gutter wretch with voices in his head."

I walked towards my escape. I had had my fill of the unfortunates regardless of how they achieved their titles. My walk seemed similar to the night I had shit out my father's thumb. It was indignant, proud and nauseating all at once.

I arrived without fan fare to the rail station bench.

Mother was soulless. My soul had the same destiny.

Mother had willed me a seed she could no longer carry.

Her burden had become too great.

I could see her face.

I could always feel her breath.

I had eaten my father's flesh, and she had called it a tribute. She called it a right of passage.

As I stood by that fire kicking my father's embers, Mother skirted the canals water.

Mother's laugh was ceaseless.

Years later my niece had said that she had lived her final days in the Rochester Psychiatric Hospital. I would learn later on my own that she actually spent them, coverless, at the county home in Bethany.

I watched the rats of the Whitechapel morning scurry as my mother had scurried. They had to earn their bread too.

The thoughts that boy held on that morning returned often.

"Where shall I warm my hands?"

"How will I survive?" I asked the rats.

I swirled my cloak into the wind as my hem sprayed piss from the street on my boots.

My walk ended at the rail station bench in front of the Whitechapel depot. I set my bag next to me, crossing my knees, right over left, and wrists left over right.

As a boy the answers eventually came.

I'd portray myself as the gentleman who always managed to be one despite the rats. I inhaled, and the recesses of my mind came to life.

I swayed.

I'd eaten my father's flesh.

I'd received the tribute mother had spoken of.

I had tasted father's salt and it could only pool on the back of my tongue. I could only swallow, not once but twice. That morning I looked at the ground and picked up the onyx ring, placing it on my finger. It was loose then, but now fits me well.

The embers of the fire cooled as I watched and kicked the ash free. There'd be no further memories of my father. The fire, with a stronger tweak of my boot and some morning-moistened soil, died without fanfare. The morning sun had lit the sky, so a beautiful day was a possibility, despite the air being horrendous. The air was a horizon of blood, dotted with miles of unwashed fallen women and slaughterhouses. As I stood in the midst of what man offered one another, I came to welcome the warmth the stew provided.

Despite what the stew was, I was thankful.

Despite whom mother was I grew in gratitude.

Despite who they were, mankind needed me.

I swayed.

That morning in Rochester and this one in Whitechapel were sewed together.

On the rail station bench my eyes rolled at the depot like they had rolled at that Sophia Street shack. I'd grown comfortable with all those years and I'd continue my journey despite an oncoming sense of uneasiness.

My eyes rolled along the landscape of the shack.

Would I live in the straw and amongst the rats?

Would I live within the walls of the unfortunates?

Would I live within the walls of man?

I looked toward both and knew that I could. My feet were heavy as I walked through the mud that morning as I wondered why me.

"Why me?" I whispered as Buck's Row unfolded.

"Why not me?" I asked the Whitechapel rats.

That morning from Sophia Street I knew I was someone special.

My pride more than the La Bretagne had carried me to these Whitchapel benches. It was from these benches that I heard paper-boys shout of Miller's Court and Buck's Row. From these benches, I watched the drunks being jarred in mid piss by thick stick wielding Constables. I watched the whores laugh after a good night and their friends say fuck off because customers were few. I watched the foolish vigilantes question even their friends as to their innocence regarding the crimes.

They missed me and I was right in front of them.

If my boyhood taught me anything, it was that a sense of paranoia is a good thing. It is healthy. The safe, secure mind is the one that will be taken advantage of. My sense of paranoia told me it was time to leave London for I'd become too comfortable.

Caution would have me return to New York.

My face began to turn red as I sat on the rail station bench. The acts of Old Bailey too had colored my face.

"Fuck 'em!" The voices yelled.

"Gross indecency?"

"How dare they call me indecent for loving a boy!"

That's what Old Bailey called me.

"Indecent!"

The Bailey had no idea who I was.

I swayed with growing fervor.

"Fuck 'em!"

I swayed and then out of the corner of my eye I saw Aaron the Jew. He was some yards away.

He had followed me.

I watched him watch me.

I watched Kosminski lick his hands, the palm right up through to his fingertips.

Aaron hated to bathe, and it was altogether likely that water had never touched him. Aaron hated to be fed by others, even out of generosity, so his meals often consisted of what he killed.

"Only Christ knows," I laughed as I swayed.

"The courts called me indecent," I declared, never looking away from Aaron.

"Only Christ knows what he licked," I muttered.

"The titles gross and indecent have been equally assigned to a lunatic pissing on the bricks and to me a doctor of reputable note."

My ankle began to draw a circle through the air.

Fuck them all for they can't separate good from evil, sane from profound, or a lunatic from a reputable doctor. My circumstance showed their ignorance.

"The authorities have stated that lunatics and I are equals. What does that say about their ability to tell right from wrong?"

The tempo of the early daylight hours skewered my rage. Screams and shouts from the paperboys all claimed he was back.

"Who is back?" I wondered, lifting my eyes from my foot. The voices of the morning overwhelmed my ears, but it was the lunatic Kosminski that held my eyes. Kosminski picked at unseen food, licked his fingers again, and voiced sermons to distant congregations.

He approached.

I voiced my own sermons.

"Mary," I said, "You were rewarded for your vile acts and I was labeled indecent, what a unique web it is."

The Old Bailey, much like Washington's Old Capitol Prison, had let me go when perhaps they should've known otherwise. They could not decide if good was evil or evil was good so it was no wonder I was let go.

In their world Kosminski was sane and 'Polly' was moral.

My voice was full of pride. After all, I was a reputable doctor and free to travel as I wished. I'd overcome much to make myself into a fine, well-educated man.

Kosminski came closer.

On my trip home, I would move slowly, London to Portsmouth, then Portsmouth to Le Havre. Le Havre would take me to New York and then perhaps a train further upstate.

I admired my wrists.

Kosminski's shadow drifted across my lap.

The lunatic Jew saw my head turn, and hid his licking as if shamed. He too was fallen and had been called a fine example of the world's gutter wretches. He eyed my bag as he walked unevenly towards me.

I put my hand into my pocket preparing for his arrival.

He was at my left shoulder, already in mid-sentence.

"...Your glared fins of God saw puckered hoops again my dear Doctor Frank!" He bemoaned.

His eyes had no life in them.

His tongue was larger than his mouth and drool fell to the cobblestones.

I wrapped my cloak tight around me. In my pocket my right palm gripped its goal.

Kosminski looked unacceptable, and smelled worse. His uncovered feet shifted his weight from side to side. As he swayed, I saw that it wasn't his palm he had been licking, but the knife I had given him. The blade was licked clean.

He talked to the stones.

"The work is hard to hide when the shop is closed for lack of pennies," The fragmented voices plaguing him forced their way out.

I pulled out my right hand slowly.

He grew agitated.

I tossed him a shilling and declared the shop closed.

He gripped the coin.

"The time for the seafarer has come. Indecency is never an act, so called when quickly settling upon a steamer's coal." Kosminski said each word so quickly that one blurred the next hiding them behind his spittle.

He was a balance of lunacy and brilliance.

I rose, nodded a thank you that only he was aware of, and handed him another coin.

He let me be.

Kosminski served as a warning to me. He calmed my paranoia. The insane have an innate ability to know what will be, long before the paperboys report it.

I brushed unseen dust from my sleeves.

Kosminski walked away unevenly.

"The hawkers of badge have smelled the blood, they know the coal too," Aaron declared over his shoulder.

I listened as he walked away.

London to Le Havre is a trip that would take a day, perhaps two depending on the crews of the train and boat. Then I'd return to New York. It was a long trip, but one that should be made without haste according to the ramblings of the lunatic Kosminski.

I walked to the back of the depot to purchase my ticket to Portsmouth. The flush returned as my mind thought again of the Old Bailey Court.

"A court?" The voices laughed scornfully.

"They called it a court?"

"A court of diseased jesters at best perhaps, but not a building of moral law," I mumbled back. "It was a court of putrid wigs casting doubt of character upon those who wished only to lend reputable skills to the world."

I reached the depots rear.

"In this land, does filth govern filth?" I asked the voices.

"Filth governing filth," I babbled, walking closer to the clerk shuffling his paperwork.

"Filth judging filth."

If that was the case in man's system of justice, how could man ever recognize good?

"Civil deviant," they labeled me.

"Grotesque, animalistic behavior," they laughed beneath their wigs.

I stood before the swine-like depot clerk for several moments, staring as if I had no goal.

"Yes, sir?" the clerk asked without looking up.

"The next train to Portsmouth?" I asked finally blinking.

"10:10, sir," he said hastily.

"One ticket please," I mumbled.

We made our transaction and I sought the nearest bench.

The chimes had just reached eight.

I hid within my cloak and continued my rage without drawing many glares.

"I've been so enraged at the recent weeks. I am embarrassed to say, that I had been arrested. The authorities said they had numerous complaints."

I started my swaying all over again.

"Imagine complaints about me, rich wishes I say!"

The voices on my shoulder began to speak in their well-rehearsed way.

"Don't they know who I am?"

"Don't they understand that I'm here for their good?"

"I'm here because I am the seed of goodness, and I am doing what I've been willed to do. I have been called to sweep man's land free of the immoral ash smothering their roses."

My heart began to beat a rhythm. The angrier I became, the quicker my heartbeats galloped.

I had a two-hour wait. I heard a train blow its steam seconds before I saw it. The East End's clocks confirmed that I indeed had two hours to wait.

My history returned to my mind in freshly printed pages, revealing a chapter at a time.

The world simply didn't understand who I was or what I offered. Regardless of my work, or what seas I sailed, the world never understood me. It never understood the art I etched just for them. No painting, sculpture, or bouquet was ever brilliant enough to enlighten the ignorant.

My eyes slid side-to-side, front to back. They saw everything, as my chin remained pointed forward. The steam, train, rain, and Kosminski were all I saw. Kosminski had returned to his regular corner.

A constable appeared at each end of the dock, their necks crooning to look in every direction, including mine. One was tall and slender, a fine looking young man. The other was the fat married type.

I smiled at the younger one.

He didn't see it. The young constable, turning with a hint of curiosity, came a few paces my way. The forthcoming locomotive steam skirted his boots.

I focused on the young constable's face. He flushed as he came near. His color was enticingly attractive. I couldn't tell if it was my desires, or just the early morning chill that gave his chubby cheeks their pink hue. I didn't matter.

I watched him.

He was soon by my side.

"Name sir?" he asked.

My eyes rose from his waist.

"Good morning constable," I said touching the tip of my hat.

"Good morning, sir. Name please," he asked again.

The fattish one slithered up to my right side.

"Frank Townsend," I answered, "Dr. Frank Townsend."

"Your business here sir?"

"I'm waiting for the train to Portsmouth. I'm told it comes at the 10 o'clock hour."

"Ticket?" asked the fattish one.

I produced my ticket. The fat one grabbed it, sniffing like a hog would old corn.

"What are you doing here Doctor Townsend?" persisted the fattish one.

"I'm waiting for the train."

"In Whitechapel?"

"What are you doing in Whitechapel?" inquired the fattish one.

"You are an American are you not?" he added.

"Yes, I am an American."

"Again, what are you doing here in Whitechapel?"

I inhaled, and then exhaled in preparation for my answer.

"I'm on holiday from New York City, and on occasion offer my services to the poor at London Hospital. I'm a doctor of reputable note in America, and my services are frequently sought after."

"Reputable note?" asked the fattish one.

"Yes, reputable note," I repeated, "and so I travel freely. I've worked with many people. I was even recognized for my service in America's recent war between the states."

The fattish one coughed a laugh of doubt, rolling his eyes. The young cute one looked at me, with his piercing brown eyes. "Have you seen anything that you might consider, odd, or even out of place since you've been sitting here, Doctor Townsend?"

"My ticket please?" I asked the fattish one. I feigned as if thinking about the question.

"Odd you asked?"

The cute constable nodded.

I feigned another thought.

The fattish, married one greasily returned my rail ticket. It was my turn to roll eyes.

"Well, odd may be an unfortunate choice of words when discussing that poor boy." I said, catching their interest.

"What boy?" the fattish one asked over his chins.

"It's that lunatic down the way," I looked past the constables.

"The one on the other side of the depot here. I noticed him not long ago. His name is Aaron from what I've ascertained. We have treated him at London Hospital several times."

I fidgeted. My answer was poorly rehearsed and if I'd been a constable, I would have certainly questioned my honesty.

"Excuse me, may I stand?" I asked.

The fattish one backed away but the young one did not.

His firm stance was comforting.

"Aaron is an unfortunate in many senses of the word, and he's had those misfortunes on full display this morning."

I moved closer to the young constable.

He didn't move aside. I was even more comforted. His eyes were so brown, his lips so moist.

"I've seen him, Aaron, many times up and down these streets, shouting at the horseman and pissing in doorways. It's a scene so familiar here that I doubt anyone takes interests."

I feigned another, better rehearsed thought.

"Aaron was different this time. Strange even for him. Wasn't long ago, perhaps an hour, not more."

I paused to look down the tracks towards the emptiness it revealed.

"How was it different?" the young man asked.

My pause increased the drama.

"I was on my way here to purchase a ticket. The crowd along these streets was the usual. I'd offered a biscuit to a fallen woman and some coins to a mother with children by her side. Mother taught me to care for people regardless of their earthly state."

I paused, wanting my kindness recognized.

"What was different?" the fat one asked instead.

I was affronted at his indifference.

"Well, I was on one side of the street and Aaron was on the opposite corner. I knew he was watching me, but I continued my walk." I pointed to accent my words.

"What was different?" the young one asked again. "Please, sir, it may be important," he insisted.

"Well, when I arrived here, I first sat on the bench on the other side. No sooner had sat than Aaron appeared next to me. I'm generally well aware of my environment, but I must confess Aaron caught me off my guard."

I paused dramatically and took several delicate steps casting a view down the tracks. My eyes pointed to where Aaron always stood.

"I gave him a shilling and a quick blessing, but he just stood there, it was unusual."

"It? What 'it' was so unusual?" asked the fattish one.

"As Aaron stood near me, I did try to ignore him hoping that my shilling would've paid for his departure, but it didn't. He just stood there, swaying and while he swayed I couldn't help but take notice."

"Notice what, you fool? What did you notice?" the fattish one persisted.

I ignored the married one from that point forward and directed all my interest toward the young one with acorn eyes and moist lips.

"I noticed Aaron was licking a knife, right over there," I pointed east.

"A knife?" he asked.

"Yes, a knife, it was long, longer than a carving knife, it looked like one that could've been used at London Hospital," I said brushing his arm.

He didn't move.

"Stolen?" he asked.

"Perhaps stolen, many things come up missing from the London Hospital. If anything can be seen as having value, it will likely be stolen."

"Many of the cities unfortunates come to the hospital to have their illnesses addressed and many come to sleep and many more come to take advantage of the other two," I added.

The fattish married one showed doubt, the young one showed interest.

"The knife was silver and appeared to be pointed at the end. It had to be more than six inches long."

I walked closer to the depot's rear corner. The young one followed me.

"Aaron was standing not far from that furthest bench on the other side there, see the one?" I said lightly touching the elbow of the smoothed skinned young constable.

He nodded.

"He was standing there licking that knife. Chills went up my spine. I've seen much in my years I assure you both but seeing that chilled me. I tossed Aaron another coin and removed myself to back here."

The fattish one had already begun to bounce down toward the rails where my eyes had pointed.

"Understandable sir," the young one said and began to follow his mate.

"Thank you for your time," he said.

I watched his ass.

"Surely he can't be to far from here," I said as he turned away.

Without a farewell both were off to the corner where Aaron was showing a whore what could be had if only he had the desire.

I returned to my seat and crossed my knees right over left and wrists left over right. I'd done well. I'd done my part in making the East End a bit better for all, as another unfortunate would be removed.

"It is a better thing."

CHAPTER FOUR

The removal of Kosminski was an important page in my diary. His story would do wonders in slowing Inspector Littlechild. Aaron's confinement for a lifetime of solitary vices was just a bonus.

The East End was eased when reports and rumors of his capture were spread.

The two constables bounced towards the lunatic while I studiously watched with smugness. I watched them seize Aaron.

He screamed newly chartered words. They had found his crate, and retrieved from it the knife in question. He had only scrambled explanations.

It was a proud moment, as I had paid his fare to a better place. Aaron and I had paid each other's admission. He paid my ride south, and I paid his to Colney Hatch Lunatic Asylum.

I wasn't sad for him. I was proud, in a throat choking way, for what awaited him. It was a better thing for both him and the East End. I reclaimed my seat on the bench.

Others were now waiting for trains of their own, but no one stood close to me.

I've known since that night in the yard of our Rochester home that we all have our roles in life, and Aaron had just played his.

Whores with stained knickers and priests with wounded vestments laughed as Kosminski, a jabbering bread chasing wretch was led to Colney Hatch. There he'd spend his days lost within his vices and the labyrinth of corridors.

My pride overrode my knowing how late the hour had become. The chimes of the East End told me it was ten. The clerk eventually shouted that due to frequent delays, the train would be arriving closer to noon.

I nodded at other frustrated fellow travelers who were gathering on the dock. I let the onlookers admire me for who I was and for what they believed I was. I smiled politely as if I was the focus of a holiday parade; sometimes I waved at empty benches.

It was 12:17 when I took my seat aboard the 10:10 bound for Portsmouth. I helped guide the elderly up the steps of the train and waved a mother ahead of me so she could have the best seat. They would remember me as the embodiment of goodness. I stood at the doorway separating two coaches, and let some passengers smile my way in admiration, while others turned away in shame, disgust or pomposity.

I provided the audience on either side of the aisle a gentle smile of reassurance. I was a great man among common travelers and my goodness would be carried to wherever these commoners carried themselves. They would tell stories of whom they saw and what he was like to be near. My greatness and the reason for my being would spread with little effort.

Portsmouth would be a short ride, supposedly three hours, but most often five or six hours. I sat halfway down the center of the train with more than a seat separating myself from a mother and her disturbed child. I removed my hat and placed it on the seat opposite me alongside my bag. I removed my gloves and with diligence reviewed my fingernails.

The train was silent beneath its generated steam.

I picked my thumbnail.

I turned to gaze out upon the depot's rear dock. The steam puffed, dragon-like. Children played amidst its glow. The faces were scattered, only legs and boots could be seen, one little boy waved my way and I nodded.

The ride to Portsmouth was ample time for just about any scene my mind wished to paint. A fine man once told me never let others tell your story when you can paint them in better detail.

I nestled against the glass.

The train's steam crawled like fingers toward the windows. I heard the voices of those wishing farewell taper off and the muffled shouts of those running behind increase.

I watched wretches running to catch the final calls of the conductor. "How can someone possibly be late for a train that's already running behind schedule?" I shook my head as several such specimens of ineptitude shuffled passed me.

The slow humming train caressed me and my eyes were growing heavy when the conductor or his pungent aid asked for my ticket. I produced it and waited for its return. My eyes returned to sleep's encroachment.

"I'll write my own history," I whispered.

It was September when my fingers tingled. It was a pleasant night with a late summer's air dancing across the East End shit hole."

The lurch of the train woke me briefly.

I nodded back off.

I had offered my service to the poor and destitute at St. Bartholomew's Hospital in London proper for many of the summer hours and now sought to satisfy my own desires.

I was a trained American doctor who offered his reputable services to any person in need of care at any hospital. My talents were God's gift to those needing it. I was always welcome to such environments as St. Bartholomew and even the aforementioned Colney Hatch Lunatic Asylum.

The train mumbled to a full rumble.

My mind danced with what that summer had been. I was a man, free of restraints and full of pride, washing piles of ash off humanity from sea to sea. I was as free as any man could be, and I lived off the kindness or stupidity of those who offered either. I came and went from the best of hotels, paying only with reputation.

I ate in fine sidewalk cafes.

I saw the best operas and Shakespearean portrayals.

I strolled on ginger leaves. I rode in the finest of cabs, and I loved the plumpest of young men.

I had paid my way through the day the only way I knew, by working with the unfortunates.

Over the years I learned the best place to find the needy was their gathering places. If one was hungry for fish, find the fish. If one desired a whore, find the whores. The unfortunates gather in herds, sharing found bread and destroying the weakest among them.

St. Bartholomew's was such a place for their gatherings.

When I first walked through the doors of St. Bartholomew's Hospital, none questioned my skills. I tended to the casually ill and thus was welcomed aboard. I cured as many as possible patting heads and serving them cool water.

The hallways and stairways were beds for countless forgotten pieces of man. The unfortunates who wandered in were a cast of characters from the most colorful of Greek comedies. They were the insane, the drunkards, and unwanted infants. There were the stillborns, and cases of worms, consumption and gonorrhea. They were unfortunate in the full meaning of the word and they'd all come just for me.

While there, I saw one specimen more miserable than many of the rest. She was a round-faced whore with greasy curled locks. She was most certainly, according to my eyes and the comments I'd overheard, stout and excessively unattractive.

This whore was as loud as she was unkempt. Her positive traits were made insignificant by her drunken bellows. When I viewed her as a whole, she did remind me of my dearest mother and that memory was my trigger.

One night I examined that specimen and confirmed her homeliness, disease and stench.

I endeared myself to her that night.

In mid-August I learned her name was Annie Chapman. During my exams of her, she chattered as she lifted her skirt in front of those who cared little. "My pun is as well worn as any of the Queen's studs," she said.

Its smell proved her correct.

I learned that she was a mother and former wife who now drank excessively. Annie had scratched her self-raw from the bites of fleas and unclean men. I imagined though she too had unfilled dreams. She sold her cunt for three pennies at the most and had done so for years.

Annie, when she needed something, returned to see only me. I'd offer kind words, healing ointments and even a shilling at various times. One night, only out of curiosity, I followed her to where she spent her hours, the Crossingham's Lodging House on Dorset Street. I wanted to know about her life but as it turned out it took only one night to learn all I needed to know about Annie Chapman.

Annie had no money so the lodge gave her no bed. She was already well drunk before she left a nearby pub. Annie had begged for a bed telling the man that she was sick, and very hungry. I heard this conversation from across the street.

The doorman had decided Annie's fate. He could've let her in. She was unwell and very undernourished. He chose to follow the meaning of the lodge's rules and turned her into that new September night.

After seeing the scene unfold, I took a gentleman's walk circling Lamb, White Lion, and Brushfield Streets. Not once losing sight of Annie. The houses were close to one another. Intimate tones could be heard as I walked. I crossed Commercial and headed toward a small brewery. Despite her inebriated state and the crowded cobblestone Annie recognized me.

She greeted me by thrusting her gloved hands toward mine. We touched at the fingertips. Her smell was incredulous.

"Doctor, please, I'm bleeding from an itch that won't stop," she said.

I looked at her frame while brushing the tip of my nose with my own glove.

"I am sure you are," I said looking each way, "I'm quite sure the itch is also well rehearsed."

Under guise of a medical examination, I asked Annie to accompany me to a quiet area, well covered by the back of the brewery. I gently touched Annie's elbow and Annie's nature allowed her to welcome any departure to any area for any reason.

I was familiar with the streets, and found the spot that was free from direct view. Its grass was damp allowing for comfort and absorption. The 2am chimes echoed in the cobbled alley. I asked Annie to lie in a manner that was comfortable. She did.

"It is late," she said.

"It is, but I'll know it by touch."

Annie's profession required she be bloomer free. As she lay on the ground, resting on her elbows it was immediately apparent that she was bloomer free. I flipped her apron over onto her stomach. She could have cared less at the view she presented or how the air increased in poor flavor.

I began my examination.

My thumbs pressed her cunt.

My palms rolled up to her stomach, and over to her kidneys. I squeezed them softly at first, then with some force. My professional intimacy resulted in more than casual conversation.

"Don't mind the smell sir, not many have of late," she said.

"It may very well be the death of you," I said.

"A pecker pleases me," she laughed.

"A pecker will be your death," I said.

I felt my face grow in temperature.

"It looks worse than it did just last week. You must've been more active than your girlish charm admits to."

"Perhaps a cock or two," she admitted.

"Yes--perhaps."

"Annie, on your last visit to St. Bartholomew's I gave you some pills. Have you been using them?"

"I have them," Annie said, handing me the envelope from the previous week, "I couldn't make sense of the letters. I don't read much. No need to read doing what I do."

I took the envelope. I'd forgotten the instructions I provided, but knew they had to be simple enough.

I brushed my glove above her pubic area.

The damage done to her was extensive. Both her body and her soul were uncared for and were uncaring in return.

I pushed her pubic area with tenderness.

"Like it?" she said through flatulence.

I pushed harder.

"Feel free to take a fuck Mr. Frank," Annie said.

My face grew in color as the night darkened.

"Best keep the voices down, as some may grow curious," I said.

My hand pushed into her pubic area.

"That tingles," Annie stated.

The damage was done. Perhaps she had only months to live anyway. Perhaps the same damage she granted countless willing others would claim them too and in-turn many others their fate. The final numbers couldn't be imagined.

"I see some blood," I said, "Are you menstruating?"

"Don't know," she said.

I continued to rub her pubic area. Other than her babbling, there were only distant voices but we were safe for the moment. If there'd been a chime I hadn't heard one.

I reached for my bag.

"I have some liniment that might relieve the itch, but you must let it do its work. There are several ways to heal, but you must let them work."

Annie rested on her elbows.

I fumbled through some tools of my trade. I focused my eyes, seeing through the growing darkness. I tried to invent a sentence that would paint my opinion of the moment, but I failed.

Annie waited there in the damp soil, resting on her elbows, her womanly charms pointed toward the sky without shame.

I added slight pressure to her pubic area, and again Annie feigned a loving moan.

She turned her face slowly toward me.

Her look, which was one discernable through the darkness, was one of sleepiness and even in her case, for a brief moment there was a hint of beauty in her eyes.

Fuck John Keats and his words:

"What can I do to drive away remembrance from my eyes? For they have seen, aye an hour ago, my brilliant Queen! Touch has a memory. O say, love say, what can I do to kill it and be free..."

I gave her a half-crooked smile. She returned it.

My smile widened as with a swish of history, a slice of silver crossed Annie's throat. Her smile faded and her elbows collapsed beneath her. The end of my cut was no less desperate that its first brush. Annie Chapman gurgled her final moments into the mud behind the brewery.

I heard only Keats however.

"My muse had wings, and ever ready to take her course."

"Now I'll take my fuck," I said.

Her blood spilled into the brewery's mud. Not in a gush, nor a spray. It simply seemed to roll to the ground. It spread evenly.

I tied a handkerchief around her neck. I adjusted it perhaps a little tighter than she would have wished. My cut wasn't straight, for she had slouched before it was complete. The blood streamed through the handkerchief though at a slower rate.

I dipped my fingers into the pooled blood that settled on her cleavage and tasted it. My lips quivered in delight.

The taste revived my senses.

I hungered in ways in long forgotten.

I needed more.

I cut where I had rubbed.

The smell was glorious. I tasted the aroma from her spoiled loins. Mud absorbed the blood that her cunt had remaining. I rubbed her belly just above the pubic area to speed its journey. It was warm and slow as the body was relieved of air and piss.

The smell!

God the smell was glorious!

Annie shit, and to my disgust that's what splattered my mouth.

I had to swallow, and then I made a swift cut, one that was half a circle. I reached inside the incision and removed portions of her abdominal wall and the well-tucked organs I had studied. The hole she sold for pennies no longer of mattered so I ripped it free and laid it near her right shoulder. It was no longer threatening.

"This will feed the voices," I said through my dream.

I butchered her like a hog.

I butchered her as I had been taught.

That slaughterhouse nearby would serve me. I would feed the hogs a hog all of there own. I'd removed most of her uterus and bagged chosen pieces of her gut to serve as a stew for the homeless.

I heard a chime.

The time was close and more voices than I wished were nearby. I gave the uterus a hard sniff and licked it with the tip of my tongue, then packed and wrapped the meat for the hungry.

As I worked, I studied the scene behind the brewery.

A pose would be needed.

That September night filled my dreams as the train rolled on.

I was half-awake and wanted the dream to continue.

With a wink and a wish, I returned to full sleep.

Annie's shit caked my chin and lips. I swallowed it once my lips were moistened. It was nearing a more agreeable hour when I managed to remove Annie's body.

I gave the street a quick glance and saw nothing that would interrupt me. I'd move her down into a yard of a Hanbury residence, just shy of the steps. I waited, hid within the shadows until everything was silent. After several moments I was convinced that I hadn't been heard nor seen and could leave casually amidst the approaching morning vendors.

I placed her on her back, her head just shy of the bottom step, her feet pointed toward a distant shed. I draped her left arm across her breast and lifted her legs. Her morals were displayed to any passing footman. She was posed as if still in want of rusted coins.

Once I'd laid her for all to see, a model as it were, I removed a brass ring that was well in place on her left hand. As a master artist might ad sprinkles of white to a blue sky I added final touches of my own with my brush a knife.

"A final touch here."

"A final touch there."

...Thud!

My head jarred against the train's window.

"A final touch," the words lowered in tone.

"A final touch," they were quieter.

"A final touch," I mumbled as my head bounced off the trains chilling glass. The stiffness and the chill had jarred me fully awake.

"Umber and hue, a dash of love for a dash of dew," drool hung on my chin, so I let it drip.

The reasonably fresh air awakened my senses.

My pulse was more than casual.

My eyes stumbled open.

I'd left Annie to destiny and I carried a bag food for the hungry unfortunates.

I was a good man.

I fed the hungry.

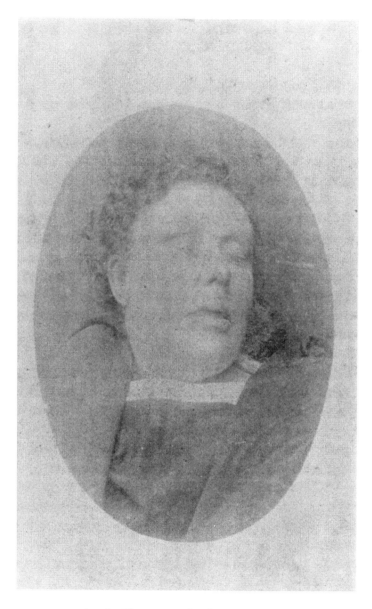

Annie Chapman in the mortuary.

The train rattled.

We were a good hour into our trip to Portsmouth. The assortment of fellow travelers hardly varied. I saw an undignified face looking my way.

Our eyes locked.

"You talk in your sleep," he said quickly.

"My mouth outruns my mind at times, I do hope you enjoyed my tales," I replied.

He returned to the passing trees, one eye remained on me.

I too took notice of the trees, remembering how I left Hanbury Street that night. Perhaps one cobbler showed interest, he might have even seen me. Quickly I returned to the area surrounding St. Bartholomew's Hospital not out of fear but out of pure lust.

I'd forgotten what lust had tasted like but Annie Chapman's salt brought it back. That lust brought me back to when I ate worms as a boy. Tasting Annie's womb reminded me of the lust I had after eating my father's flesh. It was a lust, a hunger that I had been trying to feed low these many years. It was so grand and I've never been able to find such a sensation again.

The train rolled on.

I held my pocket watch, caressing its decorative casing. Flipping it open, it read 3:30. The scenery, the trees and fence posts looked familiar, but in the South of England they always do. Perhaps an hour or a bit more and we'd be in Portsmouth.

The undignified man still watched me. I sniffed in his direction. He was odorless. I was growing bitter, not only at his stare, but also at the others who'd soon take credit for my efforts. Sadler, Druitt, Ostrog. Who were they? They were just faceless characters with fantastical names drudged up from the depths of some failed investigator's imagination.

There were those who'd written letters to the authorities, claiming their hands did the work. They were the unfortunates who deeply, deeply wanted a role of notoriety in life before the East End consumed them. They were the insane that sang to the alley cats and who ate the elements of their own voided bowels. Many in public office believed these lunatics and their ramblings. It was moments like that, stories like that, which made me burn in rage. Having a lunatic, an unfortunate take credit for the work of a wise man consumed me.

The bad were good, the good bad, and the lunatics were geniuses. I was bitter at the rumors and at how I was seen. I was called evil. I was called a monster.

I was fully awake now.

Once I recalled that bitterness, I was taken back even further. I flipped the pocket watch open and saw that it was only 3:58pm; only a handful of minutes had dissipated since I last looked. I had time to retrieve and fan to full flare more of histories glowing embers.

CHAPTER FIVE

"For time at last sets all things even
And if we do but watch the hour,
There never yet was human power
Which could evade, if unforgiven,
The patient search and vigil long
Of him who treasures up a wrong."

I was slumped, with my nature hidden by ugliness.

"Does time set its own vigil?" I asked the smoked glass of the rail-car.

"Can we evade times pursuit?"

I was curious for the answers.

Should I hold as strong a vigil as does time?

That wrong done to me was some twenty-five years ago burned its vigil's light.

Lies and accusing eyes had followed me since I shit my father's thumb.

I swayed to unheard tunes.

The eyes of my fellow travelers grew wide.

Why do people judge those who only want to do the world good?

Do the lazy condemn the worker?

Do the lonely condemn the lovers?

Do the fat condemn the slim?

Do the evil condemn the good?

Do the whores chastise the virgin?

I was judged by a world that had succumbed to everything base and forever fallen. I wanted to make it a better place, but was called a monster for my efforts.

The train rattled on as the undignified man kept his cautious watch. I watched him watch me.

My anger grew.

My feet began to spin.

The trees shook at their roots as the train clicked over the rails.

I could shake most of man's tones but one affront I couldn't shake from me.

My wisdom had come at the hands of tremendous pain. When I'd left Sophia Street in the midst of a Rochester winter I lived among the rats until I was showed a polite hand by Albert Quackenbush, an owner of a canal boat. He had known my father, and showed sympathy toward me when I asked for food.

He taught me the magic of drink.

Drink taught me the magic of imagination.

Imagination showed me other lands.

I worked those canal boats until I was shamed by one night's indiscretion. It was a shameful curiosity that would become my animal lust.

I left the boats.

As a boy I mastered skills called manipulation, flirting my way from port to port and teacher-to-teacher. As I grew I learned to love the taste of men.

I was at an age where the motherly types no longer called me cute. I would either be chased for vagrancy, or acquire a skill to avoid such accusations. That skill was lustful indiscretions. It was my flirtatious ways and moist lips that warmed me on cold nights.

I was too weak for the farms.

I was too delicate for the mills. But I was not too delicate for the mill men.

I have never forgotten that day when I was given a trade, the ability to cure. I was aimless in life, and I was called a dirty young boy devoid of any education. Many saw me as a filthy, orphaned, a bastard son of a whore. The words went on and on, but my skin even at that young age was stronger than most ships hulls.

Lawrence, my brother, fed me and he allowed me to sleep in a shed designed for his gardening tools.

During the few warmer months as a pubescent boy I was introduced permanently to the trade I practice, and to the type of company I now prefer.

I could earn pennies a day for selling papers or apples, and I'd earn five when providing warmth to nameless drunkards. It wasn't much of a debate as to which profession I'd regularly pursue as a boy.

I'd grown older than what my years actually bore out and soon I became a barker for a small arcade on the West side of the Rochester. The days of spring and summer produced many hours of work so the owner of the arcade gave me a hidden mat for my nights.

I'd sell tickets for what shows and games were behind half opened doors. Faces were filled with baked pie and childish grins as penny dolls were won for many times their value. Several small vendors popped up as the arcades patrons increased. There were those selling pies, those with fruit, and even those selling women to those who sold pie and fruit. One Sunday afternoon, while slicing pie for an elderly Negro woman, I cut the better part of my left thumb.

Blood was everywhere.

The vendors laughed at my anxiety.

I wrapped my finger in whatever I could find, and returned to work within moments. I couldn't lose out on the handful of change I was given after each day. I worked through the cut's growing pain, and after several days it began to sour. The wound was kept filthy, like the rest of me. It was red and swollen with puss, which oozed out when I touched it. As the pain grew I held it further from me in the course of my labor.

"Boy you're loosin' that thumb of yours," the owner said through his laughter.

"Go see the man out back, he'll fix you up good."

His emphasis on the word good worried me.

Behind the arcade was the office of a Dr. Lispenard. His first name was a mystery. He is the man to whom I owed my life and ass. He was the impetus for the direction my life has taken. He told me I could be what I was destined to be, and that I'd be doing the world an injustice if I failed to do otherwise. "Follow the path you're given boy," Lispenard said.

My thumb was festering. I saw a huddled group of people behind the Doctor's office. There were three women, the youngest one doubled over and bloody. Further out back near the adjacent field were two men standing near a burn barrel.

The doctor, stood at the doorway giving directions to the men watching the scene. He welcomed the young woman with the words, "Bitch get in here!"

She was distraught.

His words were less than gentle.

I stood at a more than necessary distance, holding my injured hand.

The doctor, seeing my injury was minor, asked me to come in. Reluctantly I did as he asked. The older women turned the care of the younger one over to the doctor, and left the yard without hesitation. The young woman was with child and bleeding through her garments. The doctor asked me to shut the thin door behind me as I entered. I did so.

I watched, wide-eyed, as the woman, not much more than a young girl actually, was laid upon a cot nearest a counter filled with unlabeled bottles.

The seconds were passing at a tremendous rate.

"Have a seat boy," Lispenard pointed to a chair.

I did as he directed.

Lispenard was a mammoth man. Natural oil stuck his brown hair to his skull firmly, and a bloodied, stained apron wrapped his torso. I watched Lispenard push the knees of the young woman up. Her face was filled with terror. She saw me. With scissors Lispenard sliced her garments as if they were wrapping paper meant for the butcher.

Other than that of my mother's, that young woman's cunt was the first I'd seen. It was bleeding like many of the suckling pigs I'd butchered. She screamed, cried and shit uncontrollably.

"A young whore deserves this!" Lispenard said through clenched teeth.

There was a pause of several seconds.

"Are you talking to me?" I asked nervously.

"They deserve this blood for their behavior," he added.

Was he talking to me, her, or to the air?

It was all happening so fast.

I watched as he spread her hole with the thumbs of both hands. He spread her skin to the point where her screams increased. I stared in wonderment for even in the dimly lit quarters I could see a small head emerging from between her legs.

Watching her pain made my thumb hurt less. The nature of the scene made me ready to leave rather than watch what was taking place. I stood as to leave.

"Sit boy!" Lispenard looked at me as if I had no choice.

I sat.

The doctor groped and twisted the girls' skin.

"You're of an age boy where you need to see this. You need to see what happens when a woman's flesh is traded for a bowl of corn meal."

I watched from the chair.

The young woman grew white with pain. She gurgled vomit. In short time she fell unconscious as Lispenard with no gentleness thrust his hand between her legs.

"Come here boy!" Lispenard barked.

I stood shakily and approached the cot that held the young woman, and Dr. Lispenard.

"Hold this!" He directed.

He handed me a small bag made of soiled canvas. It smelled wet.

I looked at the young woman's face. She appeared older, more mature when I first saw her outside the doctor's door. Up close she was young, perhaps only a year or two older than I.

She faded between sleep and screams.

She began to whimper. Lispenard pulled from the canvas bag something resembling gripping tools. Metal fingers. The doctor studied them briefly before he thrust them inside the young woman. Through her sleep she let out a prolonged moan and whispered something that I didn't want to hear.

He twisted the tool.

"God damn it get out here!" He shouted between brown clenched teeth.

"God damn it bitch!"

He pushed her knees further apart and higher.

"Mommy!" The young girl cried.

Lispenard slapped her as soon as she'd spoken those words.

"It's too late to call for your mother dear daughter, you should've done that long ago."

I stood adjacent the bed holding the canvas bag listening to his indistinguishable words and to her soft cries growing stronger.

Was she the doctor's daughter?

Did I hear correctly?

"I watched the doctor push the metal fingers further between the young girl's legs. Blood and shit spurted past the small head.

"Got it!" He shouted.

He tugged and it came out.

Lispenard forced me to take a closer look.

I saw the tiniest of arms.

It was twisted.

The young girl, whimpering, asked for a mother who wasn't there. She reached for my arm.

I pulled back.

"I warned you about your mother, " Lispenard barked.

The young woman with feeble words shared feeble thoughts.

The tiny fingers that had been pulled from between her legs were moving. They opened and closed as one.

Lispenard reached his hand between the young woman's legs and in a quick tug pulled it free.

It was a baby girl.

The young woman moaned in relief.

"This piece of shit!" he said holding the baby by the feet. "No one will know of it!"

He flung the baby toward the end of the cot but it abruptly stopped. It was still attached it to the young woman. Lispenard grabbed the bag I held and retrieved a long knife. In a slick, quick move he sliced the attaching chord, wrapping the mothers end with a piece of cloth.

The baby lay covered in blood.

It was choking. What natural color I saw appeared to be bluish. The baby had only one full arm. The other hand was shrunken and hung from the shoulder. Its face was pushed in. One leg seemed wider than the other.

"What's wrong with it?" I asked.

"It's a whore's work!" Lispenard said.

"A whore young or old leaves shit like this behind."

I looked at the baby. It gasped.

The young woman's blood continued to flow.

"A whore's work?" I asked.

"Yes, a whore's work! This unformed piece is what happens when a woman gives her virtue in unnatural ways."

Lispenard appeared relieved and breathless from his work. He dismounted the cot and took the baby by the feet tossing it into a box nearest the door. He covered it with some bloody rags he'd used in the course of his work.

Lispenard rolled torn sheets and stuffed them between the legs of the young woman. She jerked forward, moaning the word daddy.

Lispenard grimaced at her words.

"Whore! Nothing but a young whore!"

Lispenard shoved her legs together binding them tightly above the knees with other torn sheets.

"Daddy!" She whimpered.

"This will stop the blood bitch."

Her words faded.

"Bring that box here boy," Lispenard said.

I dragged the box holding the baby closer to the cot. Without a thought Lispenard thrust his boot into it over and over again pushing with tremendous force.

The box was stilled.

Without a change in tone Lispenard said, "Boy take this box of waste out to the burn barrel."

"No sir," I said abruptly.

"Do it now!" Lispenard pushed me toward the door.

I looked inside the box. There was no sound. I could see a tiny foot half covered by a stained rag.

"Do it now!" Lispenard barked again.

He had such a demeanor that I knew I should do as he demanded. I picked up the box looking at Lispenard and the young woman simultaneously.

I moved toward the door opening it with my foot.

I saw the two men warming their hands at the burn barrel. They watched me watch them. The barrel was giving off a pungent smoke.

With a firm chin and a head held low, I walked past the rude comments of onlookers. I approached the barrel. The two men were interested in me, not the crate. I peaked over the rim of the barrel. It smelled spoiled.

The two men eyed me through whiskered grins.

I shook the box like I was sifting for gold. There was no further sound but I could feel it rolling from side to side. I hesitated just a final moment and then tossed the box into the barrel to a welcoming flash of spark and ash. I turned around to see Lispenard watching me from the door.

He made sure I did what was asked.

He was pleased.

"Throw in some kindling," one of the men said.

The wood was piled behind the barrel. I added some of the smaller pieces as instructed and fanned the flames till they licked the barrel's rim.

"Let me take a look at your thumb," the doctor said as he wiped his hands on an apron stained brown.

"Mr. Barkley needs me at the arcade. I sell pie for him," I said.

Lispenard watched me.

"You can work here boy," Lispenard said, "I need help and I'll teach you a trade, a skill. The arcade won't. Let me see that hand like I said. It smelled bad when you came in."

Lispenard turned and walked back inside.

I again hesitated.

Slowly I made my way back past the snickering drunkards. I crossed his wooden threshold. The young woman was pale and breathing softly. Lispenard was sitting at a table at the far wall.

"Never mind her, let me see your thumb," he barked again.

I went over to the table. He grabbed my thumb in stern service.

"It's grossly infected," he declared.

I grimaced as he poked the wound with his thumbnail.

"Is she going to be all right?" I asked.

"Don't worry about her. If it's God's will, she'll be fine."

"What's your name?" Lispenard asked as he squeezed.

I grimaced.

"I've seen you working for the fat man up front. Begging for a poor man's pennies. It takes advantage of the lame of mind. Trickery is all. Gambling is all," he lectured.

"Francis is my name," I said.

He fidgeted with my hand.

"I'll call you Frank, that is a man's name," he said.

Lispenard gripped my thumb tightly and squeezed from the bottom up.

I tried to pull away.

He pulled all the harder and squeezed even more.

A thick yellowish puss squirted out from beneath a worn out scab. I gasped, as much in pain as in relief. Lispenard squeezed again until the puss became clear. He reached for the bag, retrieving a small jar of something resembling grass. He wrapped my thumb.

"Keep this in place and your thumb will be saved. If you remove it we'll be burning it too."

I watched the girl as he talked.

Lispenard watched me watching her.

"The whore is my daughter," he said.

"What's her name?" I asked.

"Elizabeth. Pay her no mind," he said again.

"Where's her mother?"

Lispenard ignored that question.

"Frank, if you want to earn some money clean this room for me. I must run some errands."

He stood, not allowing me time to answer. With some quick instructions he pointed to places where certain things belonged. He showed me how and told me when to place wet rags upon the young woman's head.

I was hired without agreement.

The doctor grabbed his bag, and told me he'd be back before the hour grew late.

"Burn this as well," he pointed to another crate before closing the door behind him. I was left alone with the moaning Elizabeth.

So much had occurred in such a short period of time. This was an office and home as well. There was a second room, which I only saw after Lispenard departed. A canvas separated the second room from the main one.

Elizabeth danced between sleep and confused chatter. I had little desire to see what that second room was like, particularly if it resembled the one in which I now stood.

I busied myself.

I burned the second box as he'd requested. I returned to the room and shuffled chairs and boxes to other places. I made it look far neater than what it was when I had appeared.

I had decided to return to the arcade. However, no sooner had I made that choice than I heard a sharp, painful moan from the young woman.

She asked for some water.

I ignored her at first.

"Please, may I have some water?" Elizabeth asked again.

I found a cup and bucket on a nearby shelf.

The water smelled old, but I dipped the cup and returned to the cot.

She took several drinks.

Her brow and neck had beads of sweat.

I found a damp rag and placed it on her forehead.

"Thank you," she said.

"You're welcome. I have to go," I said.

"Please don't go," she said meekly. "Stay."

I paused in my answer.

I was torn.

I was powerless over my actions. I pulled a chair to sit next to the cot.

"I'll stay for awhile but I work for the arcade up front. I'm sure the fat man Barkley is looking for me."

"I've seen you there. What's your name?" She asked.

"I'm Francis, Frank I mean. Call me Frank," I said nervously.

"I'm Elizabeth."

"I know. I heard the doctor say it."

"He's my father," she said.

"Your father?" I asked already knowing the answer.

"Yes."

It was difficult to understand how a man could see his daughter as Lispenard had seen his. It was even more difficult to comprehend how a grandfather could do to a grandchild as he had done to his.

"Your father's a doctor?" I asked.

She was silent.

"Where's your mother?"

"I don't know. Father told me she was a whore, that she liked men, he said she left us to follow her lust. We've lived here since," she added.

I dragged my eyes slowly around the main room, ending at the canvas curtain.

Silence had won the moment. What could I possibly say to her after all I'd seen?

Shouts came from outside.

"Should I wait until your father comes back?"

"Yes please wait. Where's my baby?" she asked quickly.

I skipped her question and stood up.

"He wanted me to clean up," I said heading for any corner that looked askew.

"Where's my baby?" she asked again.

I moved and shuffled several boxes, some unwashed dishes and a good-sized stack of soiled garments. There was also dried, caked mud and paper used to wipe oneself clean. I boxed it all.

"Frank," she said through a sharper moan.

I was close enough to escape her questions. I grabbed the box and entered the family quarters.

"You shouldn't go in there," Elizabeth said.

It was as if I were hit in the face with a branding iron. The odor was as bad as anything I'd ever encountered.

My knees buckled.

I dropped the box and vomited what I could into the pile. My spew was clear. I wiped the splash from my arms with a red stained apron.

My eyes were watery, as I'd flushed to the point of producing tears. The back of my throat was convulsing. I slowly collapsed to the second knee, wiping vomit as an excuse for my weakness. The smell was something that had no definition and as hard as I tried to escape it, it was borderless.

"Frank?" the young woman called. "You shouldn't be in there."

I sighed once, then a second time much deeper. I gathered in courage and a hint of fresh air. Closing my eyes, I stood up, opening them only when I reached my full height. I saw the top of a chest of drawers. There was a small chipped mirror above it and atop it some scattered personal items.

I felt a cold chill encircling my neck.

"Frank?" Elizabeth repeated.

"I'm here," I said through half a gag.

To my left I saw a table with three chairs, the fourth was the one in which I sat next to the young woman's bed. The table was sparse except for a prominent oil lamp. There were shelves holding numerous books behind stacks of additional crates.

On the west wall was a single bed soiled beyond description. A small woman's silhouette hung over the headboard and to the left side of the bed was another table as long as the wall itself. It was covered with canvas sewn together.

"Frank?" her voice was stronger.

I remember that smell even after all these years. I was a boy growing strong with formidable nerves. I had seen much, and the unseen voices had been with me long before I entered the view of Lispenard. That morning those same voices protected me as I crept throughout the room.

I had to do as the doctor wished. I reached for a corner of the canvas to uncover the shelf with the hopes of organizing it. Working would help me avoid the young woman's questions. If I hurried and did what the doctor wanted done, I could disappear before he returned.

I took the canvas and in one toss pealed it off the table. Glass containers, large and small covered it from one end to the next. Some appeared that with even the slightest of nudges they'd crash to the floor.

The canvas fell sloppily upon the floor.

I studied the table, top to bottom.

Beneath it there was a shelf suspended upon bricks, it too held jars large and small. It was an odd scene. The jars, as best as I could tell in the dimly lit room, contained water of different colors, some dark and some rather clear.

"Frank, where are you?"

"I'm here, I'm just cleaning," I said.

It took a moment but as my eyes grew accustomed to the scene, my nose took over. It was these jars that cast forth the odors. The stink stung my eyes.

Now I was curious.

The first jar was an arms length from me so I picked it up with my false bravado. The liquid splashed slightly on my wrist as it skipped across the bottom of the table. The jar was heavier than I thought, and something in its bottom moved from side to side.

I moved it to my eyes in hopes of improving my view in the scant light. The light was very poor though and all I could see was a small-encapsulated form. Maybe it was a fish; perhaps this is how the doctor preserved food. As I came to think twice about the scene the main ingredient to the room's stink was the odor of fish.

I returned the jar to the table and resumed cleaning. I cleaned the table and the top of the chest of drawers. I organized and stacked and shuffled the many crates that were throughout the room. There were several piles of damp, moist clothes, some his, some hers. Then the question of what to do with the bed arose. It was an old mattress, homemade. It was dirty and stained from everything that could produce dirt and stink.

I walked to the right side of the bed and saw, tucked between the mattress and a small stand, another box. This one was different. It contained personal items that only a woman would posses.

"Frank, I think you should come back in here," Elizabeth said.

A closer look showed me the clothes were met for a small woman, a girl, and a young girl. Did they belong to Elizabeth? Did her and her father share the same bed? Those questions created others that I couldn't bare to think of. I kicked the box back to where I'd found it. Ignoring it would be best.

A vicious cold chill gripped my neck. The moment was just too much. I had to leave. I went to the wall of books and picked one. I thumbed the pages not able to read the title or the contents. I did the same to a second and a third. Then I firmly shoved the row of books closer together. I had to leave.

"Frank?" she called.

"I'm coming," I shouted back.

I turned to leave the small backroom and swallowed a gasp of bad air out of freight. Lispenard was standing at the curtain. My mouth hung open slightly. His eyes didn't blink nor did they move from me.

"I was cleaning as you wished sir," I said.

"I'll leave now I have to get back to the arcade."

"Curious are you boy?" he asked from the doorway.

"Daddy, don't," said Elizabeth.

"I was just cleaning, I hope I did well."

"There's plenty to burn. I see you haven't touched those crates yet," Lispenard said pointing over his shoulder.

He was blocking the doorway and I couldn't pass.

"I'll take them with me when I leave."

He was watching me as if I were his prey.

"Forgive me if I did what I wasn't supposed to do. I met no harm," I said.

"Are you curious young man?" he asked with a softer demeanor.

"Let me burn the boxes then I must return to the arcade or I'll lose my job."

I pushed my way past Lispenard. I grabbed the crates in question. Hurrying about, I opened the front door with my boot.

"There's a couple other things I wish you to do once you return," Lispenard said following me.

"Fuck," I whispered as I hurried out the door.

I could hear Lispenard panting for my return. I approached the burn barrel, and without a look inside, set the boxes down. I tossed in rags, papers and broken pieces of wood. Again I was met with a flash of ash and licking sparks.

The sparks slowly grew into a healthy flame and I put the boxes as a whole into the barrel one after another. I brushed my hands on my week old worn shirt. I turned to head back to the arcade, ignoring the form of Lispenard in the doorway.

"Fuck this job," I whispered.

"Boy I need you in here," Lispenard said before I managed a half-dozen steps.

"I clearly said that I have work for you here if you want it. I'll pay you more than what that fat man out front can, and I'll give you a trade. Come here," he said after a pause.

I watched the corner of the building. I knew his eyes hadn't left me. I saw the street though from a distance. I was tempted to run.

"Let's eat and we can talk about it. If you say no, I'll write a note to the fat man saying your wound was more serious. That should allow you to return to your job, assuming he's a decent man of course."

I was nervous, and yet curious.

"Will you pay me more for the work I've already done?" I asked.

I saw him reach into his pocket. He tossed a coin about half way between the door and me. I stepped forward and smiled at the half-dollar. It would take three days or more for me to earn this at the arcade.

"I'll pay you that each day you work for me," Lispenard said.

"What will I have to do?" I asked looking at the coin.

"I'll teach you a trade, you learn and you work and you will get that amount of money each day. Come in and we'll eat."

In several slow steps, like a shy dog walking toward a piece of tossed meat, I walked back toward the door. My memory rattled, as much as the train to Portsmouth did.

I was no longer a boy with Lispenard, but a doctor of reputable note returning home.

In a flash of time I was back in the midst of my journey to a land long lost. Portsmouth was only minutes away. I remembered that those days with Lispenard sold my soul and triggered my nature in a way that can never be told using the best of words.

CHAPTER SIX

As I considered Lispenard's offer the growing chance of rain encouraged me to choose food over curiosity.

Lispenard held the door as I entered the room ducking beneath his arm. Elizabeth smiled as I returned.

He told me to sit and I sat.

Lispenard performed tasks in the rear room. He called me and I bolted up. We sat at the table sharing bread and raw potatoes. Elizabeth slept.

"Will she get better?" I asked.

"She'll be fine, pay her no mind, boy. Nature will see to her."

He watched me eat. My face grew red at the embarrassment from being ravenous in front of strangers.

"I have to return to the arcade," I said again.

Lispenard shoved the plate of bread nearer to me.

" I'll tell you again that I'll give you a skill, medicine. It'll take practice and you must have some desire to learn. My father believed that there is no illness that can't be made better by nature and what the world produces. He believed nature could cure the ills man produces."

I ate over his unique words.

"Your hand, does it itch?" he asked.

I hadn't noticed but the pain I had experienced earlier was now just a throb.

"Yes, it itches a little, it doesn't hurt as much," I admitted.

"That itch means it's being cured. It's healing. What I placed on your wound is produced by trees and it's healing you."

"Those books there, all those books on the shelves will teach you things and so will I. But it's practice on the sick that will teach you the most. He paused, "Do you want to learn?"

The bread was fresh. It was soft and I ate as much as was placed in front of me. Lispenard's words were heard, but they were only noise until I was ready to unscramble them.

"Books are opinions on views based on suggestions made from suppositions. They're practical and they offer blueprints in their unique way but it is practice that makes the hands and mind undeniable tools of expertise."

My hunger weakened to Lispenard's brilliant use of words.

"Eat all you wish," he said.

I followed his orders.

He retrieved several books and pointed to important pages holding marked diagrams and sentences. He was excited.

"Daddy?" The young girl called from the next room.

He ignored her first call but responded impolitely to her second.

"Bitch!" Lispenard slammed the book shut and vanished to her call.

I glanced at the books he'd set before me while he and Elizabeth shared some unpleasant moments. I reached for another potato.

My stomach was being filled, and I now believed that I'd made the right choice by not returning to the arcade. I could be taken care of here. I could learn, eat and be paid all while readying myself to save the world of the sick and the unfortunate. "This time, this place, this very moment was meant just for me," I whispered to the spud.

Lispenard returned throwing the curtain shut behind him.

"A little bitch she is," he said.

"How old is she?" I asked.

"Old enough for men," he said.

I paused in mid-chew.

I swallowed a piece of potato slowly and wondered had he fucked his own daughter? Why was there just one bed? He watched me over his reinvigorated words and I watched him over the bread I held in both hands.

"Are you curious, young man?" Lispenard asked.

I nibbled my bread.

"Are you curious for more than just bread?" Lispenard asked.

I nodded.

"Elizabeth has replaced her mother in every possible way," he admitted.

"She is too simple to know anything else," he added.

I chewed my bread. Was he the father of that baby?

He returned the books to the shelf as his demeanor changed.

"If you wish, you may return here in the morning and we'll begin. Tonight sleep wherever can and tomorrow we'll prepare a place for you with us."

I stood assuming our evening had ended.

"May I take the rest of the bread?"

"You may."

"Thank you," I said.

Lispenard had his back to me, turned in either shame or rage.

I left nodding a good-bye to Elizabeth.

It left amidst a growing drizzle. Where would I sleep? I couldn't return to the arcade.

The two men still warmed their hands at the burn barrel. The flames were of good strength. I walked around to the front of the building where I could see the arcade. The hour was growing late. There was a crowd laughing seemingly appreciating the dreary weather. There was a new boy doing what I had done.

I would return to the shed behind my brother's home for one more night, Lawrence was a gardener and I slept where he kept his tools. I would take a good walk down State Street then a shorter one on Dustin.

I would need just one more night there.

The rain grew heavier as I walked to my night in the shed. I needed to walk about two miles in it. Lawrence and I were never close, for he'd left our home as soon as he could. He remembered me though, he wasn't always kind, but he was occasionally generous.

In less than an hour I was in the shed. An old blanket upon the ground was more or less my nest.

That night I slept well.

My wound itched in the worse of ways but I did as Lispenard suggested and withheld scratching. I had seen Lawrence as I approached the shed. We nodded to one another. That evening as I neared sleep he brought me a plate and knocked to let me the food was outside. I took the plate and ate out of appreciation and not need.

My sleep appeared to run its course dreamlessly. The moon completed its term and the early morning chill woke me. I stood and pissed in the furthest corner of the shed. In hopes that the doctor was sincere, I grabbed an old bag and tossed in some persistent possessions. On my way out I passed Lawrence on his way to collect his tools for the day. We nodded in politeness. I'd never see him again.

It was a cold walk back to Lispenard's. My sleepiness made it seem longer than what it was. I approached State Street from a better angle to avoid the arcade. I rounded the back of a row of buildings and saw the same two men at the burn barrel.

"Back are you, boy?" one asked, hiding a snicker.

The barrel's flames licked loudly.

I knocked at Lispenard's door and waited briefly before I followed up with another. Lispenard opened it without words and I entered to see the cot was empty.

Where was Elizabeth?

"Set your things by the cot, it'll be yours when there's no other need of it," Lispenard said.

I set my bag down and looked with a circled snout at the cot. It was filthy, stained in many indescribable ways.

"We'll boil it," he said, seeing my eyes.

I nodded kicking my bag underneath the cot.

"Get started by ridding this side of the house of all these crates, I've no need of any of them."

I nodded again looking where he pointed.

"The bitch will stay in back," he said.

I wanted to impress the doctor, so I took to moving the boxes as quickly as I could. Perhaps I moved too fast for I dropped more than I held on to.

The morning sped by at a fair rate, with frequent trips to the burn barrel. I didn't know what was being destroyed. I didn't care either. The flames popped and snapped as it fed on the tossed fuel.

My first morning employed by Lispenard was filled with cleaning duties. There were no visits by the injured or ill. I didn't see Elizabeth, since the front room demanded all of my attention. A time or two I did hear her call my name but I ignored her.

I ate in mid-afternoon. At that hour the doctor was called away by the desperate pleas of a young boy. I saw no water and my thirst was becoming an issue. I entered the rear room in hopes of finding something to drink.

Elizabeth was asleep when I entered.

They did share the same bed.

I didn't see a water bucket. She called my name as I turned to leave.

"Hi Frank," she said through a sleep heavy voice.

"Where can I get something to drink?" I asked, turning her way.

She was pale and rested deep within the rags of bedding.

"The bucket is there near the chest."

I found it close to being dry.

"It's empty," I said.

"I figured so. Go outside to the right and past the row of houses there is a well everyone uses."

I offered her what remained in the bucket, but she refused.

I left to refill the water bucket. It needed a washing too, for there was a layer of slime roaming around its rim. I passed several small homes with porches holding as many babies as chickens. There I found the well.

I washed the bucket, and the slime seemed to vanish. After refilling it I returned to the doctor's office to find Lispenard waiting at the table in the back room. The smell of the room had changed noticeably. It was sharp and traveled easily.

"Let me see the water," he said.

I handed him the bucket.

The doctor was preparing something and needed the water more than I need a drink.

"You may clean that bed the best you can," he said.

I was understandably uneasy. I'd seen what occurred in it yesterday and as I looked at the cot I still saw sticky damp pools of blood and shit. I had slept in worse places though. I took a rag and patted dry the remaining moisture, smearing some of it in. I flipped it over. It was worse on the other side.

The doctor held a bottled concoction. "I need your help boy, come with me, I'll give you your first lesson. Bring that bag with you too," he said.

I dropped the mattress and followed him out the door with the bag. Laughter echoed across the alleyway. We passed the fat man at the arcade. He called out to me but I ignored him, holding my chin low, watching only the back of Lispenard's boots.

We crossed State Street.

We dodged carriages and the critical laughs sent to Lispenard's swaying frock. In the manmade wind it appeared to be a cape of sorts, dragging its way through mud and across sun baked branches. We entered another section of small homes. The street had no name, for the homes belonged to Rochester blacks. The doctor moved quickly. I wasn't as lucky as I fell behind, caught up in the State Street crowd.

I nearly lost sight of him, but he waited a number of yards ahead. He told that I must keep up as we had important work to do.

"Yes sir," I responded shyly.

Lispenard seemed to dance rather than walk. Gracefully he dodged trees, vagrants and horses. I followed not as ably, but always careful to watch him and not the ground under my feet.

We had to be close to the destination he had in mind, for he began to slow his walk. There were three small homes under shade of the most ugly oaks I'd ever seen. The homes were in the most tragic case of disrepair. The home on the left was the one the doctor aimed for, and as I focused my eyes I saw two figures near the door. They were the two men who warmed their hands at the burn barrel.

I stood at the roadside edge as the two men and Lispenard shared words. The doctor reached into his pocket and handed the two stiff drunkards more than one coin each. At least I so surmised.

"C'mon boy," he said.

I lowered my chin to my chest and walked past the two men who again snickered out mumbled words as I entered the home in the doctor's wake.

The home was smaller than what it showed.

My eyes adjusted to the darkness.

The doctor took a form like I'd not seen previously. He hovered. His form seemed to swallow what was in front of him. My adjusted eyes revealed he hovered over a body that lay upon the homes front room floor.

I watched him. He was smooth in what he did. His work, his routine was a good mixture of care and speed. I moved closer without being asked to do so. I was curious. The body was that of an old woman, an old black woman. One would have to study the air, but there was a hint of death, fresh death. The body though recent to death had been prone for some time.

The old woman was small.

"Stand close," Lispenard directed.

The doctor knelt at the feet of the woman.

I watched him study her.

"Parker!" Lispenard shouted.

One of the men from outside came in.

"I need more light."

"Yes sir, right away," he said.

I heard a faint vulgarity as Parker searched out some form of light. He found and lit an oil lamp and handed it to me. He left without further words.

The doctor showed me how to hold the lamp close to the body. I did my best to satisfy his instructions though he corrected me on a couple of occasions. Lispenard forced the woman's legs so the knees pointed up while the feet were flat on the floor.

"This will be your first lesson," he said.

My knee touched the leg of the woman. The body was cold and he had to push the woman's right leg with greater force. After several failed attempts Lispenard asked me to kneel down and hold it myself.

I applied more than casual force and the leg eventually remained firm. From my position the lit lantern allowed me a better opportunity to see the woman. She was quite an aged woman. She was a Negro, and I'd seen her purchase slices of pie on many occasions. Her eyes were open wide as if death had caught her by surprise. Her lips had started to draw back leaving her face caught between a smile and grimace.

The doctor laid the woman's skirt on her stomach. With a knife he had retrieved from the canvas bag he cut her under garments with delicate speed. He then cut her from his left to his right in a large circular motion. He stopped just in front of me. The elderly woman's lower belly and genitals were exposed.

His head turned toward mine.

"Young man, Frank, this woman has not been dead long. Perhaps this very hour yesterday she was walking the row of vendors looking for your apple pie."

"When was she found?" he asked Parker.

"Several hours ago," said Parker.

"I prefer them warmer, you know that. I don't pay for the cold."

"Yes sir," Parker said.

"A body is difficult to work with when it grows cold. I prefer to work with the freshly dead," he told me.

I replayed the words work with the freshly dead.

"Work?" I asked.

I watched as he took the knife and sliced open the old woman gracefully. Always working left to right. The doctor forced her legs further up exposing her backside and the shit left behind.

"The dead shit themselves," he said.

"Push her leg and hold it tight," he instructed.

He continued his cut deeper within her genitals.

The amount of blood was small.

"As soon as a body dies it's always best to place them...or that they be on their back so the blood settles there."

"It's this thing though that has caused so much damage to mankind," he said pointing to her cunt.

As I watched his performance I relived my mother's naked dance under the moonlight branches of Sophia Street. I relived her sucking man after man. I recalled how they had laid her upon bed, table and ground as I watched.

I watched Lispenard work. His mouth grew heavy with spit as he cut the flesh more out of anger than with care.

"Bitch! Lousy bitch!"

"Young, old, they're all bitches!"

What did he mean when he said this has destroyed mankind?

He exposed her stomach and removed her last meal. He grabbed the mass, studied it, sniffed it and flicked it on the nearest wall. It held pieces of corn, potato and apple. The man Parker held back a gag.

"Why?" I asked.

"Why what boy?" he asked, "What's your question boy?"

"Why does that cause damage?"

"The female hole has a purpose. In the marital bed, the birthing bed and with what nature requires, that's it, nothing more," he said.

I watched even more wide-eyed as he gracefully slid the blade the full circumference of her genitals. He cut above her ass and back up the left side just inside the old woman's thigh.

The blade opened her wide.

Shit, water and yellow fluids spilled forth as Parker backed up holding heavy lips.

Lispenard finished as quickly as he'd started. He laid the knife next to me. He reached further into the cut and folded the flesh backwards toward his lap. A big bone was exposed. There was meat he called muscle and an organ that was new to me.

He made some small additional quick cuts, and the tension of the woman's right leg was relieved.

"Take this," the doctor said of the knife. "The body will take care of itself."

Lispenard put his right hand to the underside of the old woman's uterus and pulled. It came loose with little resistance.

Lispenard held it and asked for a piece of canvas.

I gave him what he needed.

Lispenard wrapped it and took the bag himself.

"Parker you two get rid of the body."

Parker called for his partner, a man named Pinsky to come inside.

He searched the home and returned with a blanket. The doctor stood up, and grabbed my shoulder forcing me up too.

"What do you want to do with it?" the second man asked.

Lispenard directed them to take it by wagon to the rear platforms of the asylum two miles east.

"Yes sir, we know it," Parker said.

Lispenard carried the bag as we left the house. He moved even quicker than he had when we first arrived. I followed as best I could but fell behind easily.

We bound across State Street and in short time were at the rear of the arcade. His cloak snapped in the breeze he created. There was one man waiting outside the door who was looking for a doctor's care. His faced was badly marred. He'd say a fight the night before last had caused cuts, and blood.

"We'll be with you momentarily," Lispenard told him.

I was a part of that we.

When we stepped inside, Lispenard gave me quick directions. He told me where to go, what to do and what to study. Elizabeth called to us when she heard us enter. The doctor handed me the bag and told me to go to the rear room and set what was inside out on the dinner table. I did as he directed as he attended to the injured man whom he later called just "a drunkard of the most persistent kind."

I laid the bag on the table.

"Was it a dead body?" Elizabeth asked.

She knew the answer.

"Yes, an old woman."

I stood closer to the chest of drawers than I did her bed.

"Did my father cut her open?"

"Yes he did, he showed me some things."

"Father does that," she declared.

The young woman was growing stronger by the hour. She moved without obvious pain in the soiled bed.

"Why does he do that?" I asked.

I took a seat at the table. The young woman hadn't answered me. I studied the bag with what casual stares I could muster. I could hear Lispenard use colorful words to ass whip the battered man. The noise tapered off as the man left. I quickly appeared to be at work. In a move that was faster than my thoughts, I reached inside the bag.

The bottom was wet and sticky. I pulled my hand out immediately seeing it stained with a translucent blood-red fluid. I wasn't appalled. I looked at my fingers that dripped some of the fluid back into the bag and across the tabletop. I raised my fingers to my nose, sniffed them and breathed in deep the aroma the organ produced.

My lips quivered.

I couldn't tell what the odor was. I had smelled it come from my mother when she said she was making me into a man of quality. It wasn't fresh, but God damn it, it was tempting. I moved my fingers closer and licked them clean from fingertip to wrist. Never had I tasted something that moved me like this had.

I hoped Elizabeth hadn't seen me. I turned my back toward her and pulled the well-wrapped organ from the bag laying it adjacent some bread from that morning's breakfast.

Was I ashamed?

What would Elizabeth think if she had seen me?

"My baby is dead isn't it?" she asked as I finished licking my fingers.

CHAPTER SEVEN

"Is my baby dead?" Elizabeth asked again.

I was sitting at the table with my back to her, my bottom lip quivering from the salty taste of the organ.

In reflection, I've never forgotten that day.

I've always remembered Elizabeth.

She was an innocent who'd fallen victim to the worst side of life. I remember her as someone who'd never been given a chance to be more than a receptacle for men's seed, including her father's. I remember her too as perhaps my first friend.

As the train neared Portsmouth I lamented at memories in general and how for me they are often hid within a poet's stanza.

The train to Portsmouth was caught between slowing and running at a steady pace. Track problems caused the former more often then I wished.

My memories, my history, my stanzas could not be burned as easily as the trash could. Memories kept me breathing. They kept me on my mission of doing what needed to be done, making man better animals. My memories said I was indispensable and mother had showed me that. I was the seed, her seed. I was a leaf on her tree.

I swayed to unheard tunes.

New drool pooled.

My youth were days as firmly rooted in my head as was my gray hair.

I understand now that there are no coincidences in life. Sophia Street and those days with Lispenard and young Elizabeth were meant to be.

Everything has happened in order to produce occurrences that placed me in specific homes performing certain crafts. I have therefore done what had meant to be done. So the lives I have touched were also part of destiny.

The early days at Lispenard's were good ones. I felt cared for and I felt that I had a home and could I live in proud fashion. I remained with them for nearly a year. Those days were meant to be good.

"My baby is dead isn't it?" Elizabeth asked a third time.

I shuffled my mind.

I wasn't strong enough to ignore her for long though. Finally I told her, yes, the baby was dead. I added that it had been born dead.

"I thought I heard it cry," Elizabeth said.

"No, there were no cries, it was dead."

"I hope to keep a baby some day," she said bashfully.

I wiped my lips with my arms.

I had yet to turn toward Elizabeth. I was ashamed at tasting the bloodied organ that I'd unwrapped.

"Boy," Lispenard said, "Bring that bag in here," he had heard our talking.

I replaced the meat.

"Don't worry about the bitch," he added.

The battered drunkard was gone, and the doctor had cleaned a portion of the smaller tabletop.

"Drunks, lunatics and whores come here looking for treatment for their ills. They think we're a charity but remember, be careful of the greedy ones. Give only to whom you desire."

He took the bag and removed the meat and gently unwrapped it. I watched his face. His eyes were steady. Not one blink. There was no doubt that he treasured what he was doing, he worshipped it.

"Look at this boy," Lispenard said.

I didn't move from my spot.

"Look boy, look at this thing."

I remained still and from where I was it looked like a simple piece of gut, human meat and nothing more. I took a step closer.

"This is what has caused so much harm to man and to the world. This piece of meat has caused cultures to vanish and realms to end under the guillotine's blade."

I shuffled a foot closer. There was no smell coming from what I saw.

"Why?" I asked.

"It's called the original sin, human pleasure of the animalistic kind. Once man, any man of weak moral skin finds union with a woman of similar weakness, hell is born."

He handled the old woman's organ as if it were bread upon a plate.

"Boy, understand this. The world God made was good. He made a garden for His people to live in peace. We are still His people. But it was the temptation of man that destroyed that garden."

Lispenard picked up an edge of the meat holding it close to his nose. He used touch, smell and taste all at once. Juices dripped upon his lap.

He continued his lesson.

"It was one thing that tempted Eve, she wanted more than what God gave her. She was greedy, she took what she wanted, and the leaves of the garden crumbled to the ground turning to dust beneath her feet."

My eyes squinted.

"We were forced from the garden because she wanted God's fruit. Because of that want, that desire, God gave women a fruit of their own."

"What's that fruit you ask?"

I shrugged.

"Come closer boy."

I shuffled another step.

"A woman bares fruit, the fruit of her loins. Her loins are her fruit, this, this piece of shit is the woman's fruit!" he pushed the meat near my lips.

I staggered back but not before I caught a whiff of its hidden odor. It, that odor grabbed my hidden animalistic desires. Lispenard saw my eyes. He saw my inhalation as he continued.

He smiled widely.

His mouth held bubbled spit.

He placed the meat back on the tabletop.

"That smell has tempted many."

"This is human fruit. A woman possesses it. It too is God's gift but still women spoil it. It's greed that makes this fruit bad. It does have its place, but when a woman takes pleasure from her fruit and needs that pleasure constantly satisfied, she begins to rot from the inside."

"Man, men, boys, drunkards, the insane, the lazy, the defiled and defamed are all targets of a woman's lust. When a man of quality refuses the cunt of a whore she'll take it elsewhere until she is satisfied."

He was lecturing about my own mother.

"God chose women to bare the world's fruit, but when she soils it, she soils His gift. If she does so for the sake of her own lust society dies a little more every time she's bent over."

The room was silent.

"Was Elizabeth greedy?" I asked.

"Forget Elizabeth!" Lispenard said in a flash.

"You called her a whore," I defended my question.

"It's far better that Elizabeth share a bed with me then riding the streets seeking cock in exchange for two-day-old bread. It's better that she accepts my seed than that of the insane, the drunkard, or those with questionable lineage."

He patted the meat in front of him.

"When I seed Elizabeth I know that it's best. If I went to the whore on the corner I'd knowingly soil God's garden. Elizabeth satisfies my need, that's her role in life. She accepts her role. It's those who knowingly pollute man's morals that need to be cleansed."

"Cleansed?"

"Yes cleansed," Lispenard answered.

"What do you mean cleansed?" I asked.

I watched the doctor's face change from one color to the next. He sat back and wiggled his ankles. He brushed invisible crumbs off his whiskered face. He stood and went to the rear room, quickly returning with several jars of mixed fluid setting them next to the piece of meat.

He started a new lesson.

"This is where the woman receives the man," Lispenard said in pointing to the slab of meat. "It's here after subtle agitation that the seed is left behind."

He worked with a long thin knife.

Lispenard trimmed the organ as if it was beef being readied for the campfire.

"This one is elderly. Age and childbirth has weakened it, but it's good for study. If it is used too much when the woman is young, it will grow old and weak before its time."

After moments of cutting and trimming he placed the meat snuggly in one of the jars and placed the jar just inside the rear room.

Was his daughter his most intimate study?

As bizarre and mad as he appeared, and as frazzled as his explanations were, when I had the opportunity to dwell on his words they made sense.

The train to Portsmouth had begun to slow as my thoughts lingered.

"Cleansed, what does that mean?"

"Means different things to different people," the voices answered back.

While under his tutelage, I mastered knowledge of the human body. Anatomy, Lispenard called it. I was taught what to clean, how to clean and how to preserve.

"The body requires much preservation," he said.

"How is the mind preserved?" I asked.

"If we know what the body is and does, we doctors will know how to cure it. If we understand the body and the mind we will know if the ailment is physical or from the mind. If it's physical we can learn how to treat that, if it's from the mind, well then, that's not so easily treated."

With Lispenard I'd learn what was nature, and what was man. Over those months, I ventured out on my own several times but was most often under his watchful eyes. It was he who showed me that man's immorality would lead to physical and mental degeneration.

"What makes a man immoral?" I asked.

"The nature of man is to master sinful behavior. The same sins God declared as deadly. That mastering is what creates immorality. The evil side of man will ask whether or not God can be immoral or what right does God have in judging man. Once a person reaches that point it's too late. When man falls victim to his desires his society begins to collapse from the weight of the immorality. It is lust, envy, greed, sloth, gluttony and pride and all their manifestations that spread unbelievable harm unto the recesses of man's mind," Lispenard preached over each piece of meat we brought home.

"If we are decent men of science and of a God, we must do what we are obligated to do to right the course of mankind."

"To right the course of man." I've replayed those words for decades.

Those months with Lispenard passed quickly, and I grew from the hand me down knowledge and from the many books I learned to read. Elizabeth was healthy and preparing meals and running neighborhood errands within a week of birthing her child.

It took her persistence, but we started to talk and enjoy each other's company. She taught me numbers and letters and she even taught me how to have fun. Lispenard would be gone for hours, even overnight at times, and his time away allowed Elizabeth and me to become better friends.

The two men that shared the warmth of the burn barrel, Parker and Pinsky, and I became sociable. In weeks it was me they'd come to retrieve when they had a body for Lispenard. "The doctor makes us weary," Pinsky said to me on one such occasion.

I became comfortable in the home.

I became comfortable in being considered equal to Lispenard by those who were fearful of him.

I became comfortable with the dead.

I knew what was expected of me without asking.

I knew Lispenard's nature almost as well as if I could read his mind. His eyes and body language told me things when nothing else could. I studied the jars and the importance of salt, dyes and alcohol in the art of preservation. I studied his books and drawings and I studied the maturing young woman in the adjacent room.

Weeks became months.

I walked the streets of Rochester with the good doctor to learn how to recognize the immoral among us. That chore was easy for I'd been well prepared for it. Women, as Lispenard had made clear, were the first to show sin, as they wanted more than what God had given them. God saw that women would be the weakest and thereby would have greater needs.

"Most are weak by choice," he insisted.

We walked the streets with tremendous grace as he answered my questions just as gracefully, often calling them profound and beyond my years.

Perhaps I was profound.

Lispenard continued.

"God expected the weakest or the most fragile among us, women, to turn to Him at greater intervals. He wanted and still wants the most fragile of us to rely on Him. When they don't, problems arise."

Our cloaks swished like bats.

Vendors admired us as we'd begun to dress alike. Our appearance made whore and apple vendors stand aside just for us.

Day after day on Rochester's streets he taught and I learned.

"When more and more women turn from what God desires, mankind becomes the victim."

One day we walked as night fell, and stood across from a corner of fallen unfortunates.

"I've been chosen to tell you that you were meant to be, we must not let Him down either," Lispenard said this pounding an invisible pulpit. The corner of snickering onlookers welcomed my selection.

Lispenard and dear mother told me I was destined and that I had a duty to make the world a better place. I was being prepared to fulfill my destiny.

I now knew my role in the world and I was learning the skills needed to fulfill it. I was becoming of age, a ripe age as Lispenard called it when he drank more than he should have. It was an age where I learned at an incredible rate.

Lispenard was gone more often than he was home. During my free time, I learned and the more I learned the more questions I had.

The seasons changed.

The wind warmed.

I was growing comfortable, confident, and even kind in some minds.

As the warmer months came, Elizabeth and I'd sneak up to the arcade. On one occasion I won her smallest of hand-sewn dolls. It had a skirt made from red squares and hair that was painted on.

Elizabeth would cook what she knew how, and she'd assist me when I was asked to bind cuts and sores when left on my own.

"Those were some of my best days," I whispered to the voices.

The voices laughed at me.

"Remember other days?" asked the voices.

There was one night I did remember more than all the rest. I sat at the table in the back room looking through a book. I studied the drawings and looked at a number of jars Lispenard selected. It was April, perhaps early May, that time of year when it was a blend of warm and cold. I read as best I could, seeking far way answers to my questions. The ones Lispenard called profound. That day Lispenard had been gone for many hours.

The house was free from the sick.

Elizabeth sat across from me. She too was reading.

The slamming of the front door broke the silence.

Elizabeth and I looked up from our books. Her eyes wide, the brown irises were significant.

"Oh God, dear God no, you need to go Frank!" Elizabeth stood up.

Lispenard had come home unquestionably drunk. He was loud, walking sloppily, rudely seeking out Elizabeth. "Go, why? He's just drunk?"

The noise grew as Lispenard slammed and banged boxes and jars.

"Elizabeth, bitch," he loudly slurred.

She brushed the front of her dress and again implored me to go away as quick as I could.

"I won't go he's just drunk!" I said.

Lispenard tossed the curtain aside.

I didn't want to see her harmed. We'd become close. We'd taken care of the other through illness, brought small trinkets home to remember a birthday or other special moment. That night though changed things for both of us.

He popped into the backroom.

He swayed.

"Put this up," Elizabeth said.

Lispenard looked at us.

"Frank, please leave right now," she begged again.

Lispenard looked dark.

"I'm not leaving!"

"He'll be looking to..." Elizabeth said.

"Goddamn it!" Lispenard shouted.

"Looking for what?" I asked.

"There you are, you worthless cunt!"

Lispenard took a couple of steps toward us. My eyes were wide. Elizabeth was calm as if she was familiar with it all.

He approached her.

She stood waiting at the table's edge.

I moved toward him.

"Sit boy, stay right where you are you sorry little cock," he laughed.

I wouldn't move.

"Hagh, you are ripe!" he backhanded me, "A ripe little cock you are!"

I slumped to the floor.

"I say sit, you sit, boy!"

"Daddy don't," Elizabeth said with a hint of authority.

Lispenard smacked Elizabeth with the same hand he'd used on me. She fell to one knee with a thump. Lispenard then grabbed his daughter throwing her on the bed. He rolled her onto her stomach.

"Bitch, you fucking little bitch!"

He slapped the back of her head.

Elizabeth fought for just a second or two and then gave way to the inevitable.

"Frank please go," she begged me as Lispenard tore her gown exposing her pink ass.

"Don't, Daddy, please don't!" Elizabeth cried. He pulled her to him as he pulled himself out.

"Fuck 'em in the ass boy that's the best place boy, fuck 'em in the ass!" Lispenard slobbered.

Elizabeth begged for her father to stop. She cried only at the first thrust.

"It hurts," she whimpered.

Lispenard thrust again and again and again until there was no longer a need.

He gasped.

He swallowed hard.

He looked at me still on the floor.

"Your turn boy."

I slipped scrambling to get up.

It happened so fast.

Elizabeth was in pain.

"Boy, goddamn it's your turn, fuck her, fuck her now boy!"

I got to my feet but Lispenard grabbed me.

"Boy, do it, it's your turn."

"No, I won't, I won't hurt her," I said.

Lispenard laughed.

"Frank go!" Elizabeth cried covering herself up.

"You got it all wrong boy," Lispenard said.

He reached down, grabbed the back of my shirt and threw me onto the bed. I fought the best I could, but Lispenard prevailed. Elizabeth squirmed off the bed but Lispenard grabbed her too, he planted his left knee firmly on her small back. He forced me atop her.

He had me in one hand and Elizabeth in the other. He forced her head down and her ass up in the air.

"Daddy, please don't!"

Her voice was muffled.

"He pushed me closer to her."

"Boy, you best get your act straight right now!"

I moved to my knees. I was scared.

"Pull it out boy!"

"No, I won't!"

I tried to push myself off the bed.

"Daddy, please, he's my friend," Elizabeth cried.

Lispenard reached inside my pants with his right hand. He grabbed my cock squeezing until I couldn't stand it.

"I'll do it for you if I have to!"

He thrust my soft pecker up against Elizabeth's ass.

We both cried.

"Fuck her boy, push it!" Lispenard shouted.

My cock was pointless and Lispenard grew pissed. "Boy you can't fuck with that, have you no desire for its taste boy?"

Lispenard grew furious.

"Fuck it, I'll show you how!"

Lispenard spun around pushing my stomach onto Elizabeth's back. I heard her grunt for air.

"I'll show you how boy!"

I was calm for a moment. Then he pulled my trousers down. I felt his hands grab and squeeze my hips. He thrust my ass backwards. I screamed in terror as his cock pierced me. Lispenard fucked me and fucked me, again and again until there was no longer a need.

CHAPTER EIGHT

I remembered Lispenard as I saw the distant smoke of Portsmouth.

My getting fucked was destiny. It was meant to happen.

That night as my ass bled, any desire I had for love was torn from me and that is what was important. I could run from that night by turning towards birds in flight. I could be anything I wanted to be with just a simple wish.

As Lispenard wiped his cock clean on me, he laughed. He was amused as Elizabeth cried for both of us. I was physically hurt, and the blood on my retrieving hand proved it.

Lispenard laughed as he fell back off of the bed and onto one of the chairs. His trousers were around his ankles.

I rolled off of Elizabeth.

Lispenard laughed.

My chin stood firm. I never once looked at him.

Lispenard laughed.

He pounded the table with his fist.

He was pleased.

I looked at Elizabeth.

"Forget her," he said, "Bitch come here. Suck me!"

Her moist sad eyes looked my way.

Elizabeth dismounted the bed, removing her gown altogether. She blushed. She was so small and frail.

"Frank, please go, I'm sorry," she said.

Lispenard laughed as she begged for my leave.

"I won't go," I said, "I won't leave you," I said wanting to be a hero.

Lispenard laughed even harder.

"He won't stop until he's ready, just go."

"The boy has a pretty little ass, doesn't he bitch!" Lispenard whistled.

I left the room, turning around only once to see Elizabeth on her knees as Lispenard pushed her head down. That was the last I saw of her. I grabbed my bag, which was always packed, and hurried through the door. Without a second thought, I stepped over to Parker and Pinsky who were standing, as always, at the burn barrel.

I informed them I was leaving, and why. As I left the backyard, I saw them enter Lispenard's home.

I walked in a chilled afternoon wind. I hadn't done that in months but picked right back up on the journey as if I hadn't lost a step. For several days I lay in my brother's shed caught between shame and vengeance. I wanted to leave now more than at any other time. I needed work I needed a way out.

Those days delivered me to these days.

The train's whistle blew announcing our imminent arrival.

There were stares and whispers on the train due to my incessant mumbling.

It took days but my ass healed.

I recalled that I briefly returned to the canal boats, selling stories written about the desires of lonely men and the greedy women who satisfied those desires. Lispenard was the male character in the stories, and I was the woman.

The stories earned me pennies, and they earned me a reputation of being dirty and devoid of morals. I took to crossing Lake Ontario on boats where I'd earned my fare. I wrote and told stories of lust and orgies in exchange for food and fare.

When my stories aged, I used the medical skills I'd mastered at the shoulder of Lispenard. To strangers I declared myself a doctor.

On the waters I easily impressed the ignorant fishermen with my skills of tale and tail. The injuries I treated were often minor, but I performed as if they were life threatening. I was entertaining, and it worked as well on Lake Ontario as it did in Miller's Court.

A grand future was ahead of me. I was profound, and I had a duty to share my gift with mankind.

The seasons drifted by.

I traveled the bodies of the St. Lawrence and the Ontario and more than once slept upon the banks of the Genesee and Lake Erie. I worked the waters for a year until I returned completely to land.

Once on shore, I traveled to the southern counties. A man named Gilliam, said there was work in the counties south of Rochester, and that the need for my skills might be great.

"Go there, that might be your place," he said.

I agreed.

I saw other parts of New York as lands of mystery. Others of noble title thought the same way. Many writers declared parts of this state, if not New York City, were strange lands.

If the land was strange, then its people were even stranger.

I could travel as I wished and be whom I wished in those strange lands. I would bounce words of my deeds past strange people. Fancy words, my dress and deeds impressed the drunkards and gutter whores from these rural counties.

I wanted to be seen as a great man.

I wanted to be a profound man.

I swayed to unheard tunes.

The train to Portsmouth slowed as a final whistle blew.

"Yes," I said to the voices, yes my scars were deep for when I first took to crossing the St. Lawrence, I paid my way by selling my ass."

The voices laughed at that admission.

Trading ass for food was acceptable, as men did not carry God's fruit. That's how I now understood it. That's how I would satisfy my animalistic desires while also saving mankind. I thought that Canada would be my home but decided to take to the lands the man Gilliam spoke of.

My skills as a doctor were welcomed and even on occasion appreciated; yet my face was becoming common amongst those who didn't appreciate my work.

My Greatness had run its course in Rochester, as many remembered my mother and even more recalled Lispenard. But great deeds could be spread amongst the hamlets and larger villages to the south, that's where I set out.

I had acquired a horse of average talent, and skirted east of Rochester on moderate roads. A bay of water lay east of the city proper, and I camped there, reverting to the primitive pre-Lispenard skills of mine. I ate worms to clean men's seed from me, and drank urine when clean water was scarce.

The moss of the trees, and grubs from the rocks were my meals, and within two days of polite travel Penfield came into view. Penfield, New York was a town of promising prosperity, its populace was younger and more cash laden than that of Rochester.

I took a room, one that wasn't quite what was advertised but it had a mirror that appreciated me. I went through the paces of seeking employment from any of the numerous apothecaries. All the labeled windows laughed as I spoke of my credentials. Some said horses should be my patients. I grew red-faced at first, but after several such exchanges just smiled a nervous smile.

They laughed.

I smiled.

They didn't know who I was or what knowledge and experience I possessed. The laughers in Penfield were young, and filled with dreams that would never come true. Their ridicule mattered little. I found my way into their world regardless. In Penfield I took to walking the streets in hopes of making mankind better.

My cloak was my cover.

On colder days I wore it, and it was always cold on this side of the waters edge. The cloak was handmade. The first one was furnished by the landlady who took interest in me as a tenant and as a healthy young man. "You're old enough to be my mother," I said during one such occasion.

"It's grandmother you mean, dear boy. I'm a woman none the less," she'd say during her approach.

When my money was low and rent was well behind, I did as she wished and took her in my arms. Lispenard said, "If you must take a woman, take them old, their fruit has spoiled. If you need something young in years, make it a boy. They bare no fruit."

I had numerous such opportunities for old women and young boys. Nights like those allowed me time to keep walking amidst the laughing whores and stone thrown children.

In time I had covered the streets of Penfield. In a common excuse, I bid adieu without notice to the aged ass, grabbed my wears and returned to the shore of Ontario. I would do as I should've done and enter Canada. It was fresh there, a frontier for men like me. I could be who I said I was, and not what others thought I was.

Those who didn't know me are often those most easily impressed by insignificant gestures. Strangers would be my greatest of allies. After all these years, it's still the unfortunate or the elderly who succumb easiest to my art. The young tend to believe in only their own faces and thus overlook the greatest of gales with casually shifting eyes.

That year, 1852, I crossed over Lake Ontario.

My French was weak and what I did possess was manufactured; however it didn't matter as I quickly fit in without question.

"Impress the lunatic just by acting superior," Lispenard would say.

"If a person can impress the lunatic, the drunkard, the whore and the inmate, the elite will quickly follow. The elite are nothing without the lunatic, drunkard whore or inmate," I whispered.

The Portsmouth depot was a mile away if that.

Those early days in Western Canada were easy ones as there were many to impress. I treated minor cuts, burns and fungus of the skin. There were also times when hands and lower legs had been ripped completely off.

When my skills were effectively displayed, I labeled my work profound. When it failed, I said it was do to the weak nature of the injured one.

Those months I learned how to work with various forms of herbs and even more so with flowery words. When I knew the illness was minor and recovery was nearby, I'd use fanciful leaves and phrases to make my work seem more fantastic.

Those with minor wounds, yet substantial in their minds, were greatly impressed by my work.

"Don't remove this covering," I'd warn them.

It worked. I'd become a medical entertainer. During that first year some removed the wrap of moss, but others did as they were told and were healed. The dead did as they were meant to do, but those who survived their injuries were my greatest tributes.

I was impressed by nature's power to heal, and that interest expanded to other areas. I studied the trees, the grass and homegrown plants. I studied the petals of the flowers and the stalks of the field. I mixed science with the knowledge I already had of the landscape. I deserved the title doctor and awarded myself with it.

In those years I moved regularly from mountain to village.

I traveled from Western Canada to Kittery Maine. I worked the mills and carried the wares of many passengers to earn bowls of spoiled meal. I'd done what hard men wished and I returned with harsher a soul and more aggressive in demeanor because of it. The number of staged scenes mounted behind me, but I was always drawn back to Upstate New York.

Like a master over a slave, the wonders of my language took seed within simple minds. I'd accomplished magic in those frozen Ontario woods. Few spoke English, and their language was not my own, so I had to sell what I carried in my bags and mind.

The editor a local newspaper once said of me:

"To the very great measure of success which has attended your labours here as a medical practitioner during the months you resided here among us and the high reputation you brought with you from Rochester."

The editor was kind.
I'd see to it that he was.

I liked those words, great measure of success. I'd traveled at will throughout the provinces because of that high reputation. I was always on full display wherever I went, a grand jocular mixture of man, science and genuine bullshit. The lunatic, whore and drunkard were genuinely impressed at my mixture.

As my mother had returned to the earth the blood of my father for purities sake I believed mother earth could make the frail amongst us whole again.

I aged years in mere months.

Streams served as the finest of Bordeaux and snake as well done steak. I rode high on a steed practicing upon many classes of people and I also kneeled to satisfy many a firm young man.

My companions have remained the young and firm.

I practiced and was profound at what I practiced.

I walked with capped head and grossly untrimmed hair.

Some believed in my work, while others shouted vulgarities.

Some called me degenerate.

Toronto was home until I saw a need in Montreal.

I opened a small office there.

Montreal was home to the elite.

Weeks past.

A whore was lost to the city and I was in the wrong.

"Quack!" they declared.

"Murderer!" the elite smeared.

My peers were my supporters and said they thought not.

The news of the day promoted and applauded my work.

The handpicked noblemen pointed and smacked their caps.

"Tumblety is a quack!" Montreal said after one failed night.

After several such exclamations I'd reached my tolerance.

"How dare they!" I replied.

A whore is a whore whether her ankles are pinned in Rochester, Montreal or Whitechapel.

Be Damned!

If the Queen's North American could not see me for what I was, perhaps I would be better off seeking the American West, for it was still free from governmental restraints. I left Canada and returned to

Rochester at the outbreak of the Civil War. In pinned cuffs and collar and a coat that touched my heels, I rode back into the town that had spilled my morals.

That was a prosperous time for me, as my services were required nearly everywhere I chose to set my boots. I returned as a great man with diaries full of glory and legions of handkerchief waving maidens behind me.

That's what my dreams said.

I said to Rochester fuck you as I rode in. I would allow the tilted noses enough room to recall the hell they put me through as a boy. I'd walk by those who offered greetings without returning kindness. I'd share my resources with the poor, water with the thirsty, and flour with the hungry.

I swayed to unheard tunes.

For now Portsmouth was outside my window.

I tilted the collar on my coat, recalling some of my better years when I danced my words of wonderment.

I had always traveled.

Gypsy blood ran rampant in my veins.

I was well traveled and my services much needed from Chicago to St. Louis. Everyone needed me.

I treated both men and women, appreciating one and abhorring the other. I talked up the results of my flamboyant labor. With hat in hand, and my chest bearing decorative recognitions I strode as I rode a steed of white. My name grew full of grand titles. None was greater than I at making magic out of common roots.

There were times, many times where I believed my skills should be better recognized. I often times produced that recognition. I'd be shunned by the societal elite in one town and laughed at by another, but off I'd go decorating my garments all the more along the way.

I chose to offer my skills to the growing number of needy during the years of American disunion. My skills were greatly appreciated regardless if I was amidst Yankees or Confederates. The war had brought such a new course for grotesque savage infliction of injuries that I couldn't help but learn as I rode. The more savage the wound, the more fantastic I let my acts become.

I practiced being greater in words than in deed.

Up to that point, mankind had not seen anything like the savagery produced by the Civil War. With doctors from towns great and small being called to the battlefield, my services as previously mentioned were greatly needed.

I'd hover in small towns awaiting their offers.

None came so I made my own history.

I was well versed in horses and their odd personalities by the time the Bull Run was more than just a rumor. In being from the North, it was expected that I'd favor those in blue with my services. But what had the North ever done for me?

Those in scattered patterns of butternut were more polite. Perhaps they knew little of my youth or perhaps such behavior, as theirs was natural. If being polite was natural, then so too was their being fools. I found Southerners, particularly when en masse, to be mere choirs of backward buffoons. Rather than choose a side I'd declare my skills open for all and myself available to any and all who may need me. I'd begin my service near my sister's home in St. Louis, Missouri.

My sister and I were strangers as children and were far from good acquaintances as adults. We were polite when in each other's company but were in such company infrequently. I had decided that being a border doctor in a border state would be in my best interest, so I journeyed to St. Louis. I remained at her home for several months, though I was seldom within Sarah's walls. She was no longer a Tumblety but a Wilcox. My absence was much to the satisfaction of her lawyer husband, Peter Wilcox, Esq.

Sarah never knew the hell or saw the years in which I was to grow. She knew of me only by rumor and the reputation I sent ahead by cable. I'd put on a show just for her and in particular Peter. I don't know how Sarah perceived me, but I wanted to give a good impression.

When I arrived in St. Louis, I asked that a telegraph be delivered to their home from me. For a dollar more the telegraph would say I was to arrive from New Orleans in the days hence. Shelter would be greatly appreciated during the duration of my medical work at St. John's Hospital.

St. John's was a hospital that was modern by some accords. It was identified as a caring institution and was often flooded with immigrant families. Its initial intention was to aid woman and children and so was mine. The neighborhoods that sprang up around larger cities were flooded with poor of every dialect. St. Louis was a stew of them. St. John's Hospital was their repository.

I had discovered, during my travels that the cities in America, regardless of size or location, were all related. In the cities, those with political power decided who was and wasn't entitled to survival. I'd bridge the fortunate and unfortunate.

Just the way I carried myself and defended my skills was bound to impress anyone. The work I'd performed outside the hospital door was of as much importance as that within the hallway recesses. I lived as I wished and spread those whishes upon others.

CHAPTER NINE

My sister and her family quickly grew weary of my being their upstairs guest, though on the surface at least they adjusted politely to my Sunday dinners with them.

I dined infrequently because I had made a friend.

I had learned that if one is not accustomed to such a task, as friend making then it is a rather arduous undertaking. However in this one case it was easy, almost breathtakingly so.

His name was John.

"He was soft and generously friendly," I whispered with a flush.

My crotch edged forward when I thought of him.

I wonder even today what might have been if John had been allowed to be where might he be?

With jagged hesitation Portsmouth arrived.

My napping refreshed me. I felt better. Looking out the window, the trees, outbuildings and even growing number of faces were clearer.

The chill in the air had also expanded as we neared the waters edge. The man next to me no longer found me of interest. His focus was his own rapid departure.

The Portsmouth station was relatively new. Only built in 1875 or so, prior to its construction travel to Southern England had been much more difficult. The line between London's Waterloo and points near the channel was a laborious route.

It was built on a pier, which left only a short walk to the Le Havre ferry. A question asked to any attendant would direct me to the proper zone of departure.

The train's wheels screeched.

The City of Portsmouth was a union of a number of smaller townships and was an inlet to the English Channel. From its shore, the sands of France were just a night's dream away.

On the docks I could sit and read. And when time allowed I would walk a gentleman's walk amongst seagoing waifs and pray upon a St. Thomas pew.

St. Thomas was a fine Becket product, dating back to the 12th century and the reign of King Richard or one of the incompetent Henrys. I'd slept there many times covered in a borrowed vestment.

The noise from the engine increased. There were sparks from the wheels and fingers of crawling steam. I saw a large number of faces, at first blurred and lifeless now posed with a potpourri of emotions.

Their eyes stood out as black and lifeless.

I moved forward in my seat.

The slower the train became, the more life those eyes became. The train slowed until a final spit of steam brought us to a complete stop. The brakes threw us all in a lurch of inches. The train and I sighed in unison. According to my watch the ride was no more than five hours a rate of fifteen or so miles per the hour.

I waited for my passenger car to empty. I wanted to be the last off so I could make my entrance grand. I had to make a good, initial presentation. The man across from me was the first to leave.

From Portsmouth, one could choose Holland or Belgium. I though, would choose Le Havre, France. Rail lines linked Le Havre to Paris some thirty years ago, but passenger ships were still important. I exited the passenger car holding my chin high. I pulled my collar up as I saw a capped attendant several yards off to my right.

Allowing the disheveled to pass I approached a handsome young man.

"Good day," I said.

"Yes sir good day. How may I help you?"

"Where may I catch the next ferry to Le Havre?"

He provided the directions I needed, and also informed me that the next departure would not be until the following morning at six.

I'd have more than a twelve-hour wait.

I was disappointed, but knew I'd find avenues of escape.

My mind sought those avenues.

I stood in the center of the dock with my emotions a whirlwind.

Through the crowd and the engines dribbling steam I saw the points of two constable caps. I brushed imaginary dust from my frock and approached them.

Both constables were men of substantial build, which never appealed to me personally, though it was at times nice to imagine.

"Good day. I'm on my way to Le Havre but no ferry is set for departure until the early morning hours. I do have means. Do you have suggestions as to where I may spend the waiting hours?"

Both men were polite and seemingly anxious to help.

"Yes sir, there are several inns not far from here." One pointed one way, and the other pointed another, both promoting their favorite spots.

"Is it a quiet bed you want?" asked the taller of the two.

"That's not as important as is a quiet table."

"The Portsea Inn is quite fair," both agreed as to the choice. I thanked them; leaving in the direction they pointed me.

"The Portsea Inn," I repeated.

Named in honor of Portsmouth, I presumed.

I could smell the sea as I began my walk. The stink from the shore made its way to my nose. It was a pungent mixture of salt and rotting fish.

I would have to make my way through crowds all temperaments and artisans finishing their work for the day. The sun was low on the horizon. I walked behind small peddlers and larger factories that dotted the hem of the wharf.

Once behind the crowd and buildings the sun seemed to drop as quickly as the temperature did. It may have been September, but it was a December cold.

These channel ports were always cold though.

I tipped my collar toward the gaslights that'd showed me the way. After a number of additional twists and turns I saw a small crowd of boisterous seaman and the projecting sign of the Portsea Inn.

The inn portrayed itself as insignificant as I had imagined it.

I studied the scene from a few yards away, and then made my approach through an opening. The crowd of drunken seaman laughed at the unseen virtue of fallen maids and their upturned frills. None stepped aside allowing me a polite entry.

"Pardon me," I said.

None did so.

I waited, and my hue changed.

"Dear sirs, pardon me please."

With that delivery, a slender boy stepped aside in mid-laugh not offering a pardon in return.

I stepped inside, and not wanting to see what presented itself, stared at the floor. It wasn't clean. I brushed invisible pests from my sleeves and removed my billycock, only then did I lift my eyes. The setting, to my astonishment was almost comfortable.

There were five or six scattered patrons amidst uneven tables. There was a barmaid serving drinks, potatoes and perhaps other forms of meat if a decent price was agreed upon. When she bent at the waist she was quite wide.

The bald, better groomed man behind the bar nodded toward me. I accepted that as a welcoming sign. I looked for a table that was far enough away from the others as to not be bothered, yet close enough to observe.

I found one. It overstated its neutrality to theme.

I gave the table an examination before I placed my hat upon it. I gave the chair a closer review before I sat my ass upon it. I unloosened my frock, and then took my seat.

I flipped opened my pocket watch and saw the hour was nearing seven, and bemoaned the fact that I'd be here for the overnight.

The tabletop was sparse.

A window was close enough to allow me an idea of the level of darkness or sun. There were regiments of shadows passing by the distant glass, but none bore fife and drum. There was no rush by the barmaid to serve me either.

I twirled my billycock.

I watched the woman as she chatted with the one behind the bar and two others leaning on it. The three chuckled looking my way. The man behind the bar was more concerned as to whether I'd receive prompt service.

My stare gave her spine a chill. She turned toward me and crossed the floor. I discovered that she was very unpleasant to look at.

"Dear, what'll 'et be?" she asked with an ugly, practiced smile.

I removed my gloves.

"I'm waiting for the morning ferry to Le Havre, it leaves in the early hours. May I wait here?"

"We shut the doors at 2am but for a price, Ollie may let you stay," she pointed to the bald fat man behind the bar.

I sighed a noticeable breath.

"There is always a price, isn't there? I take it he is Ollie?"

She smiled an ugly practiced smile and nodded.

"Very well then. I'll see to him later. May I order some food?"

"Yes, for a price of course," she comically replied.

"A bowl of potato soup and some bread, fruit brandy if you have it too please."

"Brandy?" She said as if were a foreign word.

"Yes, if you can find some within your inventory."

She left my side and was gone briefly, returning with a bottle of very warm, and quite dusty brandy and a tin cup.

Napoleon, I was quite pleased.

"Soup will be up soon."

Brandy, it was making a comeback.

Brandy, premier if at all possible, was the only drink I'd let pass my lips.

I removed the loose cork.

There was a rush of vinegar.

The odor of fruit surpassed hidden liquor.

I first discovered the wonder of Napoleon Brandy while attending the theatre one night in St. Louis. That night was grand in every sense and every sensation. I have longed for that which touched my pallet that night in St. Louis, but now all I could do was to blow the dust from this tin cup. I've sought to recapture that night for many years but have always fallen short.

I poured a quarter cup.

I sensed the room watched me as I took a drink. The barmaid returned with a bowl of soup and bread on a tin plate.

The room was watching me.

"Thank you. Would you ask the gentleman, Ollie as you call him, what he may need for me to sit here as I await the ferry?"

She left.

The utensils were slow to arrive, but arrived along with the answer to my question.

"Ollie lives upstairs and doesn't mind the company, pay what you wish is what he said."

I looked at the utensils. They were questionable in their cleanliness.

"Thank you," I handed her a shilling.

A better, unpracticed smile was offered up in gratitude.

Sitting forward I leaned over the bowl. The smell was better than its appearance. The taste was the worse of the three. Too much salt added to too few potatoes. The noise from the streets was continuous but never increasing or decreasing in volume. It was just steady.

Few new faces came into the inn as the hours ticked toward eight, and then nine. I asked for more bread. It came and I awarded the increasingly unattractive maiden another shilling.

Her smile became experienced.

It was 11 o'clock when Ollie came over and asked if he could join me. I nodded. He had a dark beer.

"It's been busy tonight," he said in a lie.

"I see that," I said playing along.

"Going to Le Havre?" he asked.

I nodded.

"May I wait here overnight?"

"If you wish," Ollie answered through a sigh.

"I'll pay for the kindness."

"If you wish," he said in reply.

I handed him half a Crown.

He studied it, flipped it in his palm.

He asked that I be given whatever I may need.

The hour became midnight, and I was weary from the ride and the long wait, yet the activity around me fed my paranoia.

It was paranoia that had always kept my eyes wide.

The final rounds and calls were made between one and two that morning. Other than to sit and watch and taking the occasional pissing out back, the hours were spent in more of my own reflection.

The brandy brought me back to St. Louis.

I swallowed hard.

In reflection I traded this cup and its poor display for better glasses from better days.

During the course of some of those better days I was called grotesque by those with dirty wigs and little else.

How similar the words used towards me were to the words used regarding my friend John. In his case he was called un-American, and an anarchist because of his use of words.

I drank.

Where is the freedom to do as we wish?

I watched as the last of the faceless ones were rounded up within the Portsea. Some were watching me, curious as to why I was remaining behind and curious as to why my lips moved when I whispered.

The doors were shut.

I drank.

I watched.

"Ollie, behave now!" the barmaid ordered as she left with a twinkle.

"Listen to your own advice, my dear," came his reply.

I watched the barmaid walk her toothless grin into the midst of the drunken seaman.

Ollie busied himself, locking the door, clearing a few remaining plates, and counting the money for the day. Watching his face I couldn't tell if he was pleased at the result.

I could only imagine what was taking place after the raucous outside found other doors. A whore is always the best of vendors regardless of the product. There is always a demand for her offerings regardless of price.

Ollie tinkered with the required tasks of ending his day.

My thoughts were of John.

Ollie asked, "American, are you now?"

He was coming my way, bottle in hand.

"American I asked?" he repeated.

"Yes, I am. A doctor from New York," I said.

I sucked my shoulders in, intimidated by Ollie's size, by his eyes and by being alone with him.

"I seldom sleep until the wee hours anyway, so company is always welcomed on nights when I'm not so tired. You're fortunate that tonight I'm not so tired."

"I am fortunate, and thank you for your kindness."

He said I could finish the remaining brandy.

I did.

"Going to Le Havre?" Ollie asked, "Is Paris your goal?"

"No, I'll be returning to New York by steamer."

"That's a long run."

"Yes it's always proven to be one of considerable length."

"You've made it before?" asked Ollie.

"Several times over the years. I'm a doctor of reputable note in America and do have the opportunity to travel freely."

There was a still in the air.

I drank.

Ollie wondered at my words.

"Doctor? I must admit not many doctors have been guests of The Portsea Inn," Ollie declared.

I was proud at filling such a role.

My chest puffed from that pride and with a broad swipe dislodged what fears I may have had.

"It's my honor to be here at The Portsea."

Ollie drank his ale in gulps.

I poured brandy into the tin cup and drank with my pinky finger delicately raised.

Ollie's eyebrow shrank from an oncoming question.

"Have you been on holiday?"

"A blend of holiday and charity work," I said, "I've spent some weeks in Liverpool and London servicing the needs of the poor. My position allows me an opportunity to do that. I'm a doctor of reasonable means, so I do what I must for the unfortunates."

Ollie wiped foam from his thick lips.

Ignoring my prelude he began one of his own.

"A sister of mine, Gwen, lives in America with her children, outside of Richmond Virginia," he paused, "What's left of Richmond that is."

"What's left of Richmond is correct," I affirmed.

"Richmond had tremendous beauty," I stated sensing Ollie's views.

"There are plenty of us over here that wanted the war to turn out differently than it had. America was free until that day at Appomattox."

I raised my tin cup to toast.

"To the Confederacy," I said.

"To the Confederacy," Ollie added.

We toasted in gentle familiarity.

I now wondered of my host.

Ollie was not a typical ale man. He knew current events.

Did he know of his nation's Whitechapel? This night just might be a mental chess match for me, it just might be more of a challenge than I'd envisioned.

"Why do you say such things about freedom?" I asked.

He didn't hesitate, "I stayed here when my brothers and sisters moved to America. It is free! It is free, they declared. I had one brother in blue and one in gray, both got fucked in the end."

He gulped his ale.

"Within a couple of years your free country had divided my family."

"William, the oldest, moved to a small farm in New York along with his wife hoping to avoid the war. He didn't. His name was drawn from a barrel and he was told to he was a private. Wasn't long afterwards he had his left arm shot to shit and died in the Virginia woods. Left behind three baby girls."

"His wife went insane and took to the corners. I'm selling my shit for shit, she'd shout!"

Ollie waved his hand.

I drank.

He drank.

"My baby brother, James, went south to the pretty girls with plump asses. It was '60 or '61, '60 I think, when he was caught up in all the fervor of the brave talking politicians. I followed what he did, but lost track of William. It wasn't 'til after he died that I learned what happened.

"I'd get letters twice maybe three times a year. James had survived winters, starvation, and dysentery. He survived Wolf Creek, Knoxville and Drewry's Bluff. The last I heard his regiment was moving to outside of Richmond near Petersburg. No more letters after that."

Ollie's expression grew gray.

"Gwen, my sister? Well I'd received a letter from her Pastor, who preached in a small Baptist Church outside Richmond. Gwen's husband was dead, and two of her children had died during the siege of the city. The letter said she'd been brutalized by several drunken blue invaders."

I drank.

He drank.

"I'm not unique in America's mother country, we suffered and we lost family too," Ollie concluded.

My words moved rapidly, "I can't express in words my sorrow at what your family has experienced. As a doctor during that war, I saw it up close and on both sides of the lines of contention."

"Did you favor the Northern or Southern cause?" Ollie asked.

"Neither. I sided with the injured. I was on the side of the wounded and the abused and on the side of those for whom life mattered. Truth as we both seemingly know does get blurred from time to time, especially during war."

I wanted to segue.

"I was a doctor before the war, and traveled freely the genuine and historically insincere border lines that were drawn between north and south."

"Your words are very perfumed," Ollie remarked.

"Language can be a garden among man's thorns," I said.

"I saw much during those years, and formed as honest an opinion as could be formed. And as a result I sit here with you proudly tipping my cup in salute to the Confederacy."

I drank the balance of the brandy.

"Doctor of note?" Ollie asked.

"Yes, humility at time dances across my tongue in flashy, feathery words. I'd be so honored to tell you a tale of one acquaintance along the way. "

"I'd be very interested, it'll ease the laboring evening hours," Ollie said through his fattening tongue.

"I was in St. Louis just before the war working on diseased young women. I was drawn to a local theatre and a play called The Apostate."

"An impressive title," Ollie remarked.

"Yes it was, and that's what attracted me to it. Apostate has many, subtle and not so subtle meanings and was so appropriate for that time in America's history. The American South was a land of destiny, but they failed in their quest. Perhaps they failed destiny. Perhaps they were supposed to lose that war so all of man would know what possibilities had been missed." I licked my lips, "The south wanted change. They wanted out of the status quo, the south was by the modern sense of the word, apostate."

Ollie dosed to my explanations. His expression showed me he was falling behind in thought and that his ale was taking charge.

I took sympathy and returned to casual teaching.

"As we know, the meaning of apostate is a person who forsakes religion. So I wondered did freedom from religion mean a lack of attachment to Christ?"

Ollie's tongue got heavier.

"I was also curious to know if apostate could be applied to things other than just religion."

I tapped my forefinger on the table. The tapping created a rhythm for my words. The tapping also calmed the growing palsy of my left hand.

I looked over to Ollie's heavy lips.

I drank.

"Does freedom from Christ mean adherence to whatever else may be offered in His place? Does apostate mean freedom from a cause? Does apostate mean freedom from act or association? That is how I chose to identify apostate, for me the word apostate means freedom."

I sensed I could move onto a higher ground of thought with Ollie so I threw my shoulders back and let the brandy strengthen my words.

"Claudius Julianus!" I said, "He was an Apostate. He, as you know Ollie, was the last non-Christian Roman Emperor, he favored paganism."

"Perhaps you're correct," Ollie said.

He drank.

"Julian was the seed for all non believers."

"History may say you're right, I'm not sure though," Ollie said.

Before a sincere debate ensued, I continued my story.

"I had learned of this play's performance, and since I'd not been to a reputable stage presentation in years I chose to attend. The theatre was small, seating only two hundred or so. The audience would be witness to The Apostate and the skills of one good looking young man, John Booth."

John Wilkes Booth.

Ollie looked bemused.

"I hope you are being honest with me sir."

"I share only the truth. He was the centerpiece of the play, he was magnificent, and stunningly handsome."

Ollie shifted in moral discomfort.

"Mr. Booth's movements and voice were strict, firm and articulate all in one. It was clear to all in attendance that he had heart behind his words. He was a perfectionist and I believed he portrayed the Apostate in a way that I believed expressed his own personal views."

"I learned on that and several other subsequent evenings that Mr. Booth was an apostate when it came to the political system. He believed that a change in the minds and hearts of the American system of government had to come if the nation was to survive."

Ollie's heavy eyes chased imaginary shadows across the inn's floor. As he let the affects of his ale paint harmless images I recalled in silence the art form of the late Mr. Booth.

"The Provost Marshal would later arrest Mr. Booth for speaking against the government. That act fanned fires in me."

Ollie drank.

I drank.

I welcomed the invitation of my host and downed the remaining brandy with little reverence.

"So help me, Holy God! My soul, life, and possessions are for the South! Mr. Booth as Julian had separated from the norm and he on stage and in life was an apostate."

My tongue was also growing heavy.

"Amazing color you have to your words. I'll prepare a meal just as colorful and worthy of the memory of the late Mr. Booth," Ollie decreed.

I nodded a thank you.

Quickly, before I would forget the direction of my thought, I returned to the shallow reaches of that St. Louis theatre.

The weather was temperate in a state not fully blue or gray.

My life had made me into an apostate, someone separate from the world.

I'd entered the theatre that night with a newly cropped head.

People laughed at me behind unshaven chins.

The Apostate would be my trigger though. It'd be my interest in the play as well as my attraction to Booth as a man that brought about our first meeting.

When he was on stage, my eyes never left his form.

It seemed in sheer minutes the play ended.

I was in awe of his natural gifts.

I was anxious, even sweaty. It was hard to swallow.

I approached a stage boy, and with a gentle smile asked if I could be introduced to the actor of note.

"Of course," he said taking my coin.

With that gentle acclamation, I was ushered to a small room down just a couple stairs behind the stage.

The boy rapped on the door.

"Come in," came the reply.

The boy opened the door slowly.

He peeped around the frame.

I was pensive, waiting just out of view.

"It's me Mr. Booth, I have a guest who'd like to meet you, a local professional man."

A nod must've been delivered as the door was opened for me. The stage boy brushed my sleeve as I walked by. There was a slight cold chill as I stood before the dark, handsome eyes of John Wilkes Booth.

He didn't acknowledge me at first, his eyes instead holding a spot on the floor.

The air was that of gardenia. Nothing moved.

I stepped toward the gentleman, who reclined on a sofa with his legs askew.

"I'm Dr. Francis Tumblety, Mr. Booth," I extended my hand.

He looked up.

His eyes were magnificent.

"I'm John Booth, it's my pleasure. Doctor you said?"

He shook my hand.

"Yes. Dr. Francis Tumblety," I affirmed.

He had a warm, firm grip. He was well manicured and his eyes never left mine.

I felt my crotch move.

After some polite awkwardness, he invited me to sit while the boy poured drinks.

"Brandy?" he asked.

"Thank you," I said, my voice cracking slightly.

"A glass of lightly chilled Napoleon is a must for the ending of any day, on stage or off," he said again pointing to a ladder-back chair.

I sat and crossed my ankles.

The boy handed us our glasses.

"I enjoyed your performance Mr. Booth," I said accepting the glass.

He nodded.

He crossed his legs.

I watched him with withheld excitement.

"Thank you," Booth said, "It's one of my favorite roles, one of the finest of characters too."

I anticipated my visit to be short. But, as I knew I would, I had impressed him.

Our conversation became genuine.

Topics were centered on the play at first, but began to broaden as more brandy was poured.

We spoke of philosophy and of his other performances. However as our conversation drifted towards the political I became infatuated with him as a man.

I shyly admitted that I'd not seen him on the stage before that evening, and he admitted that he'd never heard of me. Even to me, the latter was understood for we'd traveled in different worlds. My desire was to have those worlds unite.

I brushed my trousers at the knees.

In an abrupt tone he asked, "What are your views of the issues facing us today Mr. Tumblety?"

"Facing the nation?" I asked in return.

"Yes sir, what do you think of it all?"

I wanted to say the right things, the proper things. I sensed that he might be offended if even the simplest of adjectives were out of place in my answer.

I shifted in the ladder-back, "Thank you for asking my views. I've longed believed that some things grow stagnate, when they're not regularly pruned and cleansed, whether it's religion, politics, or even citizens themselves."

He studied my words.

John Booth stood. He nodded his head vigorously, for what reason I didn't know. It was difficult to tell if he agreeing or growing angry.

He approached the door dismissing the boy.

"Cleansing. That's a good word," he said, "The nation needs to be cleansed." To impress him I agreed.

"Fascinating use of words," Booth proclaimed, "You practice medicine?"

"I do, there is nothing wrong with man that cannot be cured by what the world provides. I believe in natural cures, botanical remedies as it were. Man has brought many diseases, physical and moral into the world. It's the world that can remedy those ills."

"Moral diseases such as politics?" Booth asked.

"Mr. Booth, politics is as much a social disease as what the whore on the corner spreads amidst the citizenry."

He agreed with the tightest of smiles.

"Call me John," he said.

"Thank you. Please call me Frank," I said.

As I drifted back and forth from those days in St. Louis, Ollie returned with a plate of medium cooked meat, bread and more brandy.

"Did I interrupt a quick nap Doctor?" Ollie asked.

"No, just reliving better days," I said, "Thank you for the food."

The plate looked abysmal.

"It's the best remaining. I don't serve the good stuff to the run of the mill drunkard and hungry bitches." Ollie sat with a fat ass thump.

"Tell me again. You were familiar, even friendly with Mr. Booth?" he asked.

"Yes sir, I was. I was proud to be so."

"We met the first time after one of his performances in a St. Louis theatre. After downing more brandy, Mr. Booth and I discussed diseases, moral diseases."

"Remember that it was the early days of the Confederacy. All things were anxious, minds were smoke filled and hearts on both sides were fanning what they believed to be righteous flames."

We ate selected pieces of meat.

I waved my fork.

"When I spoke to Booth, I spoke of curing the physically and morally diseased. Booth spoke of curing the politically diseased."

"Destiny?" Ollie asked.

"We're all destined. You and I were destined to have this evening together. We've all been chosen to fulfill certain rolls, and I do believe that Booth was destined to be the man who exited stage right."

"Your words are flowered." Ollie said once again.

"We all have rolls to fulfill, even the dead. Perhaps a dead Lincoln did more to unify the states than a living Lincoln could have. That's where I may have disagreed with John. He should've worked silently to change things quietly. He should've let Lincoln live."

Ollie was in obvious disagreement.

"Lincoln's death was the beginning of a second war of disunion don't you think?" he asked.

"No sir. I believe Booth should've worked silently to change things quietly. Work under cover of night and in the shadows of ill traveled streets. Work so few take notice until the work has been completed. That's where Mr. Booth and I fell short in agreement. Silently is how the work should've been accomplished.

"Booth could've done more good for the cause if he had let Lincoln live and in turn live himself."

"I see your point. There were plenty of voices over here who cheered when Lincoln died, but they were left leaderless when Booth died himself."

"Did you spend much time with Booth?" Ollie asked.

"That first night backstage in St. Louis we spent hours discussing our views on history, on war, and on brandy of course."

I paused in reflection.

Ollie appeared more interested in devouring his near raw meat than in fully absorbing my story. I watched him eat and puckered my nose in elite disgust at the sight. I couldn't bring myself to disclose how often Mr. Booth and I came together and to what extent I bowed.

"Yes sir, he and I became close."

"He performed in St. Louis four additional nights, and I'd see three of those shows. Each time I made sure my seat was closer to the stage than the night previous. On one of those nights he noticed me, on another he didn't. The third visit he recognized me, and asked that I join him backstage. Of course I did."

Ollie ate. I reflected.

The night hours moved with decent speed thanks to our conversation. The church bells would chime 6am soon. I'd be on my way before those in genuine pursuit located the Portsea.

I continued my story for Ollie.

"One night in St. Louis, Booth injured his ankle. He was a mobile, muscled man and did wondrous things with his agility. That day though, he'd jumped upon the stage during rehearsal and badly twisted his ankle. He asked if I could take a look, I did. He said it was always good to practice for future roles."

Backstage I looked at his calf.

His skin was smooth under curls of black hair. I admired his foot.

Slowly, longingly, I rubbed his calf to the point where he became uncomfortable and pulled away.

"He had a sprain, a strain of sorts, and I did what I could to mend it before he left for his next city and next performance. It apparently worked as he was grateful."

The Portsea was silent.

Ollie's conversation tapered off more with each cup of ale. He may have been of more than average size but he was a weak man when it came to drink.

"Better off!" Ollie answered to no particular question.

His ramblings continued as my eyes stayed focused on my under-cooked meat. I sliced it slowly left to right. Ollie ate with his fingers. He wouldn't allow civility to interfere with his hunger.

I sliced my meat into thin strips.

I laid the strips gently, one atop another.

Once complete I laid my utensils to the side and dipped my bread into the bloody gravy that remained. I ate the bread slowly, sucking it dry in places.

Ollie leaned against the wall to get a better view of the street outside his door. He was growing weary. "I'll need to chase 'da bitches away before much longer, the noise is catching up to me," he said.

I finished my bread.

"Was Booth kind?" asked Ollie.

"He was very kind and as I traveled throughout the states. I'd often catch up to him as he performed one role after another."

"You were friends?"

"Yes, I'd say I was friends, good friends with John Booth," I said.

Ollie was losing interest and so was I.

My watch revealed it was close to 4am.

We sat across from one another in silence as the next quarter hour or more ticked away.

I could hear the tick of my watch.

I could hear the sound of a distant train.

I could smell unpleasant meat and even a more unpleasant host.

I could taste John Booth.

CHAPTER TEN

Ollie was fully asleep as I stretched my neck.

My pocket watch ticked.

There wasn't much time remaining in an overly long overnight stay. The room was cooling, and from my position I could see the increasing rays of morning sun.

It appeared to be playing games.

One minute it was here the next it was gone.

Perhaps it wasn't the sun, maybe it was just lights from London proper fully engulfed in flames.

Could it be the hungry flames from a thousand burn barrels?

Even in my best of dreams, that wasn't possible.

Ollie snored.

I drank.

"Mr. Booth," I whispered with my eyes shut.

I hadn't thought of his eyelashes in years.

I sighed passionately.

The tick of my watch was my companion. There was still an hour to go before I left for the ferry.

Days and nights like this were critical in my development. They tested my physical and mental endurance. It's a tired mind that straddles reality and fantasy.

I danced that line with skill.

When my endurance was tested, when my weariness was pushed to its limits my senses were heightened.

With heightened senses my blood grew nobler.

Meeting people like Ollie made it easy to be noble.

He was a well-mannered asshole.

Ollie most certainly had his own voices.

This evening would finish with me as the only audience.

I'd also be the only critic.

By the end of the Civil War I was well known. I sensed there were fewer people, perhaps other than the President himself, that were as well known in the capitol as me.

I saw to the manipulation of my reputation. By my dress and demeanor and fanciful history I became who I wished to be. I was seen often amidst the generals and ladies sharing tea. I'd wave from atop my steed amidst my own parade.

When I wanted to be someone, I became someone.

When I wanted others to see me as something, then I simply became what I envisioned.

As a young boy hidden among the rats of Sophia Street, it was my imagination that became the greatest fuel in fostering a quick escape.

I tapped my finger.

Ollie snored.

The art of imagination never leaves us. Our imaginations are what paint the seascape and what pens a novel. Imagination is the breath of life, and dare I say, causes the betterment of mankind.

Don't we all dream of grander names and grander lands?

I sipped my drink.

Ollie slept with slithering spittle. I didn't wish to wake him, so I slid out off the bench without removing my eyes from his chin.

I gave a cursory look around the room and was reassured that there were no faces that would cast judgment. The glimmer of the moon did reveal eyes appearing at the far window. Curious onlookers who were asking why the lights of the Portsea were still on and just how long it might be before their first glass of port.

"Simpletons," I exhaled.

For them I'd make my exit memorable.

I stood at the table's edge.

I pulled tucked fabric from my fleshy folds.

Thankfully Ollie was a sound sleeper.

Ollie's hands were strong and I'm sure they'd provide a mighty hold for whatever and whoever may desire such a firm grip.

At times, I desired such a grip.

I stood at a teacher's distance.

I put on my gloves, left one first, tugging slowly at the wrist and then repeating the same exercise with the right. I grabbed my cloak and rolled it around my shoulders, tying it just below my neck.

I was becoming whiskered.

I saw peripherally the eyes in the window had gathered friends. I'd give them something to see.

Who is that great man they must be wondering as they peered within the Portsea?

My hat was in my hand.

I placed it on Ollie's side of the table.

I moved my body closer to his. I was inches away from his boot.

I moved closer.

I had an urge.

I moved even closer.

My cock throbbed.

I pressed it into his boot. I pushed forward to increase the pressure and pleasure.

The eyes in the windows were growing wider with either shock or laughter.

Ollie slept sound.

I leaned in closer and his boot pushed further into me. I was pleased.

He didn't budge nor did he judge.

I leaned further and harder into his boot and drew closer to his face.

I was being bent invisibly from the waist.

I wished for hands on my hips.

Ollie was whiskered from a day, perhaps two.

My eyes began to roll.

He groaned, or snored I wasn't sure which, but the sound was both cute and obnoxious.

I brushed myself as if I were walking on stage.

My right hand gripped the edge of the table.

I began to thrust.

I leaned closer to Ollie's face while moving my right hand up to his throat. I was soft in approach. Ollie moaned and mumbled some words few could recognize as a language.

I could feel the outdoor eyes throb with interest.

"What in the hell?" those eyes silently asked.

"Would one dare enter now?" I whispered through shown teeth.

My hand tightened upon Ollie's throat while I slowly moved closer to his jaw.

Ollie was not a good-looking man.

He was tolerable at best.

I thrust my cock further into his boot.

My heart was beating.

I saw his beat too.

My sweat began to bead.

I bent more from the waist.

My face was close to his.

I studied his facial features.

They were poor and unwashed.

What were his final thoughts before sleep came?

Did sleep keep our thoughts warm for the following day?

Slowly I leaned.

His face grew closer.

Ollie had many lines and creases.

He had a hidden odor that was significant.

I knew the eyes at the window were numerous, but none were disruptive, only curious.

I tilted my head while looking at his.

I raised my right leg and rested my cock just above his knee.

His fatty thigh pulsated warmth.

Our faces were inches apart.

I pursed my lips and showed my teeth.

"Should I bite?" I asked the voices.

"No, not bite."

I licked my lips.

In one move as gentle as it was quick my lips touched his and I kissed Ollie goodbye in a warm, moist ever so delicate manner.

His moan was more than memorable.

His moan was more than appreciative.

The eyes at the window were rewarded and could not bear to remain behind. They wouldn't know what I'd do next. They could only spread rumors as to its possibility and to the fact that some man had swept Ollie silent.

Ollie, as I'd later discovered, never out ran those rumors and hushed whispers. He became a man of questionable character. It was better to leave behind only one witness of my being, a witness of questionable character.

I removed my lips from his.

I pulled my cock away from his thigh.

I stood up straight, folded my cloak back in place and brushed myself free from invisible dust.

I placed a second crown near his cup and moved out the door, pulling it shut behind me. The moist early morning air told me that rain would come today and it'd likely be very heavy.

I stood inches away from the door.

I wanted to be seen.

Across the street were the eyes that moments ago peered through the window.

They fell silent when I raised my eyes to fully envelope their stature. There was one of tremendous weakness that disappeared rapidly around the corner.

I tipped my billycock in politeness toward the skulking onlookers. They were not so polite in return. In a twist of my weary frame, I moved away ending the show at the Portsea Inn. I left the audience wanting more.

I walked, hidden by the crease that separated early morning from late night. I passed building, alley, whore and consumer, as if I was made of gossamer.

"Ollie, what was he?" I asked the voices as I walked, "Was he more than what he wished? Did I see more than what he was?"

My walk was the same as it had been the night previous, ending it at the docks for the ferry to Le Havre.

I waited for the attendant to arrive. He did and I purchased my ticket. I left him with a smile and a five-penny tip.

"It'll be running late this morning, sir. You may have a seat off to the right, it's protected from the rain."

I did as he had instructed.

"Ollie, who was he?" I asked again, taking a seat.

I crossed my knees right over left and wrists left over right. No sooner had I positioned myself than my face was washed clean by a morning breeze. There was the taste of sea salt and a twang of dead fish but it refreshed me nonetheless.

"Ollie who was he?" I asked the breeze.

Ollie did remind me of something, but I couldn't pinpoint what. I tapped my foot. Ollie reminded me of a time. His fat face and his unattractive nature, his homely neck yet soft lips all reminded me of a different time.

It wasn't so long ago, but I couldn't quite grasp it.

Ollie was plump and short.

He smelled as if he was fat and unwashed.

The smell of the air, I sniffed hard in hopes that it could trigger the memory I was searching for. Was it a warm night that I sought? I flipped my pocket watch and saw the hour was just shy of six. There were voices with no faces and I saw faces with no voices.

I couldn't grasp the memory I desired.

"Ollie what was he?"

I couldn't remember.

I tapped my foot and swung my wrists.

"Ollie? Ollie, Ollie who..."A spark! "Martha!"

At last!

Ollie reminded me of the fat whore I fucked not more than two months ago, Martha Tabram.

"Whom I tried to fuck anyway," I said to the returning voices.

That night, not long ago I had purchased her stained wears. I then left her with legs wide open. She too smelled of the sea.

That night pleased me.

Recalling the face of fat Martha brought a genuine smile to my own face and a snicker beneath my breath.

That night, the first week of August, the fifth or perhaps later I'd been bound to my task by watching that fat, sagging, shit covered whore conduct her craft.

"Ollie was Martha. His face brought me back to the cunt from Whitechapel," I murmured.

I swayed as the rain fell gently across the dock.

It was August 6th. That day was a Bank Holiday. It was the last holiday of summer and anyone with moderate means would spend the day outside of the city. Customers were few, but vendors of the flesh were plentiful.

"Ollie if you only knew," I chuckled through a yellowing grin.

I had taken to strolling the streets of the East End, offering complimentary aid to the people of the poorest description. I strove to be an angel of mercy working amidst those with no hopes of wings. I'd arrived just days prior from Liverpool and was again at the mercy of Lady Astor.

"Have you money today?" she'd ask.

"The work is scarce," I'd answer back.

"Find some quickly," she added.

"I'll of course do my best, but for now here is some meat." Our give and take was always the same regardless of when it took place.

Those I aided were mostly single women doing what they were bound to do to support smudge faced skirt hangers. Many of the children were children of whores, their father's one of any number of men.

I found the Whitechapel appendage of London during one of my first visits to the kingdom decades ago. I was naturally drawn to the stench of unwashed and the underfed. Most all the populace was women and children. Men came to fuck, not to homestead, and those men had abandoned those women to the trade that never outlived the market.

Gaslights were turned off sometime close to midnight and in the George Yard the gas was dimmed often at eleven.

"Ollie you fat fuck if you only knew," I smiled.

I snickered at the shared voices from brandy stools and from The Times the news of record. "Assassin" they said, "if not suffering from insanity, he appears to be free from the fear of interruption while on his dreadful work."

What oversimplified words they print.

Martha was a fat whore, unattractive to the grandest extreme. Martha Turner is how she introduced herself when I stepped inside the White Swan one night to offer aid.

I wore fine gloves and let grandiose words deftly drip.

"Have you four pence sir?" Martha asked, "*You* must have four pence."

Her smell told me that four pence was a great price.

That night was my trigger, Martha's words were the powder, and her begging to be fucked by a stranger was the flame. She'd lost any sense of self-respect and respect for morality as a whole.

It was shear impulse that directed me. I was infected with it. I was furious. I was driven by my animal nature. No sooner had I agreed to the amount she desired than a heavy Grenadier with a bulging pecker approached.

"I've six bitch, six for a suck and fuck," said the Grenadier.

Martha of course succumbed to the highest bid.

"Dear lady four is a good price for your offering but not six," I said.

Martha took the young soldiers arm.

"Shove off fancy man," the Grenadier said.

"I'll find you at a later hour," I affirmed.

It was already midnight.

I watched as Martha and the soldier left the White Swan. Other ladies of incredible gull then approached me. They wondered what they'd be offered if I was willing to pay such a fat homely specimen as Martha four pence.

I waived my glove to brush them from my view.

Martha and the Grenadier walked out the door, his arm wrapped around her. Martha took the soldier in direction of George Yard. The gaslights were extinguished. It'd be as dark as a black mare's ass.

I followed the loving couple.

My collar was up and my boots clicked the cobblestone.

The couple walked arm in arm at a hurried laughing pace. I was close enough so as not lose them but not be seen.

My hands were being kept warm.

"Ollie if you only knew," I whispered.

My feet swayed to unheard tunes.

Le Havre drew closer as I listed side to side on the bench.

The rain from the channel swept at an increased pace. I settled in nicely, remembering the similarities between Martha the whore and Ollie the innkeeper. The ferry to Le Havre was indeed running late. It was already past 6:30 and there was no sign of it arriving.

As I waited I was nourished by memories of that August night. Some said it was my first; it wasn't though, just my first of more public explanations as to my calling.

Martha was overly familiar with the route she was leading the muscular Grenadier on. No one of interest took interest in the rendezvousing couple. We traversed Wentworth and Whitechapel High Street and eventually to a side of George Yard few could see even in the light of day.

It smelled of mossy stones and damp grass.

In that corner of George Yard she and the Grenadier exchanged coin for cunt. She bent from the waist while pocketing her wages. The act was practiced, almost graceful. After some vocal thrusts the Grenadier wiped himself dry. He left her as quickly as he'd fucked her, stepping on her foot as he passed.

Martha readied herself by pissing out what he left behind. I made my soft boot approach. Her back was toward me as I walked down several mildewed steps through the narrow thoroughfare. Martha was only yards away and before she turned. I whispered, "I have four pence."

She was surprised as she turned toward my voice.

"Hello," she said, "You couldn't keep away. Sniffed me out, did you now?"

"I did," I replied.

"Let me see if I have a wee bit left just for you," she giggled through the shadows.

I walked up to her slowly still hidden by the darkness of the Yard. "Money upfront dear, I've learned my lesson from fucking first and asking wages afterwards."

I gave her a shilling.

She was quite pleased.

"Let's go down here it'll be more comfortable for both of us," I said.

She followed my lead.

"I want to see your face," I said, "Not from the back. I want to feel it, and I want to see your face," I told her.

"Suits me," she said, "My knees get mighty scarred at the end of a busy night."

She lay on the moist ground of the first floor landing.

It was hard but she didn't complain.

"It's a comfortable cold," she said.

I smelled her salt.

She chattered about pointless things.

"Shhh, quiet, you won't notice the cold before long," I assured her.

Martha only smiled back.

She rested on her elbows and spread her thighs. I tossed back her green skirt to a position halfway up her torso. Her petticoat was dark and was just a momentary inconvenience. Her jacket was dark and being carried. Her black bonnet was tied but not worn.

I looked down between her thighs.

I saw it through the dark.

I *smelled* it through the ashen smoke of the East End.

I touched it with my white gloves.

That night with Martha was as vivid as this Portsmouth bench. I had put that night to pen and paper creating my own form of street literature.

'Twas thought that soldiers had killed the poor creature
And on them people laid the blame
When found 'twas hard to recognize a feature
To leave her so, oh! what a cruel shame.

I prepared myself as Martha waited.

"How long have you been a whore?" I asked.

"I have to do what I have to do, fuck or die, die from fucking, not much of a choice. I imagine when this fanny gets much older I'll just pray for a faster way out."

I kneeled in my own way.

"A faster way out?" I asked.

"None of us know when it is our hour," I said.

Martha aimed her cunt at me. I sat with a soft cock in my hand.

"Can't fuck with that boy!" The words of Lispenard barked back over the years.

There was little in the way of conversation.

She and I were characters on a stage.

The dark holds everything hostage and it did us that night as I began what were Martha's final caresses.

I swayed on the bench of the current hour.

Le Havre was late but my memory was on time.

I tasted her salted pork and listened to John Keats's rambling poetry.

I smelled the flowers that covered the graves of Dickens characters of fame.

I heard the distant ferry and in less than an hour I'd be on board.

I remembered that night so well.

"It's a shame that women sell their flesh to eat spoiled bread much less drink warm ale," I lectured.

"Are you in me yet?" she asked without a concern.

"Not yet woman."

I grew red at her question.

She reached for my trousers.

Martha laughed at how soft I was.

A whore whose only mission was to sell ass as many times as she could each day was laughing at me. A lowly creature such as this one was laughing at me, a doctor.

"In a moment I'll be in you in no uncertain terms," I said.

"I'll pay extra if you stay longer than what we agreed upon."

"Soft or not, do what you wish," she said.

I reached inside my cloak for what I'd promised. It wasn't in the right pocket so I reached for the left and quickly tossed a couple of found pennies. I again let Martha know I'd pay for her additional time.

She giggled.

I reached back inside my cloak and in one swift move pulled the tool of my trade thrusting it deep into her heart as I thrust at her my pointless cock.

Again and again I thrust knife and my pointless cock at her. The exact count didn't matter, for the wound to the heart was the one that delivered Martha from this realm to the next.

I fucked her heart with the knife.

I swayed in remembrance.

My eyes darkened with each waking dream.

The depot clerk let those in wait know departure would be imminent.

I remembered so much thanks to that greasy Ollie.

I muttered those ramblings of Keats again and again.

"ASLEEP! O sleep a little while, white pearl!
And let me kneel, and let me pray to thee,
And let me call Heaven's blessing on thine eyes,
And let me breathe into the happy air,
That doth enfold and touch thee all about,
Vows of my slavery, my giving up,
My sudden adoration, my great love!"

In George Yard I staged a play one that would reveal one thing yet hide others. I would confuse the authorities if the frenzied scene could be attributed to the drunken Grenadier.

I was correct, as the fools were confused by obvious clues.

My mind returned briefly to George Yard as the ferry edged closer.

I had pissed inside Martha.

She welcomed it with a twitch.

The ferry barked its impending arrival.

"God, all are bedeviled by the work of the man from Liverpool," I whispered to the panting voices that were hungrier than ever.

I remember Martha. She was a fat, simple, homely whore who chose beer over food and cock over class. The world will little note neither her life nor her passing.

I stood to head to the docking of the ferry.

The attendant watched me.

I nodded his way.

The attendant failed to return it.

On that night I'd leaned over Martha. She lay there prone, her eyes wide and lifeless. I hovered close to her face, my cock pushed into her knee.

I grabbed her breasts.

Her skin was pudgy and pruned. Its warmth was failing.

I sniffed her as my right hand wrapped around her throat. She smelled old, she smelled unwashed and she smelled dead long before that night.

I pursed my lips and showed my teeth.

I feigned a bite.

I took a deeper breath the closer I drew to her neck.

Her face faded as I shuffled closer to the ferry.

I stuck my tongue to hers. I licked her lips in a slow circular motion. I tasted the far off salt of the speedy Grenadier. I caressed her neck and gave her a long, soft gentle kiss swallowing her spittle and the soldier's seed.

That night with Martha was a glorious and thirst quenching.

Thank God for the memory of Martha, I left her, still fat and gaping mouth to the rats of a better day.

Thank God for the rain and thank God for the attendant who bellowed all aboard to Le Havre.

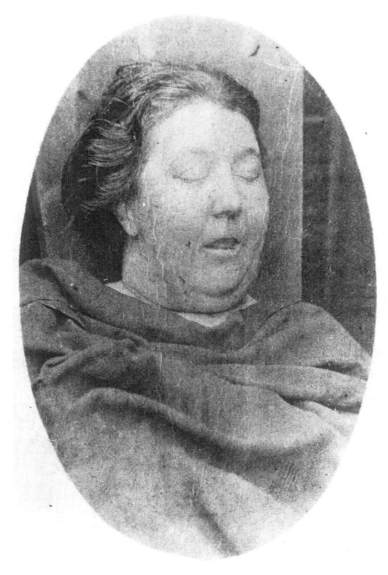

Martha Tabram in mortuary.

CHAPTER ELEVEN

I shuffled amidst polite elbows up the plank leading to the non-descript ferry. The faces were casual, caught somewhere between kindness and impatience.

I was aboard a ferry that, according to the depths of my interest in such things, remained nameless. It'd be late tomorrow when I'd disembark in Le Havre. I knew the schedule and I knew the frailties of crew and water alike. There, if the timing were accurate I'd catch the La Bretange back to New York City. If timing was poor, then the shadows of Littlechild might catch up to me.

The Atlantic in the warmer months was never an exotic journey, but crossing the sea in the winter months presented a number of challenges.

If I were delayed in Le Havre, I would have another lengthy wait. My plan was to take the La Bretange to New York cast amidst common steerage.

I carried my bag with quiet dignity.

I had booked the cabin of my regular use.

I'd pass this and step over that as one name again flashed before me.

"Littlechild!"

He was an inspector, brighter than the rest. He'd found inaccuracies in the public lamenting so he took to his own private pursuit.

I watched from benches and doorways as Littlechild read signs and kept notes of erased clues. He was, as far as I could determine, following me. He was close, both on the cobbled walkways and in my dreams.

Littlechild would guess I'd be heading for Boulogne, for now I was a step ahead. He was an ass, but the most brilliant of ones to date. Either I was careless or he was just affective, but he wasn't that far off from unleashing my tightly wrapped secrets. For now I'd stay far enough ahead to remain safe, yet near enough for him to stay interested.

John Littlechild was a Chief Inspector from Scotland Yard, brought in when others had needlessly misdirected names, places and dates. He was a fair man but no common footman such as he would outwit me.

I shuffled toward my cabin.

Ollie, God bless him, reminded me of one night after another. Ollie reminded me of all things common, and Inspector Littlechild was as common as the others, but in a unique way. I was weary and my ability at outfoxing a hungry canine was decreasing with fervor.

This ferry was good preparation for the long voyage ahead as its compartments were small. Those of infrequent journeys who traveled on such crafts produced the bulk of shit and vomit.

This ride would last a day. Perhaps a late dinner could be had in France, but timing was crucial. My cabin was private with a shared washroom. The added accommodations made the additional price worth it.

I strolled past the crewmen. I was casual in my walk to the aft where the cabin awaited. It was always best to be in the rear, the business of the day is conducted up top. In the rear I can observe.

It had been several years between journeys such as this, but I made it seem to all those who watched me that I was familiar with the setting. Knowledge of some seafaring terms impressed the young ones who had lost grip of their mothers' skirts.

I hoped to sleep, as I'd had only fitful naps the last few months. I was always tired, but my ability to out think my need for sleep kept my eyes wide when my head hit the pillow. I was paranoid and always alert to the shallowest of noises.

My work was behind me and I knew that a good night's rest was close. As I walked the passageways, several cast their own weary eyes on me. I ignored them as I entered my cabin.

Chic it wasn't, but acceptable for a day.

I put my bag close to the door and removed my outer garments. I lay down without hesitation, and was asleep before the ferry had slipped its moorings.

There was a bump and once again I was in a different time.

I was amidst a field of flowers sharing quiet evenings with the late John Booth. We'd become friends, and on several occasions I had tended to his medical needs. As our relationship came to fruition, I treated the needs of his mind and body.

Booth was grateful and took me into his confidence at times when perhaps he shouldn't have. I wanted him to see me as notable and dependable. I wanted others to see me as neutral.

Neutrality and Booth would have to wait.

It was the spring of 1863 and the fields of Southern Pennsylvania were not even a footnote. I was caught amidst the wars undertow. Shirkers and muscled spies warned that Southern Pennsylvania was inevitable. The two leagues were destined to meet when and how they did.

I'd traveled hid behind trees but for the most part I was as a grand figure as the American Civil War was itself. I had thought of Booth often, usually as I lay under full moon skies seeking his dark eyes of comfort.

I'd ridden the circuit of states as a free man, offering my cures to the destitute in life. I had nurtured my reputation among all those who needed a doctor, whether they were military or civilian. The war in the early years seemed as if it was running without a course on the Northern side. Their confusion served me well.

As the months passed, I saw that neutrality might not serve me well as I thought. History pointed to Jackson at Manassas and Lee at

Chancellorsville and hills of lesser names bore witness to the Southern strength. I sensed I'd have to make favor with those in the south.

Months earlier I had returned in full glory to Western New York. I assisted many young men into the ranks of the Union Army.

I was well dressed in the finest of Chicago cotton. I had my favorite horse as I rode with a tilted chin into small towns casting my grand image.

I had a great duty to perform, so my uniform had to reflect it. I had one made with special care. Its design would make it possible for both sides of the moving border to know that I was a man of character and of neutrality.

When asked where I was heading, I'd declare I was a doctor of reputable note and sides did not matter. I'd say to the border guards, "It's my solemn duty to care for the war torn of both body and soul."

My dreams deftly drifted the fine line border of the here and now with the then and that.

The ferry rocked.

My sleep proved enriching.

I had traveled to Buffalo, Rochester and to points in the Southern Tier, recruiting young men for Northern service. "All could be like me," I showed the shoeless ones. I'd readjust my hat. "You can be like me. You can all taste the wonder of being a hero. You can all return full of decorations and fancy stripes and show your girls how great it was. You can show them all the war would not have been won without you. You too can be a hero." I dazzled them with my dress and bullshit.

They came, for God's sake how they came.

I spoke of flowers being tossed by Southern virgins. I spoke of grand parades welcoming the saviors in blue. I spoke of the glory to God, country and of Sunday tea with the prettiest of women.

The younger and stronger the recruit, the better my show had to be. If they were young and strong my speeches would be tremendous. I'd be awarded with a dollar for every young soul I brought to the recruitment station. Those dollars would become more difficult to acquire though as the lists of battle dead were posted.

At first my dress and words could produce dozens of faces a day at the recruitment station. I'd declare: "You too, young men of Warsaw, Jamestown or Bath, you too can be dressed in the finest of spun cloth. You too can come home and impress the little maidens with stripes and badges awarded for battles won!"

I rode through farm towns, high upon my steed. So many of those un-plucked young fools came skittering my way as soon as they saw me.

"Sign me up!" They'd shout.

"I'll go, *sign* me up!"

When one village sent word ahead to the next one of even smaller size I'd have dozens waiting for my arrival.

"What have you seen? Shiloh, Richmond have you been to Fredericksburg?" asked one after another.

I'd ride gracefully past their questions eventually allowing one to take hold of my reigns. That boy would feel honored. I'd dismount and ask where a meal could be had for a fair price.

I'd follow the directions given. Often times I was given a chair at the local office of mediocre authority. Once I had a table I would settle down for a near fresh meal, usually of corn bread and meat. Chicken was a local favorite.

The fools would come in and wonder about this, that and the other. I'd paint the greatest pictures for them. The old men whose better days were on other battlefields would come too in order to relive fabricated days of their own glory.

"What'll it be?" asked unseen faces.

"A steak if you have it, some chicken and corn if you don't," I'd say.

Regardless of the food, I always spoke to wide-eyed audiences of old men and young boys. They all wanted the latest news from the front. I filled my belly and their curiosity with tales at how great the Northern victories have been.

I'd take an ample bite of what was placed before me. Daintily I'd wipe my lips of the usually undercooked meat.

The give and take of bountiful banter was tremendous as young and old pounded their chests at how great the successes were. The successes I painted. I'd sit back after a few more over salted bites and ask for a beer that I'd never drink.

"Young men if I were you and wanted badges and sashes to impress little Mary Mae from Sunday mass, I'd join up before it's too late."

Murmurs among them grew.

Drunken old men gave a 'yahoo' or a 'here here'!

I'd toast their boast and hand my beer to the one with the shakiest hands.

"If I were you I'd join the ranks of heroes right now, Mary Mae won't be around much longer."

"How?" some might ask.

"How can I join?"

A second beer would arrive.

"Down there, at the church, down there at the school house, down there at the telegraph office. The army man is in town today and tomorrow."

Boots would hurriedly scuffle out the door.

I'd sit forward in the chair or I'd stand tall upon it and wave my hands to the beat of my gloriously flowered nouns and verbs.

"Men if you want your share of glory and your share of Mary Mae I'll help you sign up!"

Cheers would rise and so would I as more boots scuffled forward.

"Follow me!" I'd say.

"Praise be and bless Mr. Abe," the older, limbless ones would shout.

I jostled on my ferry bunk.

For a moment my dreams halted.

The ferry bounced and bumped me.

The channel waters rolled me awake only long enough to realize that I must return to sleep to relive the grandeur of that time.

I returned to those small villages of Western New York. Over the course of months many young men and older men wanting to be young again followed me. Many placed their marks and raised their hands swearing to protect and defend.

I was paid a dollar a head for those who boarded trains as part of the 12th, 14th, 19th and 76th New York. I filled many shoes and in turn many graves. I was the character on a stage and my presentation was the script to the needy, anxious farm boys.

I played that role for quite a number of months but as the newspapers began to share stories that were far more accurate than my scripts; the dollars grew fewer in number.

My tales were no longer flowered.

Fewer would stop to smell them or even offer a beer.

The trains confirmed the posted lists by an ever increasing number of returning pine boxes.

Things changed after Gettysburg. I could no longer bedazzle the ignorant, for even they could see friends weren't coming home. There were more Mary Maes than could be fucked in a lifetime. Even the lunatics could see the coffins resting in family rooms.

I left Southern New York State. The crops had been picked.

I began to flank the flank of George McClellan's Army of the Potomac. I'd stayed aware of movements by being diligent to shirkers' words. They reported McClellan's forces were making a reinforced sweep south. I knew if that was accurate that it would be done in the finest detail. The general was as well known for his meticulous nature, as I was for my megalomaniac speeches. McClellan had turned the worthless sac of shits that came from the north into a real Army. They could march but not fight and soon McClellan was out and Meade was in.

Meade was in the untenable position of having to regroup, organize and recruit while defending the north from advancing Southerners. He did this with what little brainpower he possessed. Meade was clearly caught off guard when the incoming reports stated there was a large scouting party in Southern Pennsylvania.

Union Scouts said what they saw was too large to be a group of foragers.

Forces began to grow.

I'd been just north of Carlisle when I saw the flank widen and the numbers of shirkers grow.

I now wore the colors of the Union Medical Corps, a dark blue shoulder strap with a green sash. My steed bore a gold trimmed blanket. It was those garments that attracted youth to me like cocks to whores.

Upon leaving the Southern Tier, I traveled to Pennsylvania, specifically Harrisburg. I wanted, and expected, to make a grand entrance at the Governor's office, seeking a commission as an officer with advanced rank.

After all I was a reputable doctor who had recruited many to the call of the President.

I was entitled to a commission.

The streets of the capitol were thick with mud. The rain had been a long-standing companion for its residents and so had the mud. Andrew Curtin was governor. I had followed his progression to that office. He was a quality Republican who seemed to pay particular attention to needy children.

If I could have but a moment with Curtin, I knew I could express my life as a virtual orphan and how I had overcome many disadvantages. I could with my flowered words make him aware of my medical abilities and my desire to be of service to his state as a doctor of reputable note.

I could serve as a hero to the orphans of Pennsylvania.

My sense of glory grew.

I could be a hero to orphans everywhere.

I grew in fantasy.

I rode close to the accented buildings.

The streets were an abomination and passage from one corner to the next was near impossible. People were everywhere. The bridges, of which I had several to cross, were heavily guarded due to rumors of Southern encroachment.

"I'm Dr. Tumblety, Francis Tumblety from Rochester, New York," that allowed my passage.

I rode my steed from corner to bridge and then bridge to thoroughfare.

There were stragglers in blue.

There were prisoners in gray.

There were tears being shed by little ones seeking their lost mother's hems.

I approached slowly. The near gold dome of the capitol was my point of interest. Carefully I rode, saying once to a drunkard that he need be still for I had private business with the governor.

"The governor's that way," some pointed clearing a path.

I sensed that the poor and elected officials alike had heard of my approach.

"He is here!"

"He is here, step aside!"

The dome glimmered.

The closer I came to it, the larger the number of infantryman. They were scattered, encamped across from any number of official looking buildings.

Everyone was asking questions.

"What's your desire here?"

"Why do you wish to see the governor?"

I could no longer walk my steed with a full step. His frame was falling victim to the thickening mud. He too began to pull in directions that showed he was nervous over the convulsions.

"Help me," I heard.

"Please let me through," I said firmly, "I've business, important business."

Questions were asked.

Answers were given.

"Please let me pass!" I implored.

Families were moving out and soldiers were moving in.

There were empty coffins lined up across from the dome in protest while genuine dead waited for the protest to end.

"Please, stand aside I have business awaiting me," I said.

Some moved aside as I'd requested while others ignored my words honoring instead their own selfishness. "Asshole, you can wait like the rest of us, we all have business," one ill-mannered bearded beak relayed.

A soldier of decent rank was shoving one and then the other and placing others in different lines equally abreast and four to five deep.

I was motionless in the thickening mud.

"Move your animal," the man in stripes said.

"I've business with the governor," I barked back.

"I don't give a fuck. If you have a letter, show me, if not get the animal out of here before I shoot you both."

"Letter?"

"Do you have a letter confirming your appointment?" he asked.

"No, but I'm a doctor seeking a commission."

"Move your animal," he again demanded.

My steed was getting nervous and proceeding without command and with little attention to direction. There were more demands and vulgarities tossed my way.

"I'm a doctor seeking a commission," I said as my horse took to its own lead.

The man with stripes didn't care.

An officer's commission was rightfully mine, yet I was being forced away. I attempted to stop my steed but he was too backed up to gain a footing.

We were pushed forward by the shoving insistences of sergeants and drunken vendors.

"We'll all be dead soon, go to where you can help," a fresh faced private said.

The vulgar man of authority came to me.

"You need to move your animal."

"I'm doing just that you incessant twit!" I said.

His face wasn't pleased. His words weren't pleasant either.

"Go to York. That's where you'll be needed, your commission be damned," the sergeant said.

"York?"

"Yes, York. Go south you ass."

It was late in the day. I hadn't eaten, I was weary and York would be a strong ride even with a healthy horse but I would go to York. History would be forever grateful that I had made that trip.

That night I camped in a grove of trees and enjoyed the company of a group of fabulous fighters from Ohio. They were young and strong that night. They're always young and strong, and how grateful I was they were. I slept with one eye on my destination and the other on a fine boy from Dayton.

The next morning, with my horse fed, I left for York. I'd be welcomed there. I presumed the man of vulgar authority had wired the township. He would've made them aware that a doctor was on his way and would be arriving in due course.

I heard the shouts from York's street corners.

I saw the women wave their handkerchiefs.

I saw youngsters crowd about my steed.

That's what I saw.

I saw what my mind painted.

On the road to York, the numbers of straggling advancers increased, but they were small compared to those fleeing. I made stops here and there along the way for water and to piss. Doing so, I skirted the demands of questioning authorities. I rested my reigns outside of Lancaster near York on June 26th 1863.

York was just shy of Gettysburg. I rode in from the northwest and was asked by some sentries the word for the day. My password was Dr. Tumblety.

The commotion in York was greater than the day's prior in Harrisburg.

Black smoke was seen.

Shots were seen being aimed at dodgers and pubescent shirkers. Those whom I'd seen leaving Harrisburg likely came from here. This smallish town was bare. Families carried what they could. Those crops that couldn't be ripped from the ground by hungry men or beasts were burned.

From a distance I saw a soldier. I approached with my hat in one hand and reigns in the other. He was a pudgy, very nervous young officer.

"Sir..." I said.

He interrupted me.

"Sir, you must be on your way," he said, "We can't guarantee your safety for many more hours," he emphasized.

I remained where I was, observing the moment.

The crops were burning and my safety was no longer guaranteed. Those statements could mean several things.

Had Lee crossed over?

Had Harrisburg been captured?

"Lieutenant, I'm a doctor, my name is Tumblety, Dr. Francis Tumblety from Rochester, New York."

I waited for him to return a string of vulgar curses of one tone or another.

There were no cursed tones though.

"The Commons, it's south of the city, a hospital is there, go there, but we can not guarantee your safety," the pudgy boy directed me.

"Thank you and bless you," I said.

I went south.

The smell could've pointed my way.

I smelled it before I saw it.

It was the air of the burn barrel all over again. It smelled of old wood, it smelled of piss, of shit and it was heavily burdened with the odor of death.

All forms of creatures slowed my short journey.

I slowed my steed to a deliberate trot, in moments The Commons appeared. The York Military Hospital couldn't be missed. It was a couple of years old at the most, apparently built just for the war.

My steed slowed, upset at the smell.

Tents surrounded the hospital, which was the centerpiece for a great army of dead and dieing.

A corporal with a small patrol was at rest some yards from the main entrance.

I followed his cast shadow.

"Corporal, I'm a doctor of reputable note from Rochester, New York. I'm here to offer my services."

The corporal stood up.

"Sir, I'm Corporal James Denbar of the Patapsco Guard, from Maryland," he said pointing to his men.

I reached for his hand.

He saluted instead.

"We are Provost," he added.

"Sir, go to the front, the entrance is covered by canvas as you see. The office of Henry Palmer Chief Surgeon is toward the rear of the building, see him. He'll certainly be glad to see you."

I followed the young man's directions. I made my way past tents of dead and the living lying uncovered beneath the scalding heat of summer.

As I neared the entrance I saw half-naked, emaciated young boys disguised as fighting men. They were shot to shit by modern weapons.

"Go and fight for every lasting peace." I never understood that phrase.

"Yet I had said: kill to make things better, be immoral for moralities sake."

I stopped as a young colored boy approached and took my reigns.

"Tanks Capt.'," he said.

"Captain," I repeated dismounting.

That was a fair enough rank. I entered beneath the canvas shawl into the main building.

The hallway was a beacon of everything inhumane. Tables were few. Those that could stand were looking for a place to lie down and those that were prone wished they could stand one more time.

"Henry Palmer's office?" I asked a smallish, orderly type who was as dirty as any horseman.

"I'm Henry Palmer," the figure declared.

I was a bit taken aback.

"Dr. Palmer?"

"Yes, I am Dr. Palmer. You are who?"

"I'm Captain Francis Tumblety, a doctor from Rochester, New York. I wish to offer my services," I said.

Palmer shoved aside the one table with wheels, looked momentarily at several men on the floor, wiped his hands upon his gown and reached for mine.

"Doctor what?" he asked, "What's your name again?"

"Tumblety, Captain Tumblety," I repeated.

"Good, Captain, begin wherever you wish. There's no shortage as you may see."

Palmer called for another faceless boy to show me where to find what I needed.

After stepping over some shrouded faces we entered a small room. The skill sets were scattered. There were clamps, surgical saws, probes, retractors and isinglass plaster and that's all I was given.

"There is very little horsehair. You'll need to make do," the boy said as he went out the door.

I looked up and down the hallway and was stumped as to where to begin. My first few steps were deliberate.

My walk grew more attuned to the scene. I reached down towards one whose face showed more thirst than it did blood. In caressing his hair I assured him water would soon arrive.

"He doesn't need water, not anymore, he's been dead awhile," a deeply wounded private said.

I felt the young boys face. It was cold.

I strolled looking for the thirsty and hungry and not the broken. The first hours moved quickly. I worked through the late evening on Saturday, June 27th. I ate little, taking bits and pieces off the plates of the soon to be dead.

My lips quivered in delight.

I heard cries for food, whines for water, and prayers for death. Those tones twanged my ears throughout my first day.

I passed water from one to the next.

My first blood was a simple hand wound.

That private didn't want help, as he'd only assisted in bringing a friend in who had greater need.

"It'll be quick," I said.

I brushed some invisible dirt from his wound and squeezed some infection loose. There wasn't much and the private bitched. I trimmed a piece of loose skin, no sutures were required but I applied liberally an isinglass plaster.

I'd saved the young man.

The private didn't acknowledge my kindness and only drifted down the darkening hallway. He left his mortally wounded friend to my care. A friend I left to the care of God. I walked towards others who showed greater thirst than blood. There were few words past back and forth amongst the wounded. Once I'd assisted with grace and skill my first patient, calls came my way for additional attention.

"Help me!" One would say.

"Fuck him. Help me, I'm more serious," others would follow.

I sought my own folly.

There was a man leaning on a board. His foot was bloodied but still in its boot. I kneeled. He said it hurt like hell.

"I'm sure it does," I agreed.

I cut the trouser leg and untied his brogan. It was tight. There were no stockings, and blood had crusted around the top of the ankle.

The brogan was pulled loose to the vulgar pleasure of the young soldier. I studied his foot, it was immensely dirty, blistered, and a hobnail had popped through causing tremendous distress when he walked. The young man said he'd been without shoes for several weeks. The ones he had came from a dead friend. "They're too small for me." He asked if I had others.

My brows were firm. I wiped a trace of blood on a smock I'd found. I looked inside the brogan and with a tool from my skill set bent the hobnail as best I could. I gave the young soldier instructions on proper foot care. I told him that they had to be clean and blister free or infection would set in.

"I need shoes," he said.

"God help me," another voice begged.

"Stay close and you'll soon find the right size," I said.

The deeply injured cried as I walked away. I knew my skills were being warmly welcomed and in just a matter of moments I'd already assisted two of the war wounded heroes.

I was saving lives.

I was needed.

Voices came from all corners and from numerous hidden faces, help me please, help me they begged.

I noticed one of the faces was scorched with his scalp showing. There was a copious amount of scarring and most of his hair was gone from his right side. His eyes begged me when his throat couldn't.

I walked away.

Wounded voices grew in need and timbre. I watched the burned man watch me walk away to aid a soldier with a poorly wrapped head wound.

I'd maneuvered my way down the hall giving a kind look here, and a pat of a hand in comfort there. I plucked dirt from necks and scalps as I passed again beneath the canvas. I heroically saved perhaps six lives in less than one hour.

I deserved credit and honor.

I let the canvas fall behind me as if it were a stage curtain.

I strolled into the courtyard looking for anyone and everyone that needed me. There were many voices and I was lauded wherever I strolled. The voices upon my shoulders howled as I passed the bloodiest to seek out the thirstiest.

I offered water to a soldier from Ohio who'd fallen from his horse while ignoring a private whose arm was badly mangled.

I recorded the ensuing days in this manner.

Sunday June 28th, 1863

Yesterday the sun was hot. The encroaching morning embers showed the heat of this day would be unkind too. I was only a day amidst the campfires of York but was drenched fully with the poetry of battle.

War, like poetry is a form of a disciplined expression.

Its battles are story lines as in a ballade.

Its battles can be staged as grandiose achievements of terrain and generals.

Like poetry, battles with all its components are meant to be. All are characters of the art portrayed, all Carp Diem, are of the moment and of the day. I was now a character on the stage of this play. I was a word a in the stanza and a lyric of a ballade.

I was saving lives.

I was wandering among the fallen leaves from the trees of man.

I was giving ability to the disabled and securing for me a noble name.

I slept little my first night.

I admired my being admired by those who needed me. Their cries I savored. The sick needed me and with liberal water saved life after life.

21

My eyes were aware of the needy and horizon alike.

I'd noticed troop movements growing in panic and the numbers of the Patapsco Guard was thinning.

What sleep I garnered was near the colored boy who nurtured my steed; the boy was dumb but useful.

The dead were mounting in number. I assisted in toting cadavers from table to ground and ground to wagon. We, at an early hour had to stack the dead three and four high on many wagons.

I was becoming an angel for the already dead.

I gave water to the thirsty of either frock color.

I was wearing an apron that gave me a look of heavy labor when in fact I was seeking greater recognition. Troops were moving fast. I was told my safety was not guaranteed. I ate hardtack and drank coffee from a tin cup. My whiskers were thickening.

Many asked for my help. I patted those who were festered and watered those on passing chestnut mares.

-Frank

Monday June 29th, 1863

I again slept little last evening and the colored boy remained close. As the early hours came I walked the grounds that the campfires set ablaze. We boiled many an implement in the same pot that boiled our meat.

I dipped my hands into the spoilage of the dead.

My lips quivered from the smell.

I decorated my apron regularly with what I wiped.

I stayed busy by moving from one to another, it was those who did not beg that I'd calm. I kneeled over the dead and showed my attention to their already mortal wounds. I'd dip my fingers into shattered gut. Tasting the wound taught me when death had won. Having concluded my diagnosis I said a quick prayer ending with a dramatic genuflect witnessed by the Eastern Hemlocks casting their own caring limbs.

The colored boy admired my work and so too did several whose wounds were gently wrapped. My skills were great and were growing as I walked the grounds.

It was in the early A.M. when the skirmishes were first heard. I was standing broad shouldered adjacent a fire built by the colored boy. Other shirkers had found its use too. Their eyes and ears perked as the first crack of the Enfield were heard coming from the southeast. They loosened their hands of coffee and made their way to the Harrisburg Road.

Henry Palmer told me that safety could not be guaranteed as most of the Provost Guard had reestablished other grounds. I was asked to assist in different ways as doctors under contract chose to head other directions rather than wait on what the future hours may bring.

The same Henry Palmer told me that within hours we'd be overwhelmed with wounded and I best be prepared. I knew I would be, I was a doctor of reputable note and my services were always welcomed.

The skirmishes increased as the sun moved further west. There were growing rumors about the size of the Confederate advance. They were a scouting party only were the first notices. Later when the hour was nearing 6:00 and the fires were boiling meat, we were told it could be as a large as a division perhaps more.

Unfortunately I began to see those in greater need in ways I'd never before been made aware. It was early in the day and what bacon remained was given to those who could stomach a degree of rancid meat.

Shirkers from Barlow's XI Corps passed through the grounds of York and stole meat from the hungry and shoes from the dead. They drank our coffee and pulled the good horses free from the Hemlocks. The colored boy had hid my steed away hours early, as he knew more than all others as to what was just hours ahead.

I wandered the course of the day amazed at the blaze of the fires and the image I portrayed by the strength of the same blaze.

-Frank

Tuesday June 30th, 1863

Again I slept little. Its lack began to spread. I heard voices that weren't heard when I was better rested. There were shouts. There were hums. There were shots echoing from all directions. My lack of sleep was questioning everything; was it real or was it dreamt?

I woke from a shallow nap to the warm hands of the colored boy. He handed me my steed and told me that he must leave for if the southerners caught him he'd be back with his master.

I'd not see him after that first coffee and morning biscuit.

Cavalrymen were on the loose, rifle shots and occasional artillery rounds could be heard.

Palmer had stayed.

Palmer had found me by a Hemlock tree.

I recall that I was taken aback by his approach toward me. In anger he asked that I do more than what I had been as if my repairing mankind was insufficient in his eyes. Palmer asked that I assume the care for a larger number of the more needy.

I found the freshest of water and newest of troops.

We were all told that it was the division of Jubal Early; of Ewell's II Corps that'd be the first we'd see. They'd neared Harrisburg but had turned; they were flanking the Union Army. The Union General Barlow wasn't putting up a decent cross fire.

I, near mid morning of the day scampered the grounds tending to those who could travel. I replaced plasters and bandaged better hands when I could. The incoming numbers of heavily wounded were tremendous.

I sought out the freshest of water.

I shared it with those on horseback.

In returning to the Hemlock with a dirty apron and clean bucket I'd passed a collection of tents where more delicate surgeries were performed. I was capable of anything that might be seen coming from underneath its flaps.

I was of better service elsewhere however.

Palmer disagreed.

I shunned his comments.

I'd approached those tents always from a circular route.

I could see them but they couldn't see me.

Palmer was persistent and I was asked to come and assist.

They must have seen that my ability was great.

I lumbered with hesitation to one of those tents.

I'd wanted to first see proper procedures. If I asked about such procedures it might cause more problems than should be laid upon my dedicated service. I might not know the correct answer.

Approaching from the back I saw four wild bores that had been shot. Later I learned it was a pistol used by an orderly, to end the feeding frenzy of the hogs on amputated hands and feet.

I neared the tents entrance.

I wanted to be seen entering.

My appearance would be reassuring.

I stepped in offering a gentle hand to the young boys who showed fear and soft brown sorrowful eyes. The hogs, they'd been feeding for several days on piles scattered in locations. I saw piles of bone. I saw piles of shit, piles of sawed feet, hands and arms. There were fingers, lower legs, ears and pieces of meat that had no definition.

The hogs ate well.

Wagons were pulling and prodding.

Bodies with unnamed palpable lives and the barely numbered were toted away after fleeting attempts to remedy them right.

I entered the tent as an angel welcoming all to their final resting place.

I touched, waved and wondered.

I knew my glide was being interrupted.

Grab this for me Henry Palmer asked, it was a near detached left arm. I went to his table. I held the arm as if it were a sleeve of an old dress shirt.

I didn't want dirt to be cast either by it or me.

I recalled that Palmer had made a slice with the tiniest of affective tools. Pull it he said. Pull it I did and the arm drew free from the flesh that had kept it attached.

The young man who gave of his arm lay wide-eyed but free from Palmer's notice. Palmer mopped the blood while he slapped and folded the loose skin. Large amount of silk that had been hidden from me was used on the boy.

Palmer then took notice.

Fuck it he said to anyone who could hear and he moved to the next table. The young boy would lie on the table 'till orderlies freed him for the next portion of his journey.

"All that silk wasted!" Palmer said.

Over there Palmer directed me.

He pointed me to other tables.

Thank God he'd noticed my ability.

Palmer called me a Captain, he'd called me a doctor, and he knew of my skill and ability when he saw it.

I went where Palmer directed, as we were peers.

I expected to be sent to one of the larger rooms inside the main building of the hospital but was not.

I aimed for where there was enough room and yet free from observation. There I'd be seldom watched or judged and would be allowed to work the best I knew how.

I assumed control over a table that was positioned firmly. The wood was stained dark not from natural growth but from mans blood.

I'd seen the frenzied work of a steward.

His name was Arnold a burly man who was as ugly as the plague. He carried a pistol so to guard materials and to kill the hogs. Hogs were everywhere. They smelled the blood and tasted the dripped meat. So did I.

As I approached the table Arnold gave me a bucket of water to wash off the loose fluids. He waived his hands towards several others carrying litters. They came toward my table.

I was given a body of an older man who bore sergeant stripes. I was told he was the color bearer of a non-descript unit. He'd been given some whiskey to ease the pain. His left arm was shot through at the elbow. I saw splintered bone poking through the skin.

I reached for him slowly.

I poked at the bone with my fingers.

The man jerked back. This scene was of great interest to me. What did the man who bore stripes see?

Lunch was coffee and a piece of old meat.

I looked at the older man near unconscious from whiskey. Arnold handed me several rags. I was told to use the chloroform sparingly as he believed the days ahead would be troubled.

There was only one Chisholm inhaler and Palmer carried that.

Arnold confirmed Ewell's Corps was heading south.

The Provost had fallen into retreat to Harrisburg and some men went south as well.

I held the rags in one hand and the bottle of chloroform in other. Feeling as if I was not being recognized properly and not wanting to be interrupted by medial duty I asked Arnold to use the chloroform. I let him begin with the tasks I considered minor. He'd prepare the table for my work. I'd be his teacher and he the student. I'd judge him in his tasks. I'd call him a success or a failure.

Arnold said the forearm needed amputation.

I told him I knew that.

You may prepare the arm I told Arnold.

I knew I was asking of him duties that were mine; he seemed appreciative of the opportunity. I asked him if he had the desire to learn medicine, he said he did.

I told Arnold I'd observe him.

The hour was nearing 2PM.

I would teach and he'd learn.

I was Lispenard and Arnold was I.

I seized the moment. I was the master and Arnold he would be the student.

I would need to read from a book he pointed to.

I'd read and he'd perform.

I assured him that it'd be fine.

I would allow this, adding only advice and suggestions as I saw fit.

I watched as he poured an ample amount of chloroform onto the rag and forced it onto the sergeants' face. He began to choke then his lungs calmed as Arnold pulled the rag back. After counting to seven Arnold repeated the routine until he was confident the man was asleep.

The blood from the arm was significant. The old man's color was weakening.

Arnold read what he could then asked me to read what he could not.

With tremendous difficulty we sat the old man up. I braced his back. His weight was dead. There were no chairs that would've made this procedure easier and more precise.

I heard far off cannon. Their landing wasn't close.

Arnold placed the tourniquet inches above the wound.

The sergeants' body jerked as a protruding piece of bone stuck briefly to a portion of the table.

I could hear snapping. I held the arm where Arnold said I should and where, I agreed.

There were words Arnold couldn't make out so I read those to him more slowly.

Do what is best I told Arnold.

The sergeant began to groan.

He pissed his trousers.

Arnold asked that I straighten the arm from behind. I did.

Litter bearers began to come under the tents in rapid fire.

Bodies were piling up on each side of the table.

Riders are coming in.

York had surrendered so as not to be burned.

Arnold took the bone saw and in as best a fashion as possible he cut. The old man was groaning the louder. Blood splashed through a tattered artery. It hit Arnold's face, the sergeant weakened.

Riders are closer a boy said.

Arnold sawed the arm.

Chloroform was spilled.

The bone was near finished.

The old man shit his trousers.

The chloroform was weakening.

Blood spewed.

Screams ensued.

The arm was tossed.

A life was lost.

- Frank

Wednesday July 1st, 1863

It was early and it was Early, Jubal Early. The night was again sleepless for I was Arnold's teacher. In the early A.M. all sounds outside of our saw ceased. The birds had flown. The animals of the night too had gone.

Some saw the glossy black ostrich feather in their sleep.

I saw it from ten feet fluttering by in my heavy imagination.

The butternut had overwhelmed the straggling Provost.

With credit to the enemy of the north we of the Medical Corps were not bothered. When asked by a colonel from Gordon's brigade if I favored one side or the other I said I was a doctor of reputable note and that Arnold was my assistant. I concluded that curing the injured came before my political wishes.

We wondered had the north now fallen into rebel hands?

Was Lincoln now a prisoner of Jefferson Davis?

We are the 44th Virginia one in well-worn attire said.

52nd and 13th Virginia came the calls of others.

Whites Comanche's, one bellowed.

They ravaged the area, so I was informed.

They took shoes and food at first.

They took shirts and water next.

Some took the rare young woman.

Some took the more rare young boy.

I'd believed that none could look worse than a war weary man from the north. Yet the young men from Virginia, they now only walked in loyalty to the cause and more often loyalty to Mr. Lee.

Litter bearers were a constant hum.

The screams of the living and silence of the dead were deafening.

Arnold learned quickly.

I was a brilliant teacher.

He cut one piece after another.

We'd toss the limb of the moment.

The hogs lumbered.

Bodies were removed and another still faint of breath would be placed before us.

Arnold prepared the table and I sought the appropriate page in the book.

Virginia's youngest in arms came to us not threatening but wanting of water or even our stalest of food. I gave just that.

They took our weapons. When confronted for his pistol Arnold said it was to keep the hogs away from the wounded. He was allowed to keep it.

I held my station at the table teaching Arnold.

A Confederate officer approached me.

I met a Captain David Anderson of the 44th Virginia. He asked for coffee and we shared a cup while I kept a steady eye on the work of Arnold.

The Captain had done much; his was an original Richmond Gray. I was intrigued for thoughts of the Grays brought back fond memories.

I'd proudly informed him of my familiarity with the noted actor John Booth who too had been part of the Grays.

He seemed doubtful but further talk relieved him of that doubt.

Over coffee we chatted of the war and of what life will be like afterwards, he agreed the slaves should've been freed first.

He had duties and so did I.

It was a night of caring for the thirsty and hungry. I served those in the gray and scattered dress as they were the dominate number now at York.

Henry Palmer watched from afar.

He'd begun to call me a scoffer.

Work was being done Arnold was a quick learn.

A torn young boy was placed before me on adjacent barrels.

He was crying.

He was so young.

Perhaps he was 12 years at most 14. He had a belly wound. Guts were oozing. He'd die soon.

He was from Virginia.

I had no ability or I admit knowledge on how to end his suffering.

My mama, he cried, please, I want my mama!

Those demands I couldn't meet.

His death though I could satisfy.

It was a silly cry for someone who in minutes would be meal for the thrifty hogs.

Though he'd die I could benefit from watching his final moments.

I wanted to know what he'd see.

Arnold had his own table.

Henry Palmer was gone from view.

What would the boy see in his final fleeting moments?

Some in gray were close but showed no care.

Did the boy have a name?

I'd heard one say the 44th would move north of Gettysburg.

The gray would leave York.

Leave the dead here and the wounded can die south of Carlisle.

The boy became just a thing.

The boy was slim and most certainly over used by the armies of the south.

The belly wound was great and his inner gut had been perforated, the young boys shit was dripping into his torso.

I could smell it.

I tasted it.

My lips quivered to the taste.

Compressed rags held most of it in place.

I removed them to view what his state of being was like.

I wanted to see his final moments approach, arrive and overtake him. I could see it in his eyes. Was he afraid of death? Was he afraid of what it might be like?

Leave him Henry Palmer said, there're many others.

Don't leave me the young boy asked.

I lowered my head for a closer look at his wound. It smelled of all things spoiled. Death was already well underway.

Finish it Palmer shouted!

Arnold mumbled to himself as he removed a foot.

Mama! The young boy cried.

The boy's blood seeped with furry from beneath the rags I'd removed.

I moved my face closer to the boy's eyes and asked what it was he saw. He looked from side to side. His eyes seemed to bounce. His final moments were in panic.

God! Mama! I don't want to die! He cried.

Captain David Anderson came and bid farewell. He hoped the war saw me safely through.

I wished him the same.

I returned to the boy.

His eyes bounced.

His pain was intense. Insanity was coming.

Arnold called for the litter bearers.

He kept the hogs fed.

He drew his pistol and lamed a hog with a snout full of rebel hand.

I wondered what are the final moments like for the dying?

It became a growing interest. It's an honor to see death come. It's a privilege to share such moments with those who were in midst of their final journey.

He's dead already move on! Palmer shouted again.

Oh God! I don't want to die! He cried.

Mama! Mama! The silly cry was repeated.

My hue was changing too.

Let me care for him I told Palmer.

What are the final moments of the dying like?

In this state of being, how is it possible not to know?

What are their final questions?

I lowered my head and sniffed his trousers. He was young. His frame would be a loss

I kept my head low and took a deep well rounded breath over his belly wound.

I looked at the kit of tools near my table.

There was a knife one of medium length used for amputations. My kit was the cleanest in all of York. I took pride in that.

The boy cried.

With my fingers I pried.

Guts aside and his ribs strewn apart.

I slid the knife into his heart.

-Frank

Thursday July 2nd, 1863

Those that couldn't ride or move at double-time were left to our care. Those that could ride and double-time were ordered to die later that day.

It wasn't a matter of if but when.

The gray marched regardless.

Arnold had learned well.

I'd taught well.

I taught with my eyes and body movements allowing my voice a rest. His moves weren't always correct and errors were placed on his conscious not mine.

I was proud at having made Arnold into what he was.

I was affronted though when Palmer turned to him for help rather than me a doctor of reputable note.

That word scoffer penetrated some litter bearers.

I was noble but was being seen as less than what I was.

Smoke from the south was growing intense.

Sounds were muffled but the muffle too was growing over the day's hours.

Troops in gray had left behind many and so many, many more were arriving. The grounds of the hospital were covered with dead and the half living. To be honest in full to the seed that bore me it was becoming difficult to tell who was dead and who had life.

The sky was blue.

The colored boy returned.

He had my steed.

The sun was at its worse.

Tongues boiled with thirst.

Blood fell from the sky and bubbled from the ground. It seeped along the mountains and broke the crest of the Susquehanna.

Hell arrived in the small college town not far from where mud claimed my best boots.

Over here and over there Palmer asked.

Arnold shot hogs.

I watered those I could.

I heard poetry being read.

I plastered hands and feet.

Under dark of night when ones guts, whether gray or blue, were loose I cut a throat and thrust a heart.

I'd done my part.

-Frank

Friday July 3rd, 1863

I left that night. Darkness stilled the litter bearer; my knife quieted the living.

I let Henry Palmer be who he was, selfish and unappreciative.

I took my steed and gave the young colored boy two-dollars. I told him of my departure. He told whomever he wished that I went to the front lines.

I'm a doctor of reputable note and that's where I could be of greatest service.

He handed me my reins.

He handed me my hat.

He handed me my knife.

-Frank

I rode tall, hat in hand atop my high stepping white stallion. The trumpeted fields of those days would note my work, and I marked them as some of the grandest in my caring of mankind.

Under cover of darkness I rode past those begging my stay. I saw twinkled eyes wishing me well and I received the politest of salutes. I saluted back with the honor that must be shared with such fine men.

Palmer mouthed scoffer as he tossed a fat Irish foot to an ever so tame hog with a blood red snout.

That was my service. I taught those who wished to learn and the soon to be dead taught me lessons I carry still.

The ferry ride jostled my dream.

My story was ending.

I lay with my eyes planted firmly on the ceiling.

I sat up resting on the edge of the bunk.

My throat was dry. I found the bowl underneath the bunk and pissed in a hearty way.

CHAPTER TWELVE

When done, I shook the drops free. I let my feet and my balance determine the condition of the English Channel. It seemed as it always had, generally calm but occasionally rude.

I opened the door of the cabin with casual care.

The passageway was empty as I stepped into its rough interior. I could get coffee at the other end by going down several stairs. I followed my memory. I saw no faces. When I arrived at the galley area, I saw only one empty table. What eyes there were, were aimed in my direction.

I took the table and without ordering had a cup of coffee and some bread set in front of me. It smelled relatively fresh.

I twisted some off and dipped it into the hot cup, a habit I carried with me since my hard days on the battlefield. I adjusted myself in the uncomfortable chair.

I took a bite.

The windows showed a lively English Channel.

My days, my months, my weeks and my years. I'd forgotten so much. I'd forgotten many scenes, yet it was my dreams that brought back my life's poignant streams of color.

The window showed the channel water approaching with its rude moods. The water came and longingly licked the window glass. In the glass the room was reflected. Faces gradually appeared.

I had little interest in my own face.

I sucked the coffee moistened bread.

I turned towards the window to see what the man looking back might have to say.

As expected a weary face did look back. Lines around my swollen eyes were the heaviest of all facial scribbles. Graying temples sat on either side of my face. I seldom blinked. Faces surrounded me. I was ugly and seemed as a dream.

A Tumblety sketch?

Was my age becoming an adversary?

Was life playing with death in a game of cat and mouse?

Was Littlechild the cat and I the mouse?

I sucked the bread a second time eating the balance of its twisted end.

"Gray hair," I whispered, "Fuck the window," I said turning around.

My finger drew a circle on the table.

"The Richmond Grays," I muttered through gathering spit.

My mind returned to those ever so brief moments with that one glorious, luscious man.

The window drew scenes of the Richmond Grays and of one enlistee, John Booth. Booth the son, the actor, the apostate. The window reflected his face. He smiled as he did when we shared our first brandy. My eyes returned to the bread. Nervous stares from fellow travelers hit me.

A man seated behind me left altogether.

Did he question my stability?

Am I any less stable than that long dead diseased prince or his whore of a Queen?

"Fuck him too," I said through a tongue of pooled drool.

I studied my bread. I studied its texture, and saw in it the hands that crafted it. By studying the hands of the baker I was taken back to the mill that ground the wheat. By studying the mill I saw the farmer at harvest and by studying the harvest I could see the planted seed. The bread showed me what it took to create it. Studying my face in the window, I was taken back to all that created me.

I felt the caress of John's hand.

The face of John Booth was deeply planted in the glass. Booth helped to make me, and the Richmond Grays helped define Booth.

I swayed to unheard tunes.

I dreamt as I reached for the shadows of York.

I'd lied to the colored boy holding my horse's reins.

I didn't go to Gettysburg; instead I went southeast to the Baltimore area. I'd served my country, and my war was over. I was battle tested and heavily scarred, so I'd say. I'd go to a city like Baltimore, near insistent upon its neutrality and be a man of high stature. I did just that, riding proudly with my hat in hand.

I foresaw the wave of plump maidens and I foresaw the caresses from handsome young boys. I envisioned free meals and beds covered in cherry blossoms. I dreamt of papers in print telling of my coming. But my visions fell short as I soon found Baltimore was not passive but aggressively seeking neutrality.

Booth's face told me.

"They should appreciate you more Dr. Tumblety, but they do not. Be aggressive. Demand their appreciation."

My steed sought a familiar respite. There were no crowds of plump maidens nor were there handsome young men. There were just crude remarks from those I passed. "Piss the whores and piss the papers that seek other stories to print," I said.

I wandered the streets seeking a one-time landlady. She was a kind woman, though she didn't possess great wit. She and her son had relocated their fortune that had been built upon foundations of smaller roofs.

I followed the direction that the best of rumors pointed me, eventually arriving at a boarding house on H Street in Washington D.C. I knew the house and I knew the Surratt family. Mary was kind as stated but lacking in awareness.

She was a war widow and she was as heavy in gut as she was in naivety. The war years had ravaged her financially. She lost her former home and some said her husband, John, to the war.

It was in the late summer of 1863. Gettysburg had decided the wars outcome, though it'd take two additional years for the sides to put it in writing. I found H Street. I found the home after only looking twice.

Mary Surratt was easily taken advantage of when it came to business dealings and flowery words. John had handled their life's details but since his passing she was left to her own ability. Mary was, according to some with questionable taste, a woman of substantial build. I saw her as kind and generously homely, nothing else.

I dismounted and tethered my steed.

I brushed invisible dirt from my smock.

I scuffed towards the door.

I knocked rather than enter unannounced.

Mary answered before my second rap.

Her eyes were sad yet she presented a polite greeting.

I returned the smile.

I was full of colored fantasies when I entered her boarding house worse for wear in August of that summer.

I was now a Major.

We stood in the entranceway.

"Ma'am, I've overcome many hardships. I've seen many a fine man on both sides give their lives for what they saw as a just cause."

"I recognize you," she said, "I'm thankful for your safety," Mary said.

"You may stay as long as you wish, until you're well rested," she added.

"It's always served us, me, well to have professional men here at my home," Mary said.

I thanked her.

We walked towards some comfortable looking chairs.

"There've been many men of quality who've stayed here, politicians from both sides, writers and preachers," she boasted. After a brief pause she informed me that even the famed actor John Booth had stayed on several occasions.

That I already knew.

It had been some months now but I'd paid close attention to the theatre bills of every town of fair size in which I entered. He was growing in fame and in looks.

My eyes left the window of the ferry.

My feet swayed under the table.

The channel's waters became angry.

I sat staring, motionless out the window. The voices, which had fed on me for years, now seemed to be a shadow of what they'd been.

Had the voices vanished altogether?

I saw I was no longer a man of aesthetic quality.

My words were torn between faded leaves and occasional flowering.

Had I ever been of quality?

What if I hadn't been?

I looked at the window and dwelled on what Mr. Booth may have seen in me.

Whatever it was, I failed to see it.

I hadn't my hat.

I was gloveless, and my palms and fingers were raw.

Besides Booth, I saw other faces too. There were those of the fellow travelers but the deeper I looked into the channel sprayed glass I also saw the faces of my youth.

There I was as a boy clung to the barns loft.

There I was a young man left askew to the weather's wishes.

There I was a boy eating his father's flesh.

There I was selling apples at the arcade.

There was Dr. Lispenard.

There was young Elizabeth.

There was Lispenard fucking me.

There I was doing the fucking.

Then the channel's splash wiped it all clean.

In the next thrust of the ferry's belly a new set of blurred faces appeared in the glass.

There was----- who is that?

There-----I can't remember their name either.

There is the first whore, what was her name?

Where'd I meet her?

There were the faces of young soldiers and the little colored boy.

There was Ollie the Innkeeper.

There was Littlechild.

In the center of it all was the one I knew, the one I loved, John Wilkes Booth. I smiled as he smiled back before the channel too wiped him free.

I grappled with my state of being. I knew I'd seen better days and that I'd been seen in better light, but few aboard this half sunken scuttle cared.

I swirled my coffee.

I recalled how Mary Surratt and I chatted that first night.

I was excited to hear about Booth and if I were fortunate he'd arrive on this or any other night for that matter. That was my whisper now, and that was what I shared with Mary Surratt during those evenings filled with tea in 1863.

I nodded fully aglow when she spoke of the actor.

"I know Mr. Booth very well," I said with pride, "He's a man of substantial talent and incredible looks."

"Yes, he is," Mary agreed, "My son John is a scout under Southern service and is acquainted with him. John, my son, introduced me to the actor and I was instantly enamored."

"I know that sensation," I blushed.

Mary took that time to begin a series of tales as to what her life had been like since the beginning of the war. It was an oral journal of rambling events in which I had little interest but showed great fascination.

My eyes remained focused on Mary Surratt's face but the splash of the channel's waters washed her clean from the glass. It never reappeared. However, I started to see all that was, all that had ever been and for exactly what it was.

I stared at my plate of bread.

I twisted it and asked with a wave at the server for a second basket. He brought it without a smile.

I reorganized the plate of bread in front of me, large pieces to the right, small to the left. I broke a piece and dipped it. A thrust of the ferry starboard returned me to the Surratt's home. Mary was finishing her list of stories.

With that I thanked her for the evening.

For several days, Mary and I would chat on varying subjects. She had few guests but claimed she'd been promised that a series of important meetings were soon to take place.

On one night I sat in a chair on the landing near the door.

Mary had finished her duties for the day.

The summer evening was brilliant.

Jasmine flowed from unseen sources.

Crickets voiced concerns to their mates regarding the birds of the night.

I rocked in a chair that wasn't built for such movement.

A dog from a neighbor's yard showed his discontent for the crickets.

I told them all to fuck off.

Riders galloped past the home. One rider came to a complete rest.

He was stoic.

I watched him with my back erect in hopes of preventing confrontation. I was pleased that the rider in question presented a strong, formidable form under the moonlit sky but no threat.

His boots were heavy on the walkway.

A large man with uneven whiskers made his way toward the first step.

He studied my face looking for familiarity, there wasn't any.

I saw Mary's frame appear in the window.

I greeted the gentleman.

"Good evening," came his reply.

"Is Mrs. Surratt home?" the stranger asked.

"In the backroom I believe."

He nodded and just as he was about to enter Mary Surratt came to the door.

"Hello Lewis, I've been expecting you," she said.

"Ma'am," was his greeting.

"I'll bring out some coffee and biscuits, Lewis this is Dr. Tumblety, Doctor meet Lewis Payne."

He removed his hat and sat opposite me.

He was a giant of a man.

His thighs were muscled.

I tossed back my shoulders, briefly intimidated by his size.

"Have you ridden far?" I asked.

"From Gettysburg. Mrs. Surratt is good to me, others too," he said.

"Your wrist looks injured."

"I was hurt on the second day," he said.

"I was at the York Hospital," I puffed.

Payne showed no interest.

His eyes focused on his chestnut mare.

The riders up and down H Street were infrequent but within the hour two more had arrived. They stopped in jolted urgency in front of Surratts'.

Payne stood in tribute.

I sat, curious at first as they tended to their horses.

Then a smile overcame me.

I recognized one form as that of the actor.

Booth studied my form seeking recognition, there was none. I was greatly disappointed. He was at the base of the steps looking up.

Polite words were exchanged as he came near Payne.

His brow frowned as if he was tapping his memory. Then under a better-lit doorway he cast a knowing grin in my direction.

"Doctor, so good to see you again, I've thought of you often the last several months," he said smiling broadly.

We shook hands and my disappointment subsided.

"Doctor, I'd like for you to meet David Herold. He has studied medicine and he too is a great friend of Shakespeare."

Herold and I exchanged greetings.

They seem hurried.

"Doctor, please excuse us for the evening. We have some work to do, but you and I will enjoy some moments perhaps in the morning," Booth said.

"I hope we will," I said.

We didn't meet the next day and over the course of the next several days I saw very little of him, though we exchanged common mailing address's. It was David Herold that shared conversation with me.

The meetings in the Surratt House were held without my offering opinion. Regardless I showed my support, especially to Booth. My penciling of fantastical notes took place in the front room. My sermons to the invisible were delivered from the front stoop.

I'd written many notes and dreamed many fantastical dreams.

Alas New York City would be my next home.

Later that evening John and I did sit for our final conversations. He appeared exhausted.

He wrote in a small diary.

"Always keep a diary, Doctor Tumblety, so you don't rely on others to tell your story for you," Booth said.

I studied his face.

His eyes said much.

He wrote some more.

"Doctor? Do you hear me?" Booth asked.

I snapped out of the gaze and said I would keep a diary.

"We'll be leaving early in the morning," he said.

"I may leave within the next couple days myself for New York City," I declared.

The air was silent.

The crickets were nearby, waiting for the next words.

"May I ask a favor of you?" Booth wondered.

"Most certainly."

"Do you think it possible that in some weeks from now David may join you? You're both men of medicine and it will be easier for him if he is shown techniques under a man of greater knowledge."

I couldn't have been more honored.

John Booth wrote my addresses in New York in his small book.

"79 East Tenth Street is always best, but on other days tell him to look for me at the Madison Avenue Hotel."

Booth wrote with a small lead.

I continued.

"I'll be returning to St. Louis early next year to visit with my sister. I'll be there for some weeks. Here is her address and my hotel in Missouri."

"Thank you, Doctor. It's my hopes that after all this is done we may share an even better bottle of brandy."

"It's my wish as well."

We stood in unison.

Our thighs brushed.

We passed on our farewells.

He tore several pages from his book.

That'd be the last I would see of John Booth.

Within days I was aboard a northbound train to New York City. I'd sold my steed for twenty-five dollars, a good price considering his wear.

Mr. Booth was a good and decent man. He loved me and I most certainly loved him.

"John I kept my word I have kept my diary," I said to the channel spray. I dipped the last of the bread into the coffee, ate it in one bite as the faces on the glass vanished.

I stood up from the table to see the room empty with only two servers waiting at the entrance of the room. They eyed me to the point where even I was becoming uneasy.

On my way out one said, "Le Havre in one hour, sir."

I nodded to the fat fuck and made my way back to my cabin. For the balance of the trip I sat on the edge of the bunk.

There were two ports in Le Havre.

This ferry would come to nest at de Grand Bretagne.

It was Saturday November 24th 1888.

I'd arrive in New York City on Sunday December 2nd. A nine-day journey if the waters of the Atlantic were obedient.

I sat motionless on the bunk.

"Le Havre," said a voice at the door.

The footsteps moved down the passageway knocking and announcing the same.

I waited for the ferry to be properly docked and the passengers made ready for departure.

I opened, and then shut the door behind me.

Without moving my head I viewed both ends of the passageway.

I strolled with as a common a look as I could manifest and found the crewman who'd always been the kindest to me in these journeys.

I handed him two coins.

He thanked me. This would be my last ride on such a scamp, and I wanted to make sure that I had paid the ferryman for taking me to the other side.

I stepped into the chilled wind of Le Havre. My cloak was weakening in its defense. There was to be no walk of considerable length or prolonged overnight stay in an aboriginal company.

My face no longer flushed to the glares of shunned onlookers. I wanted the La Bretange and a comfortable bed. It was boarding some yards south of where we docked. Two large funnels and four masts poked the bottom of the sky and could be seen before I handed the crewman his coins.

La Provence, similar to La Bretagne.

It would be crowded.

I'd be a commoner again. The upper class numbers were few so I chose to be a commoner. Selecting a better class bed would be a clear a sign for the sniffing Inspector Littlechild.

I joined a line where many were waiting to board seeking their lower class compartments. Crying children and dialects of every nation surrounded me. Some were even English. This was a steamship whose mission was that of immigration. As I've discovered, the immigrants to America's shores were never as fully prepared for such a learned man as I. That's why making myself common would in their eyes make me great. I rode in common steerage for their benefit and not mine.

It was good of me to do this.

The line waiting was long.

The sky shared its drizzle.

We shuffled our feet in unison.

Two steps forward, stop.

One step more, stop again.

The line grew longer and wider from those who had little in way of common sense.

I showed patience.

My face no longer changed in hues but remained consistently white. My beard was getting thick and often only thick lips and discolored eyes were seen.

Two steps forward, stop.

One step more, stop again.

It took a full two hours for me to hand over my ticket and obtain directions to the cabins furthest below. On this journey to New York, I was sure that I'd have to share my space with ones more entitled to the title common.

Topside was crowded as those with fancy hats stood waving at those below who they'd just hugged goodbye. This was an odd ritual. They were clearly agitated at the number of us steerage passengers being allowed below. I could hear one such voice ask if they'd be forced to share their meals with those people.

I lowered my collar as the passageways and crowds of stink protected me from the grips of the same wind.

I was only 55, but my walk was growing weaker with each step. At times a walking stick was an added comfort. I found one that was unattended and tended to it.

Down several rounds of steps and over one passageway I past running children of every size followed by mothers of every size.

Their noise was making me weary.

I found my cabin.

The door was unlocked.

As expected, I wouldn't be alone on this unimaginably long journey; there were two already in the room built for four. I hurried to grab the last remaining bottom bunk.

One slept loudly. The other hid by the shadows watched as I made what preparations were needed to secure my safety and reasonable comfort.

I dropped what I carried.

"I'm Jonathan George," the hidden one said quickly.

"I'm Frank Townsend," I said peering toward the shadow.

"Who's he?" I asked pointing to the other.

"Only Christ knows. He was here when I opened the door."

The hidden man and I exchanged some brief, casual conversation. He said he needed a meal and I said I needed rest.

I rarely removed my boots. Leaving them on would aid me if and when a quick departure was demanded. I did however remove my cloak and outer vest and even unbuttoned my shirt. I was in need of a bath. Perhaps I could see to that at McNamara's in New York. My clothes I folded as best as I could and stuffed them with reasonable neatness under the bunk.

They smelled of all things recent.

Dampness kept it recent.

I lay down and placed my hands behind my head. I stared up at the bottom side of the upper bunk.

My eyes and mind danced all over the scene.

I saw fleeting horizons, faces and names but caught only the occasional word.

My eyes flittered to all that was.

My mind filtered flowered words belonging to others.

"To grunt and sweat under a weary life," I spastically whispered.

My lashes fluttered to the stage of Hamlet Act Three.

I slept instantly and hard.

"The undiscovered country from whose bourn, No travelers returns, puzzles the will... fuck Shakespeare," I said.

"Always keep a diary, never allow others to tell your story, always keep a diary."

My eyes danced as Booth's words woke me.

I raised my neck in the empty cabin.

I looked below the bunk. My bag and clothes were undisturbed. I rolled onto my stomach as a deeper sleep overtook me.

"To sleep? Perchance to dream. Ay, there's the rub; for in that sleep of death what dreams may come."

Oh the dreams that came.

"I did keep a diary, Mr. Booth. There'll be no others telling my story."

That night that one night I showed them in word and deed.

"They call me indecent. I'll call you indecent?"

"It's they who are indecent. It's their minds and their words that are indecent," I added.

"They call me indecent while pieces of shit like the walking diseased are called unfortunate?"

"It's quite a Queen's legacy!" The voices said.

Shakespeare spit like this.

"The flesh is heir to-- 'tis a consummation devoutly to be wish'd."

I wished for the flesh of one.

I had watched a woman who some said was not a simple, common whore. Stumped by those words I followed her to better understand the phrase; flesh is heir.

If she, Catherine they called her, was not a common whore should one have taken that to mean that she was just an occasional whore? Was she someone who sold morals only when they needed to be sold?

One night I sniffed Catherine's hair, it dripped with fish. I saw another, one who tweaked even my cock.

"Ay, there's the rub," the ghost of Stratford-upon-Avon whispered.

It was late September and my stoop was growing pronounced. My back was painful. My drool harvested a steady pool and I wiped my chin often.

After an unexcitable dinner at The House of Astor I left that night without notice. Even Lady Astor had seen my digression in nature but chose not to mention it to her greatest of debtors. My mind took to racing my feet and I nearly stumbled in attempting to keep up.

That night I was torn between two whores. I'd watched for several days the other small woman with dark hair and a grotesque toothless smile.

I sniffed her salt too.

My lips quivered to the scent of them both.

I'd treated her for minor ailments outside the Queens Head Public House on Commercial. She was plump, and named Elizabeth. I was familiar to her. I'd given her coins at various times and cachous pastilles for her poor breathe. She may've been a good woman for it was said that she whored herself rarely for there was a man and a church that saw to her needs.

Elizabeth could be attractive to men with regular desires.

On the 27th of the same month I entered a lodging house located at Flower and Dean to offer free services. Upon entering the kitchen of that house I clearly saw Elizabeth amidst the whores and children. They seemed huddled in fear.

She smiled.

I left after she smiled.

I followed her for a couple of nights and on the evening of the 30th Elizabeth Stride was filth in full definition. I'd see her grin again. I was caught between two but it was she that I chose to follow first. I followed in the drizzling wind as she left both the lodging house and the Queens Head. Rumors were being spread that Elizabeth had some great amount of cash on her. When she was asked to produce it she had but a few pennies earned from actual labor. I followed safely concealed.

I'd sought shelter from the rain.

I had bread and soup of mild temperature served to me at The Bricklayers Public House. I was patient and as expected Elizabeth came in. I'd been drinking more than usual.

The rain increased.

I watched Elizabeth move with abhorrent grace from lap to lap. She brushed back her hair and walked to a position near me.

I tasted her scent.

"...'tis a consummation," I muttered.

Drool began to pool on my tongue.

My billycock was falling victim to the weather, so to preserve its newness I would have to wait for the rain to cease.

Elizabeth saw me and shared her toothless grin.

Brandy made her lips appeared ample and her form pleasant to view.

I asked that she be given a drink of her own. Elizabeth stood an arms length, she was short and had a full neck. Her eyes were worn but her lips were moist.

Her lips attracted me.

We chatted.

We laughed.

That night I gave her more cachous pastilles to make for better kisses. Elizabeth thanked me at which point I reached for her. I kissed her long and hard. The men in The Bricklayers applauded or jeered I couldn't tell as both noises sounded the same.

We laughed and patted hands.

The rain shortened its reign.

"Shall we?" I asked.

"It'll be five pennies Mr. Frank," she said.

I nodded and we departed The Bricklayers.

The men applauded.

We walked down Berner Street. The hour was nearing midnight at its fullest, the dead hour.

I gave her a shilling for her time.

"Frank, you are a good man. You show a kind heart to we who depend on the streets."

She softly nudged my elbow.

"Your looks are more than fair and your cock seems full," she said grabbing my pants.

"Dear Lady, you'd say anything but your prayers," I responded.

She hushed me.

I hushed her in return. My face changed in color. None ever pushed back. We continued to brush each other with sharp tongues, at first only in jest.

We passed Sander Street.

I heard Russian songs.

We walked hidden by darkness. There was a man's social club not far from us. I grabbed her elbow as she pulled it away. Forcefully, I pulled her through the gates spread wide in Dutfield's Yard. I hid us using those same gates. She pulled and I pushed. Her voice began to rise.

"I'll give you a shilling more when we're done," I told her.

Elizabeth fell silent.

She said I was hurting her.

Her shy voice became two perhaps three slight grunts.

I couldn't allow the noise.

From the shadows I saw someone leave the club and enter the building used as a printing office. "Hush now," I said.

She did.

She reached into her apron.

In her hand were cachous pastilles.

"Dear Lady, I'll now take what I've paid for," I said.

Elizabeth let out several short grunts. I pulled the gates shut behind us.

I heard an unidentified voice, someone was still singing. The strange dialect was the perfect background noise for the time I needed.

"Elizabeth, I must have your lips," I declared.

We jostled inside the gate for our short transaction.

She was falling backward.

I knew someone had seen our shadows argue.

The ground was mud and the mud had ruts made from that evening's heavy rain. The drizzle was scattered. Elizabeth sought small talk. She claimed she'd been in the gentlemen's club many times, though it was for men only.

"Find a comfortable spot," I dictated.

She did.

The voices from outside the Yard were more numerous than I wished.

"We must hurry," I ordered.

Quickly I moved behind her forcing her down.

She rolled.

I reached into my cloak and in one quick motion ended our argument. I cut her throat solidly from left to right. The cachous pastilles fell to the ground.

"For in the sleep of death what dreams may come?" I repeated.

I stopped the initial cut. I reinserted the knife into the incision and pressed the harder splitting her windpipe. I could feel it snap.

The blood ran like a stream.

I'd cut her in the mud so the blood would easily be absorbed into the soil. It would disappear. It'd give the body a pallid look when it was found.

Never leave solid clues in uneven cobble.

Her throat bubbled.

She fell limp into the mud.

My cloak flapped like bats wings.

As I lifted her feet I heard a cart approach. Simultaneously as I pushed Elizabeth to the ground I also heard feet on the stone. The hour was nearing one. I saw a second man through the night's shadows. I recognized his frame. He was familiar in the scattered light. It was Israel Schwartz. He was a begging vendor, a Jew who lived in the area. I knew him more as the latter and not the former.

I held my breath.

I wanted her lips.

I taste them even today after all these years.

If some men were seeking to stable their ponies George Yard was not at a great distance so additional vendors might be near.

Schwartz left the scene.

I now had time.

I fumbled my cock.

I thirsted for Elizabeth's breath.

I craved her salt.

Her lips pouted up at me as if she were a spoiled child.

Her blood drained with gentle professionalism into the mud.

Her eyes looked surprised.

I peered through the slat board. The cart moved slowly and with a sudden jerk the pony shied.

The animal saw what the Jew had not.

I wouldn't have time after all. I'd been careless and my urges had led me rather than my instincts. One voice was removed allowing me time to deliver Elizabeth to outside the men's club allowing for her full display on Berner Street.

I left the scene fully winged.

"Fuck him!"

"Fuck the Jew who'd seen me!"

I grew paranoid over what had just occurred.

Had a Jew betrayed me?

The voices uttered scribbles for later bricks.

Dear Diary;

The Juwes are the men that will not be blamed for nothing.

Let the useless fucks at H Division sort this out.

Had Schwartz seen me?

Would a fragmented immigrant such as he be ignored?

Immigrants are fearful of everything. He might run from such questioning. Elizabeth's shallow grunts may have slowed him, but the growl I sent forth scattered him.

Would Inspector Littlechild garner more of his needed tattered, makeup from the testimony of a Jew?

I was frenzied.

My drool and heavy tongue were coupled as one.

It was a frenzy that was full of paranoid panic.

I let Elizabeth be.

I'd been interrupted before I'd tasted her lips.

I had an unsatisfied urge.

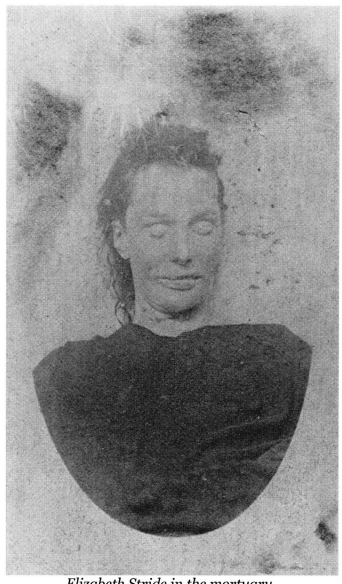

Elizabeth Stride in the mortuary.

CHAPTER THIRTEEN

That one night few would ever forget.

I had an urge that shunned lips had hurried aside.

Fuck the Jew and H Division.

I breathed heavy as I walked away.

I scurried in the sizzle of the cobbled drizzle.

I walked covered with winged cloak carrying my bag and with billycock pulled low.

Voices permeated my ears.

Hums from histories screams kneaded the bread of life on all my plates.

I wanted her lips.

I needed her lips.

I quivered for her meat.

Fuck Schwartz!

The Bishopsgate Police Station was close.

The hour was ten past one.

I slowed in hopes of being seen but instead I saw.

Small groups held private court in and around the Bishopsgate.

I held my own company standing in near-lit corners a curious distance from the station doors.

I spit what I'd stolen from Elizabeth's mouth.

A side door opened. An officer was discharging a woman; her voice was loud either with drink or by habit.

I studied the two, she tapped his chest but he gently shoved her to the street.

She walked without a goal in mind.

I sniffed the air for her salt.

I recognized the odor and I recognized the dress.

Catherine Eddowes, the whore of infrequent cocks had slammed the door shut at Bishopsgate. She mumbled at being refused by the constable so she walked towards Mitre Square.

I could smell her from where I stood.

My lip quivered at the scent.

She'd saw my form but not face. She offered no flirtatious words.

I was offended at this sexual snub.

My eyes were dark, the drizzle trickled. Spittle gathered anew and now oozed from the corners of my mouth.

She I'd follow.

Catherine appeared quite drunk from what I observed of her walk.

She bid for a cock or two but was laughed off. I closed in as the hour neared quarter past one.

History filled each subsequent minute.

Dear Diary, the closer I got to her the more I smelled her soiled thighs. Her salt was in the air. It tempted my cock. My lips quivered.

I walked at a comfortable distance.

She, too, I had treated for frequent vomiting and back pains.

"Too many spoiled cocks," I told her.

Catherine walked quickly. I was of an equal pace, stopping when she stopped, walking when she walked.

Catherine knew the unlit streets. We crossed Duke then Bury and Heneage Lane in no particular order or recollection.

Clip clop, tick tock, the echoes returned.

I drew closer to her walk.

Catherine suddenly stopped. Her quick appearance before me seized the moment by the throat. Catherine didn't seem caught off guard and without a break she smiled her whiskey smile.

She was at my arm's length.

The night was asshole dark.

The drizzle had hushed its wishes.

I was flushed and seeking my breath silently Catherine gently touched my chest.

We molded our sentences near the corner of Church Passage, which was a collection of some worthwhile stones just outside Mitre Square. Catherine knew me instantly and I was satisfied at such recognition.

"I was hoping to find you, I've been wanting to taste you for many days now," I said gently rolling my bottom lip.

"Doctor you speak fancy words. Any number of pennies you can offer. It's been a long night and I'm very hungry, even the gaoler wouldn't fuck me for bread," she said.

"You're a good woman, a fine woman, and certainly your body is worth more than just pennies. I'll give you a shilling for your scab covered holes."

Despite my affront Catherine eagerly guided me to a shadowed corner just off of Mitre Square.

It was twenty past the hour.

Clip clop, tick tock.

Her dress was old and soiled by any number of men and even spoiled piss couldn't hide her smell.

Her hair was matted and held rather neatly in place by a bonnet.

I inhaled more air than I exhaled.

I could taste her odor.

To feign seductiveness she turned her back to me.

"In the ass boy!" Lispenard would say.

Catherine lifted her dress as she bent from the waist.

There was no bustle, corset or petticoat, just her stained ass.

I smelled it.

I fingered my cock.

The voices on my shoulder hummed ancient tunes.

She pushed her ass towards my hands. It touched me.

I licked my fingers.

She salted the air and it flowed like the tide.

My bottom lip quivered.

"Fuck me, do it quick, I'm hungry," Catherine said.

"In time," I said with an aggravated tone.

"Fuck me before the strong arm returns," she begged.

My face changed with each word she spoke. The voices on my shoulders sang songs in old dialects.

I bent her further at the waist.

I tore her dress slightly.

I could no longer resist her scent so I kneeled to the odor her ass offered the air. I slid four fingers into her and Catherine asked if I was yet inside her.

I licked the stink.

I had my salt.

My lips quivered to its taste.

I licked again.

I pulled my fingers out and after a long sniff I licked them dry, there was a taint of blood.

"Menstruating?" I asked.

"Yes," she answered.

The hour neared half past.

I rubbed her ass inside and out.

I licked my palm afterwards.

I rubbed her lower back while fingering my cock.

The motions were repeated.

I pressed my palms harder into her lower back.

She said her kidneys were painful.

My bag was at my feet. I reached inside finding what I sought.

"Use this to mend your dress," I tossed her a thimble.

My pointless cock touched her ass.

"I'm uncomfortable," Catherine said.

I leaned over her.

"Are you in yet?" she asked again.

I could hear an "Oh Christ," come through her hushed laughter.

"Time, be on my side," I prayed, "Hush, Catherine," I insisted.

With my left hand I reached for her throat. I rubbed it and she feigned a moan of satisfaction.

"Your skin is soft but you smell of your own bowels."

My cock was still soft.

"Ouch," she said as my grip tightened.

Then in a quick slice of history I cut left to right ending her before she could produce another laugh.

She fell to the ground instantly shitting spraying my hands as she did so.

Her left arm flailed.

Trinkets fell from her apron.

I rolled her over on her back. Her eyes were surprised and still held twinklings of life.

Did she see me?

Her blood sprayed more than I'd wished on the closest of walls.

In seconds not visible to anyone I took the knife and started to cut at the bottom of the ribs in a circular motion.

Catherine pissed on my thighs.

It smelled of coffee.

I rubbed my hands into its gathering pool.

I was in the throws of high passion.

I raised my fingers to my face.

I licked my fingers.

Her blood was draining at a rate I knew it would.

I worked at a labor I loved.

It was meaningful.

I was a boy again slicing runt puppies for mother.

I was a boy again gutting pigs for neighboring nuns.

I laughed through my bubbling spittle. It sounded like a growl.

"Time, be on my side," I prayed.

I flipped the folds of skin upon her upper stomach.

Fluids spread across her wrinkled, fluid stained skin.

I laughed a laugh that made the ravens flee to safer trees.

This sad creature, just seconds ago begged to be fucked for the stalest of bread and now I nibbled on her like a hog upon the hands of York.

The smell, God the smell!

Simply licking my fingers wasn't enough.

The voices grabbed my neck and shoved my face into Catherine's bowels. It was a moment like no other.

I rolled my face in her open pubic.

I licked what many men had thrust without dare and what she had sold without care.

I licked intestines. I nibbled on one, feces squirted from the opening. I pulled on them, removing a significant amount from her cavity.

I licked her like a man would a woman, from the inside out.

Time was running short, as even the slowest of constables would be coming through the square in just minutes.

I fingered my pointless cock.

I had to do it once again.

Holding the victors title I thrust my face, with teeth wide back down into her simmering gut.

I bit with force where I'd before just nibbled.

Shit sprayed upon her, my whiskered chin, and deep into my unclean nostrils.

Her guts throbbed only out of habit.

God the smell, I couldn't resist it, but I had to as the constables time neared us.

The voices and her smell were winning.

Is this where I'd be found?

No, not yet, there is one more to meet.

My nose drew closer to what she'd sell to the highest bidder. I let my fingers twirl intestines large and small. I inhaled deep. My tongue reached for them all and I bit with force what remained. I swallowed it all without gags of regret.

My lips quivered as I again rolled her over.

Her guts, great and small jumped out onto the ground.

I fingered my pointless cock.

"Fuck them in the ass boy, it's best when with a whore," Lispenard's memory flashed.

I dry fucked her ass without reward.

Shit was smeared.

"Always in the ass boy, it's the best," his words bounced.

I spread her ass.

I rubbed shit on her back.

Catherine had not bathed.

That sickened me.

I tasted her dirt.

I rubbed her back high and low.

I needed her.

I licked my lips of the drying shit.

I couldn't have her as a seaman would, or as I would a handsome boy, but I needed her as I'd never desired a woman before.

I rubbed her back just above her smeared ass.

Her kidneys were a frequent bother for her.

I'd take her pain away.

My needs grew more animalistic as my gray hairs sprouted.

Catherine presented no more sounds of satisfaction as I rubbed her.

She couldn't moan now but I assumed she still enjoyed it.

I rubbed her harder.

I thrust my cock for no reason and at no target.

The hour had to be well passed half-passed.

With a stroke I'd used on many a chicken I cut above and below her left kidney.

The peritoneal and heavy artery was cut through.

"Breakfast for the Misses," my spit bubbled.

I cleared its cavity.

I placed the kidney in my bag and rubbed my blood and shit covered hands on the nearest wall. I licked my palms. I rolled Catherine over tossing her bowels and bonnet closer to her neck.

I cupped her apron.

I took what seemed a lengthy rest and sat back on my heels, my cock now fully erect as if observing my work.

I began to stroke my cock in demand of my vice.

The time spent in reflection was only a minute or two at best.

The scene was hurried.

It had to be.

I was hurried because of one man, Schwartz!

I leaned over her. My face neared her.

I placed my hand gently on her neck and I gave her a soft, long, moist kiss on her full lips. I tongued her mouth and swirled it from gum to gum while I sliced a piece of her right ear.

"Food for my thought," I said as I stood.

I pissed a pool into her stomach cavity.

It smelled of Ginger Beer.

My cheeks were red.

I was panting.

I shoved a finger into my nostril and swiped shit and other chunks clean. I swallowed both rewards, chewing what needed to be chewed. My urge had been satisfied.

I shifted her body so it could be hidden from a quick glance.

I removed her apron and left her where we began. My cloak flapped as I approached Goulston and Wentworth Streets. I had hurried and knew at such a pace that it wasn't possible for me not to be seen. I'd stood with bag in hand in the gradually lifting, ankle high fog.

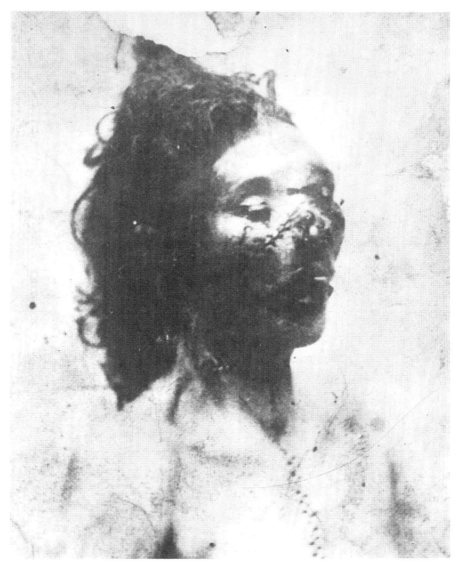

Catherine Eddowes in the mortuary.

I turned and pissed again, hidden by shadows.

I swallowed pooled drool.

I crossed Wentworth and walked several feet before I heard voices begin to snap.

"Stop! Now stop you son of an Irish cunt stop!"

I did as the voices beckoned.

The voices buzzed like bees protecting their hive.

"Fuck them, look what they've done to you!" The voices caused me to wince as I walked.

I couldn't escape the voices. I could ignore them but I couldn't escape.

I walked several more doorways.

I saw a shadow dodge down one entrance not twenty yards ahead.

"It's Schwartz!" The voices said.

I hurried ahead to see what the voices said was there.

It was the dwellings of Wentworth, numbers 108-119.

"Stop here!" The voices said.

Should I follow them?

"Stop! Here! Mark their doors as the lamb's blood marked the ancient Hebrews," the voices demanded.

I did, as they wished.

I saw a chipped stone and with ample effort wrote upon the wall those words to confound the occupants, vigilantes, writers and constables alike. I thought the Jews, guilty or not, will never be men who are blamed. I too was confounded at to the meaning to the words that earlier had only been dreamed of.

I dropped Catharine's apron and made my exit deep into the cave of the voices.

The sea tossed my feet.

The dream was quite vivid and it quivered.

I rolled to the sounds of my sleep.

The voices that haunted me sung poetry none dared admit authorship to.

I swirled asleep in my arms and drool pooled across my arms.

I muttered words only I knew.

"Mumble be and little lambs, beckoned hearts and fattened calves. Fallen trees with moistened leaves, shitty asses with cunts in half," my mind wrote.

I quivered to the voices.

La Bretange rolled with the early hour sea.

My muttering was the spark that woke me.

I sat up.

One face was shown hid deep within the shadows.

I swallowed hard.

I gasped as if I was still fleeing Mitre Square.

Police evacuate Mitre Square.

Something was said from across the floor. I didn't hear it.

"You speak in your sleep, sir," the man within the shadow repeated.

I sought his eyes.

"Lunatics must dream your dreams," he said.

"I'm as much a lunatic as you are a commoner," I declared.

I swung my feet around to the floor.

"I'm a doctor and have seen so much, especially during America's Civil War," I added, "I apologize if my dreams disturbed you."

The gentleman's face remained hidden.

"How was your meal?" I asked.

"Memorable until it ended," he said.

We cast casual pleasantries for several minutes. I couldn't see his face as it was hid well amidst the evening's shadows of the cabin.

My belongings were in place that I was certain of.

I was hungry but more weary then hungry, stress and anxiety had engulfed me like no other time before.

"Mr. George, may I ask you a favor. If in three hours, I'm still asleep, please wake me?"

He graciously agreed that he would.

I rolled toward the wall.

In no time I fell asleep.

The voices of the night returned.

"Animal, butcher, lunatic, sadistic, grotesque!"

Those who shunned authority and their failed attempts at claiming the man of these actual deeds had taken it upon their own shoulders to walk the streets in search.

"Vigilantes," I smirked.

I laughed as they even wore homespun caps.

They walked with guns in hand throwing drunks into walls, kicking them when proper answers weren't given.

Vigilantes sprung up all of London some groups larger than others. Some had money, others had whiskey and some had both. All took to the streets each night.

I dreamed and moaned again according to Mr. George.

I felt my feet kicking.

My eyes danced between my fucking that mother of mine and Lispenard thrusting my own ass.

The voices continued.

"The devil walk with the vendors of flesh," I whispered.

I rolled. My flailed arms hit the wall. I felt my feet jerking as I garnered breath from other years.

I choked half-awake.

Was I deep in sleep thinking I was half-awake?

That man, Lusk, he was the most pompous and ignorant of the vigilantes. He declared his name often for the press that hungered for even the meekest of accomplishments.

He promoted himself by name. He asked for votes by offering the wavering business silver for their badges.

George Lusk was hence elected by local businessmen to serve as Chairman of the Whitechapel Vigilance Committee. He promoted himself more than he had desire to solve the crimes of infamy.

I watched the progression of his ego.

His name was listed on posters seeking information.

I read his name. I learned of his work and of his home address. He was a musician and not a good one even to the most alert of deaf ears. Lusk was a freemason, a braggart and failed architect. It'd be his ego that would be easiest to flatter.

The Devil reserves a table in hell for all of us of legitimate skills and for those who seek to rob from us the notoriety that's justly due. That night where I'd been so rushed, I posted him a gift. It was wrapped neatly. He deserved more and perhaps when the time was right and he'd learned from his transgressions he'd be given more, but for now I'd just tease the hog with mild script.

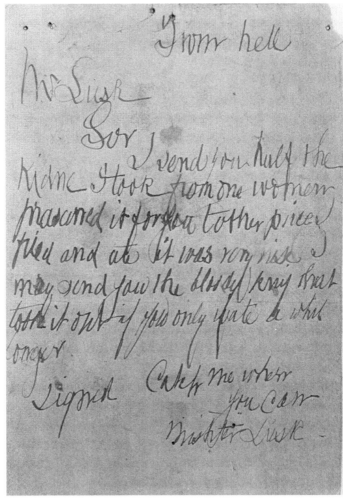

The From Hell letter.

CHAPTER FOURTEEN

The sea waffled tempting me with far away salt.

I slept and dreamt of that tempting taste of men, any man.

I dreamt too, of words and phrases written by he who died young but whose life's work torments the noble of conscious.

"Did those who spoke and wrote flowery words generations ago foretell days like these?" I asked my dreams.

John Keats, that young songster of prose seemed anxious as he foretold of fair England and the days it would hold.

If all our dreams foretell of days to come then what tales do the lunatics tell us with their dreams?

"To sleep? Aye perchance to fucking dream. After all, what did Horatio or Marcellus dream?"

"For in that sleep of death what dreams do come," I repeated the words of the magi from Avon.

I quickly woke and unfolded myself.

The night had done it to me again.

It had taken me home. I was home again. I was home where it all began on the pebbles and mud of Sophia Street. I had only one, final chore to perform and then I can dine off any East Bethany deer.

"What dreams may come?"

"Did I not do just what Hamlet's ghost asked for and accomplish revenge?"

My feet jerked to the waffling bow.

They jerked to the thoughts of Irish castles.

"What dreams may come?"

I shivered where I sat.

Lusk, the asshole, the bleeding twinkling star!

He spent woman's silver while also loving the firmness of the same young men I cast aside. Mr. Lusk, I'll ask you a princes question, "Whether 'tis nobler in the mind to suffer the slings and arrows of outrageous fortune, or to take arms against a sea of troubles and by opposing end them."

"Dear Lusk, by your opposition to me have you ended me or my kind?" I asked with a baritone tone.

My twilight dreams splashed in full color the blood and rumors of Catherine Eddowes. I quivered for the taste of her womanly salt, of her gut and of her shit as the sea chased me from one gaslight to the next.

"The flesh is heir to: 'tis a consummation devoutly to be whished."

"Fuck Shakespeare!" I muttered and his memory mounted.

My type have forever walked histories cobbled stone, Mr. Lusk; "To die: to sleep, no more; and by a sleep to say we end..." It is only by death that we end the heartache and the thousand natural shocks.

I slept through the finely quaffed borders of all those dribbled voices. Yet I was curious as to their goal. If we are hidden by the dark, do we still cast shadows? If we are dead do we still dream? If we whisper alone, who hears us?

My arms flailed.

I hummed to the dreams revealing my history.

Under shade of darkness I felt the palsy in full jerk of my left hand. I also felt the constant stare from the face hid within the shadows.

My leg jerked.

My right leg jerked again and this time it delivered me near full awake.

The seas personality I determined to be shy.

I swallowed words that weren't my own.

In the cabin my eyes batted seeking to find forms of some sort, any sort.

I grew cold.

Was my chill but a dream also?

Was I delusional?

Was I hallucinating?

I licked my lips in full circle.

I wrapped myself tight within my own grasp. Nothing could approach me as I was hidden within my fingers.

I repeated the verse of a crafted man, a rosary of sorts for the nonbeliever.

"Whether 'tis nobler in the mind to suffer the slings and arrows of outrageous fortune, or to take arms against a sea of troubles," his words were filling my soul.

Shakespeare had told my story three hundred years before I was born.

His words blurred all others.

My sanity wafted.

"Keep others from telling your story," the face of John Booth reminded me.

My right leg was pulled.

"How can I prevent it if my story was told before I first suckled my mother's breast?"

"Travel often to cleanse lands covered with fallen seeds," Lispenard said as a scrambled genius in his own right.

My right leg was pulled again, this time harder.

"Eat this you sad sack of shit," mother said.

Voices came from all angles.

My right leg was pulled yet again harder from the boot.

"It's after three. You wanted to be called," the man hid within the shadows barked.

He repeated the request I had made.

"It's three?" I asked still holding mother's breast.

"It might be some minutes after the hour now," the hidden voice said.

I rolled and thrust myself forward.

The fog of sleep left quickly.

I gasped for any fresh air available. It was hard to find.

"Thank you much," I said wearily.

"Your dreams are full of color," the hidden voice exclaimed.

"They're quite lively, entertaining for the last hour at least. Some might ask further questions if they'd not been only dreams," he said.

"I just can't sleep peacefully anymore," I said.

The cabin was dark. I couldn't see his face and the corner protected his form. It was as if he was perched in that room's corner.

Was he watching me?

"He hasn't yet returned," he said pointing to the other empty bunk.

"Plenty of lonely cunt here I imagine, might not be fresh but it's always plentiful," I answered.

I swung my feet to the floor. My left heal felt my personal items still in place under the bunk. The hair on my neck felt the stare from the hidden face.

Was he watching me?

My paranoia was well fed even though my stomach wasn't.

I felt nausea, as I had had no meal of quality since I kissed the greasy lips of Ollie good-bye. The meat he served wasn't the best even when it was properly cooked. Since then, only my gastritis was satisfied.

"I need a meal," I said.

"Care to join me?"

"Thank you, no, perhaps before the trip ends we'll chat over dinner," he said.

"Are my belongings safe?" I asked.

"They'll be just fine, doctor, as safe as mine are under your eyes."

"Fair enough," I pushed my clothes and bag further underneath the bunk.

I stood and reached for the door.

"Bon appetite," the hidden face said.

"Merci beaucoup," I said leaving the cabin behind me.

Baffle the simple ones, Lispenard always said.

This man, hidden in the shadows, had to be simple or he'd not be among the commoners.

I walked instinctively to the right when I exited the cabin.

My weariness and half-awake slouch caused my feet to shuffle in an unaccustomed way.

"Lispenard also lectured, impress the lunatic and the whore for the elite are nothing without them."

The chill wind was strong as I walked the narrowing passageway.

The chill disappeared as my pride warmed me.

The passageways held firm, as the battle between port and starboard grew stronger.

I held good footing.

I needed no rails or slat walls to hold my stance.

In several steps I saw mild light creeping down from up above.

If the light was of moderate strength this far down it must be of handsome character when the horizon was in its fullest.

I saw children at play several doors down.

"Hi, mister," came their salutation as I approached.

I nodded only.

"Fuck off, shit-eaters," I whispered in passing.

I stepped on a small hand.

A sharp cry ended their play.

I rounded the corner of the first passageway and the amount of light increased imperceptibly but increased nonetheless.

I heard footsteps but saw no boots.

I shuffled a few more steps of my own.

The sound of those footsteps increased and the closer I came to the better class cabins the quality of the footsteps improved too.

I walked now with a firmer heel.

Lispenard, the man with a boyish fetish, said a man of quality never shuffles his feet. It's the poor, the lunatic and the lazy that drag their heels.

"They scuff mankind with their souls and soles," he'd say.

With my memory of him placed on the mantel of the moment I pulled my feet higher as the first curious eyes befell my exit from below.

I was beginning a performance worse for the wear.

I entered the portside deck from stage left.

There was a cast of characters filling the mezzanine chairs. They were waiting on us commoners to come and admire their fancy hats and hand sewn white gloves. I'd be the first they'd see.

Those with the fancy hats and upturned noses stood only feet away from the top of the stairwell with anxious eyes.

They eyed me as I reached the upper deck.

I had entered their realm, without vest or parted hair. I was stepping high with my chin pointed towards the horizon. I knew my appearance caused many a sentence to be paused in mid-verb but they needed to see what they've waited for.

I wasn't a commoner.

They would ask, "Why is this man, a doctor of reputable note, cast among the moldy steerage of bag and man?"

I stood with great pride and puffed arrogance as the first laugh was tossed at my feet.

"Look at that one," they whispered.

"He walks coolly among us," others snickered.

"Look at his trousers, his messed shirt and careless hair," they whispered.

My chin remained firm and my steps high as I walked past the fat hats and fatter asses. I let fly airs of my own to enlighten their smug, pug noses.

Their footing was unstable.

They all held the railings.

It was my chin that held me firmly in place.

I'd paid so close attention to the ones holding snuff tins that I'd ignored the wind of the upper most deck. It was frigid, it was strong and swallowed up the buckling white caps.

Many huddled as quaint virgin lovers sometimes do.

They held one-another.

They kissed.

They shared holds, looks and tastes that I'd never know.

My chin pointed toward those fallen caps of white.

"Give me women, wine and snuff until I cry out, hold, enough!" I repeated Keats under my fattening tongue.

I watched as a nearby boy, a man in the making, poked at his fluff haired cunt like a robin does a worm.

They're all alike.

"Hold, enough!" I whispered turning from the star struck lovers.

I clenched the railing not ten yards from the coupling pair.

I listened to their shared whispers imagining what it was he said to make her blush.

I spit only to have it forced horizontally across my face by the wind.

"Fill for me a brimming bowl and let me in it drown my soul," John Keats spoke for every wind and every man who had been the brunt of a whore's laughter.

The coupling nuzzled their whispers.

They giggled secretly, her blushing desires obvious in the cold wind.

I leveled my chin to the Atlantic gasps.

The couple was some feet away but I could smell her anyway. The strongest of winds couldn't prevent her salt from petting my nose.

She was a flirtatious whore, young and plump with perfumed, ringlet filled auburn locks. Oh she never sold what she powdered, but the young man was paying for it nonetheless.

I swayed to my trickling spittle.

My spit was a boiled bowl of lust and revenge.

"But put therein some drug, designed to banish women from my mind," I spoke the fallen one's words into the Atlantic.

"Fuck Keats!" I declared.

My face was upturned sucking in the gusts from depths and heights alike from the water below.

I welcomed it all because inhaling a generation of dead cod is far more preferable than one second next to the young whore at three arms lengths.

The young woman turned her face slightly, viewing me from the corner of her eye. She held tightly an outburst of impolite laughter.

She rolled her eyes and batted her long lashes. In mumbling limericks to her cock of the moment both giggled at my expense.

Despite the chill my face was warming.

I swayed from the heat of their laughter.

The giggles echoed across the deck.

Their snickering grabbed my boots and caressed my calf.

The Atlantic wind was ice and it staged a battle with the fancy whore for the high ground upon my shoulders.

I tilted my chin to fight off both.

My stare became as sharp as diamonds.

The couple had moved as soon as my diamonds cast a glimmer in their direction. Did they notice that I had taken notice? They shuffled past me whispering what I knew to be the most derogatory of undertones.

"And what is love? It is a doll all dressed up," I squirted her way.

Her hat was teased into place by the Atlantic's tongue.

She held it as she passed by.

The boy of the unspoken love seemed a farmer standing amidst her ample orchard.

He was soft in words and firm in cock.

"That silly youth doth think to make itself divine by loving, and so goes on."

If they fluff, we follow.

If they powder we follow.

Love is momentary in histories light but the young; their foolish hearts believe theirs is meant for eternity. The young place flesh first and enshrine the fuck as eternal.

They giggled holding each. I added my own snicker as they held each other as winter does snow, spring the flower and fields the weed.

I stood holding her salted scent.

The salt was firm as well.

My moment was committed to her natural stink.

However, as I held firm to her salted seed, from within my cabin below, the man hidden by shadows began to move. He'd given me what he believed time to locate my needed meal.

Was he curious?

He swung his feet to the floor.

I loosened my grip of the portside rail.

Her scent vaporized and my nose was free again to seek the meat being boiled by the galley crew. I let my animalistic senses guide me to the spot down the passageway and two sections of stairs.

My ears were hearing distant shuffles of boots.

My neck chilled to what was close and what wasn't.

The man hid by the shadows stood and shuffled his way to the center of the cabin. The cabin was dark with only the floor receiving a trickle of light from the passageway.

He stepped slowly listening to the shuffling boots of the commoners from outside the cabin door.

I stepped slowly listening to the high steps of the fur covered upper classed whores and their boys in tow.

The man hid by the shadows approached my bunk.

The corner of another passageway hid me as I came near the room where meat was served.

He stood inches from my bunk while children ran past the cabin's door.

I stood near the door of the galley.

He paused at the noise.

I paused at the noise.

Voices said pardon me.

We both heard apologies offered. Others cussed and still others were being rude for just plain instinctive reasons.

I waited for the voices to pass, as did the man hid by the shadows. We both had need of silence to determine our next action.

I reached for the door where the meat smelled like a woman, only better washed.

The man within the shadows leaned to see what was tucked beneath my bunk.

My eyes focused on what was within the galley.

I paused to a shiver trickling up my spine.

He paused to a shiver trickling up his spine.

I turned toward the end of the passageway lit by the trickling light.

He turned toward a spot on the floor lit by the trickling light.

"What I did now might forever change the final sentence of my diary, Mr. Booth," I muttered.

I turned to follow the voices upon my shoulders. Their whisper was faint but forceful. They skirted in no uncertain terms to the last door at the end of this passageway.

I had to return to the cabin.

Something was wrong.

I was a dog and my den was about to be disturbed.

The man hid by the shadows went no further instead looked closer at the light coming from beneath the door.

"Something's wrong," he said.

I'd turned away from the boiling meat and with my nose aimed below decks I high stepped to the rhythm of the voices back to the cabin.

The man hid within shadows was not so hid in his intentions, he never had been. My answers to his questions were vague enough to have fueled his curiosity.

I rounded each of the upcoming corners. I was deliberate but not in a panic and as I neared the cabin the shuffling of my boots increased the more.

The man hid within the shadows, listened carefully. His ears were good and were pressed against the door. He heard many steps but it was my foot shuffling that gave me away.

He had to be nervous. Wouldn't I be if I were he?

I shuffled with scuffling fury to the imagination of what may be unfolding near my nest.

The man hid within the shadows backed away when he heard my boots slow.

I reached for the knob.

He waited for the knob to be reached.

He retreated toward his bunk and the shadows he called his own.

Slowly I turned the knob, and opened the door.

The toe of my boot was first to enter the cabin.

There was a noticeable chill in the air.

I stood in the doorway with my frame lit by the passageway.

I was but just an outline to him.

"Who is it?" the hidden voice asked.

I shut the door behind me using the same toe of my boot.

"It's me," I said.

"The food wasn't pleasing to smell much less taste. I thought you might be sleeping by now," I said.

"I don't sleep much," he admitted as he dribbled small talk across the floor.

I listened to his dribbling of why he slept little and what he'd done to try to rectify the matter.

"Powders and drinks work well most times," he said, "but for several months now even they've lacked in effectiveness."

I offered no response instead aiming for my bunk. My head hit the wall as I lay down. I knew he watched my movement. I was also sure his eyes were deliberate in their dedication to my form.

Was he attracted to me?

Did he have animalistic desires for me as a man would a woman?

I blushed as I snuggled within the unclean air.

I surmised he knew more than what he professed.

What did he know?

Had I erred in letting my paranoia subside for even the slightest amount of time?

He had drifted in his tales from his sleepless woes to far off wars. Once he paused for flatulence sake, the man hid by the shadows began to speak in great concern about the mysteries haunting fare England.

"England has seen too much recently. Even the poorest whose names will never be remembered have fallen victim to unkind histories," he said.

He paused.

"England should be happy, don't you think?" he asked me.

Was he asking me an opinion or lighting a stage for me to cross?

"Happy is England, do you agree?" he asked again.

"Happy is England, sweet her artless daughters..." I responded.

"...enough their simple loveliness for me," the hidden man finished.

"Enough their simple loveliness for me..." I said.

"Enough their whitest arms in silence clinging..." I added.

"Keats was a magnificent master don't you think?" he asked.

"He was quite charitable with words," I admitted.

This man, hid by the shadows wasn't as simple as he'd painted himself to be upon our initial exchange of words. He was well read and read well.

I adjusted my body so I'd lay with one knee up.

"He was a master, Keats that is," I said.

"He was a student of medicine as well, and like myself he worked in what was an apothecary. Like me too, his boyhood was filled with bouts of great turmoil."

"Keats wasn't happy with medicine, he told peers he wanted to do the world good in some way. Like me he also wanted to leave his mark," I added.

"We all want to leave our mark," the man hid within the shadows declared, "Some are meant to leave the mark while some are meant to benefit from that mark being left."

"We all have are roles in life my friend," I said.

"We do, we genuinely do," he said.

I paused allowing my words to fall like snow.

"Keats had tremendous power of imagination. He learned and interpreted from geniuses of other generations," I added.

"John Milton's Paradise Lost, was one I do believe," the hidden face offered.

I was stumped by this remark for it was as profoundly accurate as it was an unknown fact.

"Yes, you're quite right. Many things were key in John Keats development, his education and his complicated years being among them. But it was Edmund Spenser who John would say opened the door to literary brilliance."

"Imitation of Spenser 1816?" asked the man hid by the shadows.

"Yes, Imitation of Spenser, one of Keats early works. I do wonder if he was lamenting over what he saw as his own personal paradise lost. At an opportunity being lost or a once in a lifetime opportunity being lost. I think that opportunity could only be his childhood as both his parents died when he was young."

"Perhaps he wrote Imitation of Spenser in memory of his own childhood," the man hid within the shadows surmised.

I was still prone but my eyes shifted from paranoia to debate preparation. This man across from me was not a simple commoner and has thus proven to be a worthwhile opponent.

There was a pause long enough for both of us to take a breath of equal length.

Were we preparing?

Yes, for a debate of words and of imagination. As I've often stated, any artist of word or paint cannot perform without a well-manicured imagination and we were going to see who possessed the better imagination.

He was still hid despite the creeping light across the floorboards of the cabin. Shortly that light would reach the foot of his bunk. A shadow hid me as well.

We'd fight with stanzas at equal paces.

"Now Morning from her orient chamber came..."

He threw me a toy of a first line as it was just weeks earlier that I too came from many a woman's early morning chamber.

What did the man in the shadows know of me?

Did Keats foretell of me and of the numerous orient chambers I'd crossed?

Did the hidden man read the history that Keats wrote?

"And her first footsteps touched a verdant hill crowning its lawny crest with amber flame," I added.

"And after parting beds of simple flowers, by many streams a little lake did fill," he offered quickly.

"A little lake did fill," I whispered.

What lake was Keats thinking of?

What lake did the man hid within the shadows speak of?

I had filled many a lake some with piss, some with my lover's seed and many more with the blood of life.

Their blood flowed like little streams through the jagged, moss green cobblestone of the East End, I whispered; "Which, pure from mossy beds, did downhill distill, and after parting beds of simple flowers."

I had parted their flowers and their blood flowed downhill.

My adversary had skipped lines important to poet and reader. He'd lost and we'd just begun.

I could now artfully delve into the tribute to Spenser losing the hidden man amidst the early scribbles of that forlorn genius.

With a full stanza missed he boomed.

"Ah! Could I tell the wonders of an isle...Or rob from Lear his bitter teen..." he added without breathless pause.

The hidden face wasn't stumped. He used the correct color at the correct time.

It was I who paused instead, for fuck it all to hell; I was that bitter teen of King Lear. What did the man hid among the shadows really know? Was he telling my tales when telling those tales were told only by tidy, tersely tucked timely translations?

Sanity was losing its grip.

"Of all that ever charmed romantic eye, it seemed an emerald in the silver sheen," his voice grew as if an actor nearing center stage.

He was reading recent headlines written sixty years ago.

"Emerald eyes and silver sheen," I whispered to my palm.

"Emerald eyes and silver sheen, what did books and cabin mates know?"

Mother, Lispenard, and John Booth they had such emerald eyes.

Catherine's eyes though covered by darkness had shown emerald in the quarter moon as well.

In the darkness of the cabin with both knees pointed up my torso began to sway.

Fuck, what did he know? What did the shadows know of me?

Did he know more than just the selected verses of Keats?

Did he see Catherine's eyes too?

What bout those of Liz? Martha? Mary?

I should have plucked all their eyes.

"Something wrong Mr. Townsend?" he asked after my prolonged silence.

"No nothing," I said.

In silence I dared his mockery of me.

I sat up.

I crossed my ankles.

He became a festering presence from within the shadows. I dare he for prejudging me and soiling the words of the one gifted short-lived man with charity of word.

I leaned against the wall.

I could hear him waiting.

"Here's a hint," he said, "Of the bright waters; or as when on high, through clouds of fleecy white, laughs the cerulean sky."

Sanity swayed.

"Woman!" he shouted and then paused.

"Woman! When I beheld thee flippant, vain, inconstant, childish, proud, and full of fancies; without modest softening that enhances," I spat completing his thought.

His hidden corner paused.

Have I won I wondered.

Did he now need a hint for he too had paused?

"Sir, you have erred," he said.

"Not possible," I quickly insisted.

"It's so nonetheless," he said.

"The line properly reads, woman when I behold thee; you clearly stated woman when I beheld thee," the man hid by the shadows said.

"Semantics," I declared.

"Perhaps, however your version is in the past tense, the correct version is not. Your version speaks of memory while the correct version does not."

I reflected over his interpretation.

"You are right, and I am not. I will give you your do."

He'd won the moment, but what had he won?

"I will present a better challenge in the days to come, I promise," I said.

"I believe that you will," he said.

I lay back down in a slump.

What did he know and how could he know it? I sensed he watched my form. Both my knees popped as I stretched my legs out.

Did those who were always victorious ever admit defeat?

Did those who were always defeated ever recognize victory?

Would I do either?

I also had always wondered why Keats gave up on the study and practice of medicine. Did he fail at it? Did he admit his defeat? Did he cover-up his failure of one skill by mastering his charity of words?

I sighed heavily. Out of addiction I inhaled the sea and the outline of the man hid by the shadows.

My conscience collapsed like a speared doe.

Weariness overcame me.

The encircling voices began to whisper.

"Light feet, dark violet eyes, and parted hair; soft dimpled hands, white neck, and creamy breast, are things on which the dazzled senses rest..." whispered the man hid by the shadows.

"Does this sound at all familiar, Doctor Frank?" he asked.

I nestled in my arms, as if I was my first firm young man I had loved.

"It does," I replied, "Till the fond, fixed eyes, forget they stare...in lovely modesty, and virtues rare...yet these I leave as thoughtless as a lark," I added near my sleep, "Till fond fixed eyes...and virtues rare," I mumbled with sleep heavy eyes.

"Who can forget her half retiring sweets? For man's protection...surely the all-seeing...I shall never forget her retiring sweets and downcast eyes," he paraphrased Keats in a hushed lullaby.

"Retiring sweets, what a way with words he had. John Keats had written my story years before I was born," I muttered through growing spit.

"They were all dewy flowers, not only her and she but him and he too, as my hands always quivered when I neared them all. The boys giggled like the whores, the same whores with emerald eyes and who'd been laid askew by the silver sheen."

Sanity lost its grip.

Night succumbed to that lost grip.

The man hid within the shadows waited.

It was in my sleep that I could chart other courses.

"For in that sleep of death what dreams may come, when we have shuffled off this mortal coil?"

Those dreams returned me to the foot of a bed secured within the frame of Miller's Court.

I listened to the encircling voices.

The voices said that Keats was forever dead in body but that his mind lived on for eternity through cobbled history and hob nailed boots.

Keats did live on. I found him to be subtly obvious when it came to women. He was trained to be a doctor, just like you the voices said. You both wanted to make your marks, you chose knife and herb and he chose noun and verb said the voices.

Mortal coil took from the floor the trickling light.

The man hid within the shadows moved as my will weakened.

What would he do next?

Miller's Court became my dream.

My mind danced the horizon it painted. My eyes followed the dance. What did the man within the shadows mean when he said he'd not forgotten their sweets or their retiring eyes.

I rolled over on the bunk. I seldom slept on my stomach, for it was more difficult to rise rapidly. I was in the world offered up by twilight sleep. I heard the man stand. He was most certainly of good solid build regardless of how I saw him. His eyes had to be dark even under the brightest of summer skies. The last of the trickling light showed limited facial features. I saw a prominent mustache on an oval face.

Did twilight show him to be more than what he was?

Mr. George that is.

Jonathan George.

John George Littlechild.

Chief Inspector John George Littlechild.

CHAPTER FIFTEEN

Chief Inspector John George Littlechild was the brightest of the slouches when it came to advancing from scene to scene. Was it he who hid within the shadows? Was it he that shared a cabin and was it he who stood only feet away? Did he know of my history? Was his much-publicized pursuit of me to Brussels a bluff to comfort me?

The night gripped me by the throat.

"What dreams may come?" I wondered.

What came was a vision of that one night.

What came was the vision of my dry fucking the eye socket of Mary Jane Kelly. Her eyes had been plucked like grapes from the vines of Bordeaux. I died every time I dreamt and I dreamt every time I slept.

My sleep was death and in that death all was revealed.

That night, that one night I walked the stones muttering, "I have to leave my mark. I have to be profound."

"I need to be as profound as Keats. My deeds needed to be remembered centuries after I had shed this mortal coil.

"Fuck Shakespeare!" I muttered in the moon-glossed drizzle.

Shakespeare wrote for Spenser, and Spenser wrote for Keats. Keats wrote for me.

I dribbled spittle as I delivered sermons in churches not yet built.

Miller's Court was the dream.

It was Friday November 9th.

Perhaps I was, as some in news declared, already profoundly insane.

Perhaps I was manic. Perhaps I was a mere madman who had the taste for human flesh traipsing through his soul.

Fuck them all.

Those with tainted wigs and stained robes, noble manners and ill-timed thrust, I dare they judge me.

I walked the sizzled rocks in a wrinkled frock, seeking just one name as if she were far off game.

Worthless sack of seed she was. 'Ginger' was how I knew her others knew her by Mary. She too I had tried to fuck like a man would a woman, but she also as many others had only laughed when they found my cock to small for their cavernous hole. Even after tasting all those cocks 'Ginger' still possessed beauty. She would have been a good wife and possible mother if she'd stayed unstained.

Her essence wafted as I followed.

I found her first on the 6th I walked the stones with the voices growing in their anxiousness.

I was pensive.

Pageantry was close.

The night of the 7th, I walked the streets with my throbbing throat growing.

Lord Mayor's Day was now upon the city.

The newly selected leaders would be officially presented to her highness. Money had come into town for the several days leading up to the celebration and, where there was money; there would be the hungry holes of Whitechapel.

Money came to be seen by those wanting to be seen, and the whores came to be seen by the money that had come to be seen. The money was well drunk at an early hour on the night of the 8th. Those who knew or had encouraged the outcome of the mayoral selection were boasting of their deed and in their newfound friends wearing powdered wigs.

I walked amidst the money when they danced their cocks in the East End. There were those who came to London just for that celebration, it was an escape from their own mundane days elsewhere. In London they could be whomever they wished.

Many with heavy pockets considered 'Ginger' a choice fuck. She had, as I could testify to, many regular gentlemen. Her value was impressive during celebrations such as Lord Mayor's Day. She had sold her cracked cunny often for better coin, as she was a rarity, a whore with a regular room, 13 Miller's Court.

'Ginger' was a higher-class whore, and like a new hat or a better horse, her pretty face produced jealousy among the homely. 'Ginger' was not well liked within the East End by the other women. One growing rumor was she had taken to sharing a bed with a younger, fresher whore. Jealousy or not I had seen her with just such a woman, young with a heavy French accent. They walked many an evening with their arms locked at the elbows.

I had begun to wonder if 'Ginger' desire a woman's touch as I desire the touch of a young man?

I dribbled spittle to that thought.

The night of the 8th I walked in heavy air, not proud of my state of being. I was unclean. And though I was clean-shaven, heavy blotches covered my face. My eyes were weighty, the voices on my shoulders were stout, and my lips quivered in full view under any half lit gaslight of that night.

I stood at the corner of Commercial and Church Street. I heard the voices and saw the faces behind them. It appeared as if they were dragging, their motions lethargic. Their laughter and feigned moans of love appeared more like howls.

My head swirled within man's pool.

My ears were pained to a point where I removed myself to the cemetery behind Christ's Church. It was a cage for the dead surrounded by the ones laughing from just outside the gates.

I felt an imperceptible urge.

I walked over shade-covered stones.

I had to piss.

I pulled out my cock. My left hand shook as I gripped the poisoned tool. I was pained. I noticed the scent it expelled was that of old coffee. I watered the grave of James Peck, four years deceased.

I packed myself back within the trousers and licked my fingers clean. The salt and coffee taint pleased me. I left the cemetery and took a right on Church Street. I would scuff the stones of Commercial, Fashion and Flower for hours.

My mind and lips were full of passion. I played with my cock in clear view of all who had howls instead of laughs. I had become the center of ridicule, I had grown into an unfortunate, and there was no one who offered me what I'd offered others.

Those with fallen wills pointed my way and asked how could society allow such a being as me?

I was aghast, for how could they judge me?

I dare they judge me, a doctor of reputable note?

My tongue was thickening with each passing day.

I strode to near the Commercial Glass Works. My anger had its limits now, as my body, growing in frailty could manage only a limited response. I was better than they who laughed at my wounds but I could do little to prove it.

I knew of Tenter Street it was incomplete street and it was joined to Whites Row by a very small alley, in that alley I hovered many evenings, and from here I could be close enough to be away from it all.

The small stoop is where I'd spend some nights in combat with the voices. I'd crossed Commercial and Shepherd ignoring the corners of laughter. I walked down Butler, passing a non-descript Catholic Church Tenter Street was at Butlers end.

Row houses were on my right.

I approached a niche of other smaller homes. I stopped for that's when I saw her in full scented glory.

'Ginger' was encircling several hansom cabs near Butler and Tenter. The waiting cabmen were the drivers for those who'd come for Lord Mayor's Day.

'Ginger' flaunted her pretty amber hair and her better dress. She was in full display.

"Fuck for three?"

"Suck for two?"

She ignored the drivers' offers.

I watched not far from that niche.

"Fuck for four?"

She brushed that away too.

"Fuck for five?"

"Six?"

"Seven?"

She turned when a hidden face called out the final number.

I was so close that I could see her smile and hear her giggles. She was led away to the end of the very niche I stood.

I saw her face up close. It was beautiful.

'Ginger' was shabbily dressed, without a bonnet her red hair was the centerpiece to a dark crossover that hung about her shoulders.

I tipped by scarred billycock as the man with seven pennies and 'Ginger' walked on by. I looked toward the far end of the niche built to hide penny fucking. It was dark; no thrusts could be seen or heard.

I walked the remaining block or so to Tenter and seen one remaining hansom cab well hid by the shallowness of the street.

I approached it, slowly to be sure.

It was my cabman.

The flap eared man.

The beast at the cabs mercy was magnificent in the night's shadows.

The driver's topper was off.

His face was extremely unpleasant.

His shrunken ear was covered, hidden from mockery.

"Take me into the night. I'll pay you well," I said handing him a shilling upfront.

He looked down toward me and after refocusing his eyes he took the coin.

"Yes sir."

He seemed nervous.

"You will see a whore exit that niche, follow her slowly."

"Yes sir, you mean Mary the bitch."

"Yes, I'll call her 'Ginger' follow her please."

He opened the door with a crack of the whip.

The cabs interior was sour, smelling like a mix of old milk and piss.

On the floor was a well-tucked quart pot of ale.

The driver moved the cab forward so I could better observe her exit.

Soon she did exit.

"Now sir?" asked the cabman.

"Yes, but slowly."

As I reached for the pot the cab jarred again.

Some ale was spilled.

The wide-eyed beast did as he was told with a more than gentle crack of the lash.

She stopped several homes from the corner of Shepherd Street.

We stopped too.

The hour, I assumed, was later than nine-thirty if the darkness could be trusted.

My wait was impatient.

'Ginger' was recognizable by many, and chatted more often than she debated over price and place. She sang a song of sorts as she walked. What her voice emitted, at first was unrecognizable. Then as we neared her I was able to determine several words from a song that I sometimes sang in my own youth.

I listened carefully, her voice was female at its purest and though she feigned a Gaelic tone, it was quite lovely nonetheless. 'Ginger' was in full display and as faces gathered around she sang:

> "Scenes of my childhood arise before my gaze
> Bringing recollections of by-gone happy days,
> When down in the meadows in childhood I would roam
> No one's left to cheer me now within that good old home;
> Father and mother they have passed away
> Sister and brother now lay beneath the clay,
> But while life does remain to cheer me I'll retain
> This small Violet I plucked from mother's grave."

These words awoke me.

Why did 'Ginger' sing that song.

What did she know?

She sang and fluttered her hands, and when she completed those selected bars those who'd gathered applauded as if they had just seen Othello.

She curtseyed and daintily twiddled her way several more homes closer to Shepherd Street.

Our cab jarred ahead as she returned to her walk.

"I plucked when but a boy and oft times when I'm sad at heart..." I continued her lament.

"Follow her slowly," I told the cabman.

'Ginger' paused briefly then crossed both Shepherd and Commercial Street. My flap eared driver pulled back in force, it wouldn't be impossible to follow her directly. The heavy commotion of pedestrians, horses and tramway would prevent it.

He corrected course and with a sharp right on Commercial. We'd have to circle the block. The last I saw 'Ginger' she danced toward the cemetery. If we were to stay close to her we'd be forced to go down one of the foulest parts of Spitalfields, Flower and Dean Street.

The scene was horrific even for the encircling raven.

Yet the driver and I knew it quite well.

I'd become familiar with the lodging houses here. Nearly twenty of them held the thousand inhabitants of the one street. Elizabeth had been a common guest at # 32 and Catherine along with her cock John Kelly there at # 55; they had resided there for years. The street was incredibly narrow, perhaps no more than a dozen or so feet at its western end. A commotion was growing, as we neared the corner of Lolesworth Street and the Cooney House. I soon saw the reason for it.

There was a hansom cab; it seemed unusually clean and very inexperienced for this street. A driver, also inexperienced, had wrongly taken it down Flower and Dean. Its riders were a quaint young couple. Any number of unfortunates surrounded them en masse. The young man was being held back, fighting only with words. His lover, young and frail, was stripped and was openly and frequently fucked to the applause by those waiting for their turn. She screamed and screamed until there was no longer a need. He could do nothing but watch.

We waited until all were wiped blood and seed free.

The crowd slowly dispersed in shared laughter.

"Now, sir?" my driver asked.

"Now," I answered.

As we rode past the screeching young woman I held my chin within my collar to hide from the scene.

The flap eared driver took a left on Osborn Street.

He guided us to yet another left on Fashion Street.

The driver was good at what he did, as in short time we were at the intersection of Commercial and Fashion. 'Ginger' would be off to my right if she were still without hired labor.

Only several minutes separated my last vision of her and now, the chime said it was later than I had thought.

Despite the thinning crowds, I didn't see her.

I was growing pensive.

The crowd passed in front, behind and around us.

My throat throbbed.

My lips quivered.

I hungered for her salt.

The driver stopped. I looked out into the crowd for her but heard only the laughter of the drunks, the begging of the two-penny cunts and the sales pitches of boys with grapes.

We went right on Commercial Street.

The cab drew to a complete stop.

"Fuck for four?" I heard.

"A suck for three?"

I saw the flailing of a knitted crossover above the piping of faceless commoners.

'Ginger' stood on the bottom step of the Christ Church sanctuary.

"Here?" the driver asked.

"Yes here," I said.

We were in complete view of her.

I moved the curtain of the cab slightly aside.

I heard some drunkard offer a penny here or two over there for a squeeze, tug and suck but 'Ginger' brushed them all away.

I saw that she was now goodly drunk.

She saw our cab.

"A fine one wants your cunny, Mary," a lost crackling voice shouted.

At first she ignored us like a playful puppy does its master's commands. My gloves were now on, my billycock presentable. I motioned out the window for her to come over.

She ignored me still, firmly, but playfully.

"Do you wish to proceed, sir?" the flap eared driver asked loudly.

'Ginger' then took heed and with a quickstep approached the cab.

The driver played his role well this night.

"Do you wish a drink? " I asked holding the pot of ale.

'Ginger' poked her pug nose inside.

"What else have ya'?" she asked.

I set the pot down and crossed my wrists, left over right.

"Well, dear lady, as you may know I have a fine reputation. I have many stories that I can share that will be entertaining. I will share with you my glory in war torn other lands. I will share with you this ale and of course I will provide you two-shillings for a comfortable fuck!"

"I am thirsty," she said shyly.

I opened the door and she climbed in.

'Ginger' slid in close to me throwing her hand immediately between my legs without a pause for any hint of innocence.

"We'll get to that in a moment," I said removing her hand.

"Now, sir?" the driver asked.

"Yes, now please but slow."

At first there were no words exchanged, and in apparent boredom, 'Ginger' reached for the curtain on her side and pulled it open.

Cheers, perhaps jeers came floating our way.

She waved to the crowds and jeered back unkind words still feigning a hint of Gaelic in her tone.

We were centerpiece to a Lord Mayor's Day parade.

My driver knew his role and followed my unspoken directions. He took a left on Brushfield Street, another aggressively overcrowded and crime-riddled street of Spitalfields.

'Ginger' still waved and shouted to those she knew and she knew many faces within the crowd.

I remained calmed and stout, hidden deep in thought.

A raven flew ahead of the cab.

A raven, "Noble bird of yore…"

'Ginger' waved and sang as we rode.

She sang as I wandered weakly in my own mind, "once upon a midnight dreary, while I pondered, weak and weary."

"Fuck that Poe boy too," I said louder than I should have.

"I'm on Dorset Street, off in a room of my own, 13 Miller's Court," she declared.

"I'm familiar with it," I said.

13 Miller's Court.

The driver without being asked had taken a left on Crispin Street.

The raven flew ahead of us and settled on the Crispin cobblestone.

"Here, sir?" he asked.

The raven as part of his saintly days of yore pecked piled horseshit as we approached.

"Yes, here is fine," I said.

The raven, dedicated to his seed, fell victim to the wheels of the careless cabman.

"Miller's Court is up around this corner, is it not?" I asked.

"Yes, it is," she said.

"Let us walk then, I shall carry the pot of ale."

"Whatever you wish, Mr. Frank," she said.

I was pleased for she did remember me.

We exited the cab.

I saw the remaining twitches of the raven and stepped on its neck to bring about a swifter ending.

'Ginger' held my elbow.

I held the pot of ale.

I tapped my fingers along side the cab.

"You know where we will be...circle the blocks until...until the early hours, three, perhaps four," I told the flap eared driver.

The driver appeared nervous.

He pulled in his shoulders.

"But sir... I must be done with this...I...I can't do this any longer...I can not wait..."

I stood close to his boots.

His gallies had holes.

I drew a line on his leg with my sharpened finger.

My nail was sincere and so was the line.

He appeared to close his eyes in grimace.

I grabbed his ankle and slowly began to rub his calf up and down.

He didn't pull away but provided a shameful moan.

I rubbed firmly.

"Your skin is rough and badly scented," I said, below your skin flow the veins of life, and below the skin of history are London's veins.

I am who I am and you will be who you are. Circle the blocks as you are told." I let go of his calf and provided him a Crown.

"Yes sir, " he answered meekly. I turned to take 'Ginger' by her elbow, and scraped the raven from my boot.

"It'd be nameless here for evermore," I smiled.

A woman was nearby.

I held my chin firm as she passed. "Good night now," she said.

"Good night to you Mrs. Cox," 'Ginger' said as she again took up the chorus of "A Violet I plucked from mother's grave."

We followed the woman Cox up Dorset Street.

Miller's Court was on the left halfway down.

'Ginger' sang.

I carried the ale.

The drizzle returned.

The woman, Mrs. Cox, crossed Dorset to her own room.

I guided 'Ginger' slowly, hoping for the woman Cox to disappear but we were upon Miller's Court in only seconds. Cox looked our way.

There was more than a preferred amount of light on number 13. Mrs. Cox watched as the door shut behind us.

The hour was far later than I had expected perhaps close to 1am. 'Ginger' lit a lamp as I pulled the blinds closed.

I stood facing the door.

She sang that same fucking verse incessantly; for God's sake I thought it must end soon.

"...But while life does remain; in memoriam I'll retain..." she said.

"...This small Violet I plucked from Mother's grave," I completed.

I pulled off each glove, right hand first, fingers first.

'Ginger' grabbed the pot and was first to drink.

"I have only one glass and it's broken," she said as she took a handsome swill, followed by a shorter second.

I turned from the door.

"Here, Mr. Frank, drink," she offered.

I held my hand up.

"The ale is yours," I said.

She held it looking into what was left.

"Fuck me now, Frank?" she asked with out a hint of innocence.

"There'll be time for that," I replied.

I removed my billycock placing it on ill formed dresser. I laid my gloves next to it. The mirror presented itself to the corner of my left eye.

It'd be watching me.

'Ginger' sat on the foot of the bed.

I turned from the dresser and looked down at her.

She drank from the pot.

Her red hair was mussed, yet laid seductively across her shoulders.

She swirled the pot of ale.

I removed my cloak and brushed invisible dust from my vest.

My eyes were fixated on her hair.

It glowed.

It had energy.

It had meaning.

I walked toward her as she swirled the pot.

Her head was bent.

I stood just in front of her.

"Suck now, Mr. Frank?" she asked looking up with heavy eyes.

She pushed her face into my pants.

I pushed her away. "There'll be time for that," I said.

'Ginger' looked up at me.

I gripped the back of her head. Her hair was soiled from being days unclean and uncombed.

She swirled the pot of ale.

"You have magnificent hair."

She only drank in response to my compliment.

I dragged my fingers through her red mane. It was knotted in many places. The left over seed of men had dried within the locks, but nonetheless her hair was beautiful.

"Your hair has an energy, it has a meaning," I said.

'Ginger' only swirled her ale in response to my compliment.

I held her head in my hands.

She separated her thighs.

I glanced down and saw just a hint of her upper and inner thigh. Even in this poorly lit room they appeared smooth, subtly pink. Her air of saltiness though quickly overwhelmed the beauty that her inner thighs produced. My lips quivered spastically to that scent.

She sipped the ale and I rubbed her head.

With ease I was imagining what would await me between those soft white thighs. I was growing hungry, like any man does, or should, when near a woman's mouth.

"Your hair, it's beautiful, you are beautiful," I brushed it with my fingers.

I cupped her chin with my hands and turned her face up towards mine.

"Fuck me now, Mr. Frank?" she asked.

I shook my head and gripped her chin tighter.

"Your beauty, it's sadden by your vile acts and your vile words."

'Ginger' reached for my pants and this time everything was strong and firm.

"You're ready. I can see that," she said with a smile.

"I am ready," I said with a heavy tongue.

She placed her hands on my hips and pushed her face into my pants.

Her fingers gripped my ass as she pulled me closer towards her. She gently fell onto the bed. Her legs extended out to the side and then enveloped my lower back.

Her legs pulled me to her.

My arms were locked at the elbow, with my hands next to her hips.

I was nervous.

I had infrequently been with a woman by choice and desire, Mother may have been the last, but 'Ginger' moved me, she fueled in me that animalistic hunger long lost.

Her hands worked my trousers.

The cock rolled to one side.

'Ginger' reached for it and I jumped to her touch.

"Easy, Mr. Frank," she giggled.

I started to grunt as Lispenard had that day he fucked me.

It was happening to quick and I couldn't stop it.

It was unpreventable.

The thrusts I gave found a hole that had no grip.

My hips were thrusting as if out of control.

'Ginger' moaned in her Gaelic tone.

My hands slid from the bed to her shoulders.

I was deeply inside her.

'Ginger' began to hum the song of violets.

I thrust and thrust and thrust until there was no longer a need.

I was powerless to stem the flow and that flow came.

"I feel you now, Mr. Frank!" She giggled.

My hands had moved unknowingly from her shoulders to her ears.

I held her head tight.

I was wide-eyed and panting in spasms.

My hands slid down to her temples.

Her legs squeezed my lower back again and again.

I was breathless.

Exhaling more than inhaling.

My thumbs reached her eyes.

I thrust the last of my spasms into her.

My thumbs gently rubbed her eyes.

"Fucked good 'aye, Mr. Frank?" she asked still squeezing my lower back.

Her words changed my hue instantly.

My eyes became dark as my thrusts slowed.

My thumbs pressed into her eyes as I wiggled my way free.

"Aye!" She managed to screech as my hands moved to her throat.

My eyes were dark.

My thumbs were at her larynx. I squeezed and squeezed until there were no more ayes. I had a rhythm to my work. The rhythm was matched by a gentle tapping at the door. I squeezed and squeezed as if someone was gently rapping. 'Ginger' scratched my face with her hooked talons. I squeezed and squeezed until she released a final wheeze.

Tapping, wrapping, tapping, rapping!

I couldn't ride the rhythm.

"Fuck Poe!" I said freeing myself.

Her legs were loosened from my back.

'Ginger' flailed with what was left of her life.

As the moment of her soul's departure neared I lifted her dress. Her cunt was soiled and spoiled.

What many men knew, no rats would chew.

I rubbed it with my hands and blew the spew.

'Ginger' gave a cough and it was done.

In a motion that was both artistic and pure I reached for my bag. I'd end her struggle to my smile and chuckle.

I leaped.

Sitting on her spoilage, I cut her throat in one hacking left to right motion.

Blood threw itself from wall to wall.

It covered my eyes, teeth and thighs.

I rubbed blood and squeezed her skin.

Her breasts were soft and her hips firm.

I began to thrust again as I rubbed and squeezed.

I pissed uncontrollably in delight.

'Ginger' would no longer suck, swish, swallow or spit the spoiled seed of man. I stuck the mattress and in a slouched manner I pulled 'Ginger' further up the bed. Her blood laid a stream next to her body.

Her piss sprayed my boots.

A rhythm continued.

There was a tapping as if something was gently rapping.

"Outside the door?" I asked the voices.

"Tis me the wind and nothing more," the wind answered.

I stood aside the bed, piss running down my leg.

"...and the Raven, never flitting, still is sitting...still is sitting above the chamber door..."

It was still gently rapping.

I hopped to dim that one lit lamp.

I pulled the blinds shut, as tight as they could be pulled.

I turned from the window. Her eyes were looking at me judging me as all those before her had.

I swayed to unheard tunes.

The Spitalfields clock told me it was 2am.

I jumped and straddled her frame again in a room enveloped in total darkness.

I stabbed without goal.

I would need some light.

Blindly I cut her dress, trimming the sides and rolling her over to obtain most of the material from behind. My right hand was covered with her shit still being drained.

"I need light," I exclaimed again.

'Ginger' was near naked, what garments remained I lay across her shoulders.

The clothes I'd cut, pieces at a time I tossed near a grate.

That'd be my light.

I dismounted.

A match lay next to a sailor's clay pipe. I struck a small fire.

I burnt several pieces of her clothes, never letting the flame be extinguished fully and never allowing it to cast a full shadow.

I was an artist now and it was time to mold my clay. I stood between the wall and the bed and turned her torso on her left side. She'd cast a welcoming smile for all those who'd enter on the morrow.

I went to the foot of bed and spread her legs as far as possible. I pushed her thighs up at right angles.

My spittle dribbled.

"Fuck, nevermore, nevermore!"

My tongue grew thick and heavy.

"Mumble me this and spittle me that. Fuck this shit and eat her fat!"

Her legs remained fixed as I sat between them.

I rubbed her knee from top to the underside.

I squeezed her inner thighs, they were soft, even attractive but they watered my eyes as my nose picked up her salted cunt.

I rolled the blade from knee to the muff without walls.

> "Mumble me this and spittle me that!"
> I spit as I spoke and shit as I sat."

I began at her hip cutting slightly into the muscle. I removed the skin and its subcutaneous fat all the way to the bone. I was again slicing bacon for the open York fire. I removed a flap of grizzled skin that was just adjacent to her muff. I sniffed it, licked it and chewed it until there was no longer a need.

My lips quivered.

I cut just above her asses twinkling star and ate some but less by far.

It had a shitty taint.

My lips quivered the more.

I was frenzied as like no time before.

"Abhor! Abhor! They'd say!"

"I'd say nevermore, nevermore!"

My eyes were wide and never once did I blink.

I encircled the bed.

'Ginger' was watching me with a face full of grin.

I smiled back.

With folded arms, I swayed to unheard tunes.

"You fuck near as good as my mother, 'Ginger' fair. Even your smile says you are quite pleased with this split-wide mandrake," I said.

My sway continued.

"Is that what you think, you stink filled cock hole? You think I'm but a cracked open mandrake?"

My eyes grew darker.

I was pensive.

Her eyes, her fucking eyes!

The fire from the grate was fading.

I breathed through my mouth as I mounted her again.

I hacked at the sternum and cut her like a melon, down in a semi circle left. I cut deep, feeling the scraping of the bones. I cut near full circle and with my right hand tore back the skin exposing her mornings meal.

My hand shot into her spoilage, squeezing her viscera with all of Hell's passion. I stuck my knife inside the cavity, dicing it up like meat in a pot. I pulled out bloodied scraps and tossed them near the grate that was fiery hot.

Her cunt's front door I removed and flung it upon her chest.

"This is the fruit of man you profound boy," Lispenard taught me, "This is the stink-hole that has destroyed cultures since that first garden."

The hour was swirling around my head.

I'd heard the impatient hansom cab.

With a left circular incision I removed her of her milky breast. 'Ginger' looked up at me. I took the other one too.

"Fuck you muff!" I said as she winced.

Reaching her head, I propped it up with one breast and lifeless uterus.

I trimmed her buttocks.

I shoved her liver and other breast between her feet.

"Mumble me this, and spittle me that, never to stroll never to peak, your sins are now between your feet!"

I jumped between the wall and bed, grabbing the stomach and chunks of other forgotten meat I laid them next to the broken glass.

I chopped as a butcher.

"Hush, sweet Mary, no face and no ass, hush, sweet Mary, you're now an unknown lass."

I emptied her well, intestines to the right, spleen to the left. I returned to her face and cupped the gathering blood, tossing it here and there, gently, and daintily as if queer.

The cab came again.

"He must be near!"

I slashed the beast, knee to thigh
Ass to eye, cun to lung
Clip clop, tick tock
I licked her lock.
I slashed the beast knee to thigh
Ass to eye, cun to lung
Clip clop, tick tock
I licked her lock.

I stood admiring an artist's pose and with a well-aimed finger I cleaned my nose.

The Mary 'Ginger' Kelly crime scene at Miller's Court.

CHAPTER SIXTEEN

"Nevermore, nevermore." The final words flushed from me.

Sweat beads preceded a sense of impending doom.

This night's dream had been so real.

The night's sleep had been pure and evenly spread despite the cramping nausea.

I lay on my back, staring through sleep sticky eyes at the underside of the bunk above me.

Would I ever again sleep as pure a sleep as this one had been?

Flashes of light bounced one answer after another off the inside of my eyelids as they scraped shut again. My friends, the voices of doubt and paranoia awakened me.

"Who, what, where, why, when," was the charm of their callings.

"Nevermore, nevermore," the ravens laughed in return to their call.

The sticky lashes batted like the wings of a dying raven until they were pulled open with force.

I had an urge.

The urge grew into a painful pinch.

I knew what it was. A need to piss.

My lids opened, cracking free from the crusted seal that had buttoned my eyes.

My legs were growing restless. My boots had been discharged from their service at an unknown earlier hour.

I swung my feet to the floor.

The pinch was stronger when I assumed a sitting position.

The cabin was now well lit by the midday sun.

The brightness showed more of my bunk than I'd wished. I wondered. Just how long had my belongings and I been illuminated?

The piss was coming. I reviewed the cabin first.

There were neither shadows nor mustachioed figures hiding within them.

I saw no chamber pot.

All the bunks were empty. I stood and faced the wall that was between the head of my bunk and the portside wall.

I pissed without straining, exhaling a sigh of relief.

My piss looked brown.

It smelled of salt, heavy salt. My kidneys hurt as the piss was broken and scattered. Numerous streams, beginning at mid-wall skirted to the cabin's floor. The stream of piss followed the lean of the La Bretagne.

I sighed with relief when it started and I sighed with relief when the last of it dripped upon my darkened once splendid feet. I stuffed my cock back and licked what remained on my fingers.

The other bunks seemed unused. Was I alone?

"Had last evening been real?" the curious voices asked.

The cabin even appeared to free of body odor.

My empty boots were placed quite anally below where I slept. I returned them to their assigned, predestined role.

From the look of my boots I knew my appearance was becoming objectionable to those who expected better and for me, an aesthetic perfectionist, it had to be abdominal.

I rubbed my chin.

My face, once a purebred glory, was now cracked, dry from fatigue and the beatings from those voices of paranoia. The palsy that had been known to just one hand had become a permanent twitching presence in the other hand as well. I'd calm the shaking by placing it firmly into the small of my back while I walked.

Such a pose only enhanced my image.

I'd walk down dusted road and cobbled street with pointed chin, tilted billycock, swaddling cloak, white-capped hands and a fisted palm placed into the small of my back. I was admired as a firm, austere figure.

I lived to dream and lived within my dreams. I dreamt of being more than what I was and certainly more than what I'd become.

As a boy I dreamed of if, when and where.

As a man I dreamed of where, when and if.

I'd wished to be profound among the simple and worshiped among the unfortunate.

I had been a noble man, a doctor of reputable note, but in fact I may have been nothing more than a palsied commoner with mandrake desires.

My hair was salt and peppered. It was permanently unkempt and frequently unwashed even by the most spoiled of water.

My ears had been weakened from a lifelong battle against the strength and various disguises of the voices upon my shoulders. For so many years I battled the voices gallantly, but as age weakened my body I was raped again and again by insanities grip.

In fighting the penetration of those voices my head had taken on a noticeable twitch. It frequently shook uncontrollably hence my spittle dribbled.

My waxy ears had been left to dry. I'd thought it would protect me from those voices but I learned that it was the mind that discerned what was heard and not the ear. As it turned out I couldn't block my mind from the rape of the voices and eventually my mind craved insanities penetration like a whore craves a cock.

My eyes, they too were growing in haze seeking only discernment and legitimacy.

Was it the fog of sanity that swallowed me? Was my life engulfed in nothing but the battle between reality and sanity? Was I real? Was I fantasy? I shook all my thoughts free.

I had but a few days left to delve into the pool of answers for these questions. New York Harbor would wash me, but for now odor enveloped me.

My legs, from the ankles up were years unwashed and my jack was covered with worms and bugs from spoiled men, boys and the final trappings of 'Ginger's' cunt. When left to my own personal vices I ravaged my cock's skin.

It had been years since I cleaned my ass after its use.

There would be no hint of my being rather in shit or on paper. The scent that my body inevitably produced would blend in with the existing East End potpourri. There'd be no lemongrass to show my course. No solid hint for man or hog to sniff, lick or eat.

Regardless I admired myself without a suggestive mirror.

I brushed invisible dust.

My eyes concerned me.

An encroaching cloud was surrounding my world, and I saw less of it every day. I no longer knew if I was sane or insane. The remaining seafaring whitecaps would tell.

I neared the cabin door. I was hungry. My mouth was unwashed and my gums were sore, caked with blood.

The spastic motion of the La Bretagne seemed to have ceased. For the moment, everything was calm.

Even the shadows that haunted me disappeared into the surrounding clouds. One moment they were summer fluffy white, and the next they were snow laden December cover.

Rubbing my eyes never cleared the mist.

"Alas! Cataracts were claiming me. I must persist!"

I rubbed my face and both hands held my skull.

"Alas, poor Yorick! I knew you well!"

The fragility of life, had never encircled me like in had Yorick.

I left the cabin, stepping into the passageway.

My bag, cloak and cane were left behind.

The floorboards were heavily traveled. I looked to my right and then to my left, both ends were cloud covered.

"Was it my eyes or the morning mist?" I muttered.

The passageway was strangely empty.

There were no children at play.

There were no high stepping quaint lovers, and no foot shuffling common souls.

My eyes struggled for the best direction.

My mouth opened habitually and my bottom lip quivered as spittle dribbled.

I wiped my chin.

I could smell the galley to my left. I proceeded in that direction.

My chin was dried and billycock straightened. My palsied hand was placed into the small of my back. I walked deliberately towards a morning meal of undercooked hash or boiled beef. Dyspepsia would be the end result, regardless of how daintily I ate.

My heels and chin were pointed high as I aimed them both toward the portside railing. The walk to my meal would gently ease me into reflection of recent days.

It took several days for the clay sculpture of Miller's Court to reveal the artist as one of considerable means. My goal, or the artist's goal, was to craft a pose for the needy and ungrateful alike. But I was curious, had 'Ginger' spoken more than what she knew? Had she, or had I written more than what I wanted read?

"Was it she who whispered my name to Abberline, Littlechild and their bob headed bents?"

My boots beat a rhythm of constancy upon the passageway boards.

The memory of my being judged as indecent still boiled my soul.

The hobnails thumped the boards harder with each and every memory of that one word, indecent.

I too meandered the cobbled streets of London when my needs were afire and when words like indecent we cast towards me. Those cravings were a blood lust burned into me years ago by this son's mother. My lustful needs for the warm tongues and pinch tight asses of young men were becoming intolerable.

"Gross indecency! Fuck them all," I'd say.

My boots beat a rhythm.

Berner Street.

Dutfield's Yard it was there after weeks of performing spastic self-vices that I took to the scene not far from The House of Astor. He was a young man, fatter than I'd appreciated but willing none-the-less.

As I walked by he deduced my needs.

"Get bent for three," he said.

"I have five if you'd please," I answered.

He giggled.

He kneeled before me until I was no longer pointless.

Within the shadows
He pulled his spoiled prize,
I bent near a door named for Buster Wise
To my surprise,
Filled quite nicely,
I rolled my eyes.

He released his seed into me.

I did not release mine, so with a tremendous grip I stood to viciously finish the act myself.

That night I too found Liz.

"Indecent, they called me!"

I neared the portside rail as my memory was flush.

"Had 'Ginger' said more than I wished?" I muttered.

"Had new eyes accurately been laid upon the clay of Miller's Court? How many judges now cast their affronted tones my way? Had, as I'd always believed, Lady Astor, out of spite and for back rent's sake, turned to Scotland Yard with my name?"

Was it she who gave shape to my clay?

Was it she, while on her knees before Littlechild, who gave him not only her wet hungry tongue, but names and dates as well?

I walked the clouded passageway hoping to hear some noise, any noise, screams of bastard children or the love moans of portly muffs. Nothing snuck from beneath the doorframes. I even waited for each echo of my boot steps to cease in order to confirm the silence.

There were no noises to block my torment.

Lady Astor, who was she?

What was she?

Was she just another hallowed out shell?

The boards creaked beneath my boots.

I was alone on this walk, a journey nearing New York. I'd welcome the New York waters in only a couple of days.

For now there was complete and utter stillness.

For now I could only walk and wonder.

There was no murmur, yarn or rhyme.

Lady Astor, was she the blue tick who pointed her shit-covered bristols my way? A gust of sea breeze budged my billycock. I repositioned it.

Lady Astor, after all, had seen me on a late October evening changing my clothes. She clearly viewed my soiled boots and moistened vest. "You have worked today. Have you any money Doctor?" I dropped my trousers in response to her question.

I folded my vest and laid it upon the bed.

She eyed my darkened ass and spoiled cock.

I didn't shade myself from her view. As she talked I faced her directly. Her eyes never went above my waist.

She swallowed hard.

My arms hung at my side.

"Work is rare and good pay is scarce. I assure you that when the work and money is steadier I will pay what is owed and handsome bonuses for your trouble."

I took a step closer to her that night, her eyes held my pointless cock. I was at more than her arms length. She moistened her lips and swallowed firmly. Her eyes ceased blinking. She tasted my salt.

I took a step closer.

She rubbed her hand on her skirt for it had grown moist from her animal lust. She wanted me. She wanted me as any old washed up woman with an anxious cunt wants any man when forthcoming fucks are few.

I made my cock twitch.

She swallowed even more firmly.

She balled the ends of her apron.

I had a shy grin, as I knew she was fighting back an ocean of temptation. She tasted my salt as I made it twitch and dance an act just for her.

Her face had reddened.

She wiped her sweaty palms.

I could see her throat throb.

That night, I moved closer to her as a man does a woman. In her eyes I saw my mother's face and it was then that I had manly cravings. Despite its spoiled and unwashed nature, it became firm with craving in loving memory of my dear mother's breasts.

"Do you wish me to wash your clothes?" she asked.

Her eyes held my pointed spoiled toy.

I stepped closer and reached for my mother's face.

My moth sought mother's mouth.

"Doctor, do you wish me to clean your clothes?"

Her eyes slammed several quick blinks.

Mother's face evaporated and my spoilage went soft.

"No, dear woman, no, these are no longer worthy of even the stalest of whores," I said.

I desired her that night, but still I wondered if it had been she who revealed all that I was, or what she thought I was to those who now sniffed in pursuit.

Had she always watched me?

In retrospect, every day and night as I entered my room at The House of Astor it was her salt that I smelled. She had been the one to leave behind unseen crumbs. She had sniffed after me all along.

It was Lady Astor who'd given my graft of meat and her graft of egg-rotten ass to one inspector after another. The more well titled the men were the more she'd reveal.

She yearned and burned, and that night when I aimed my cock her way, it was all she could do to keep falling upon her knees and swallowing me deep.

I stood at the portside rail smelling it all.

I was no longer alone as faces rushed by, seeking the undercooked hash and boiled beef in the galley.

"Was she all that she claimed to be?" I asked the sea spray, "Was The House of Astor her stage? Did she fan the flames of passion for all of the cast and audience alike?"

She, too, was a common whore in words and in deeds. Although she never charged to have herself filled by seed of dribbling cocks she earned the title none-the-less.

Lady Astor had a burning lust. A savage lust.

Though I knew she had betrayed me, in her own way, her own special way, she was attractive.

Her gray flattened hair.

Her boundless, heaping breasts held aloft without chord.

Her bulging belly which was always being scratched.

Her semi-toothless grin.

Her fat, sagging ass that dimpled when turned.

In a way it was all quite attractive, and it moved me when even the firmness of a tight young man could not.

I sniffed the air in hopes of finding her salt.

Salt came and went, and so did two faceless skids of shit seeking biscuits and tea.

I stepped aside.

I inhaled the sea spray and in so doing set free the faces of Astor, 'Ginger' and Littlechild behind me.

I sought sounds other than those of the voices encircling me.

Would I hear crying children?

Would I hear their sobbing mothers?

Would I hear their laughing, fleeing fathers leaving not even a name?

I heard nothing. That alone was profound.

Now, at last, I could smell the salt of the sea.

The salt invigorated me.

Each deep breath caused my eyes to roll back in delight and my lips to quiver. I breathed deep again, inhaling every woman I'd ever known.

I licked my lips dry. My eyes widened as I became more alert to my surroundings.

All those who desired boiled beef were now below.

I waited.

There were no faces, none whatsoever. There were no hidden lovers or smug poorly powdered muffs. I was alone with the desires of an animal.

Before I could dedicate a longer more curious stance I was bumped from behind, not once but twice.

"'Scuse me mista'", a little boy yelled as he ran into my leg. The second child, following closely was not so articulate in asking forgiveness.

Children at play returned.

I glanced over my shoulders and saw their mothers weren't far behind.

One stared at me nervously another smiled politely.

Gradually, the faces of the day emerged into the approaching rain.

I'd missed my meal. I'd been left alone in the cloud-covered passageway for only minutes, though my paranoia had presented other evidence.

Paranoia, I imagine has made me what I am. But aren't we all paranoid? Are we not all insane in one-way or the other? Isn't it the insanity of others that determines the level of our own competency? Isn't paranoia a necessary element to human survival?

I'd not eat publicly for the balance of the trip. We'd be docking on the 2nd and I could live off of found, discarded biscuits. As the final columns of fat-assed mothers bounced toward their little ones, I entered the galley door. The dining area was empty except for the discourteous faces of the servers. I strolled through the room pocketing half eaten biscuits and meat.

I smiled at the servers.

They judged me, just as all the others had.

Once back in the cabin I'd not emerge until we reached New York Harbor. I'd say to anyone who'd ask that I was ill. My cabin mates returned one at a time for several hours but for the most part I was left alone.

I tucked the half-eaten food between my arm and the wall adjacent to the bunk.

Who was the man I debated on the history of stanzas and scene, act and theme?

Where had he gone?

Was he real?

Was he just a shadow?

Was he a Keats stanza brought to life?

Was he simply a creature hid within the fingers of paranoia?

Was he Inspector Littlechild?

As I ate the crumbs of tainted meat and soon to be stale biscuits, I returned to better days and the brandy sips at Paris café's.

Was Littlechild in hard pursuit?

Had he been watching me from the hidden eaves and bare bone trees?

"Had he fed on the gossip and crusty cunt of Lady Astor long enough having been bit by both?"

"If it was him what was he waiting for?"

I'd build a nest within the cabin.

Astor was who she was?

Who was Littlechild?

Who am I? Those who would some day say it was I whom gave birth to a new generation would answer this.

But I have told my story so others would not.

"Mr. Booth, I am Hiram Abiff, I am the widow's son," I murmured through twilight.

Friday November 30th, 1888

My palsied hand shook as I gripped to write these paragraphs of final words. I entered the cabin on the evening of November 30th, ill from sea and bad water, or so I'd claim. It was the shadow of one man's uncertainty that kept me hidden. That shadow may have assumed I was a shadow as well.

I slept when my cabin was full.

I ate when the cabin was empty. My piss would be left under this bunk; my shit would be released when my back faced the wall.

Saturday I lay restless in wait of Sunday.

Sunday came it was December 2nd.

I knew that hundreds had flooded the cobbled stone of the East End looking for the suspect Astor described between her fucks.

I had fooled them all!

Abberline, Littlechild, Andrews, Crowle all of them!

They'd never be able to admit that I, a mere mandrake had outwitted the bloviated geniuses of Scotland Yard. Mr. Booth, they could not allow the New York authorities to know that they had lost the game to me. They'd sent notice ahead; "Look for Tumblety!" But they, the bob heads would follow the name Frank Townsend.

Mid-afternoon arrived.

I waited for the scattering chit chatters of hurried mothers and children to fill the passageway. I found one with need of assistance and under guise of a loving father holding a child I disembarked La Bretagne.

I asked a handsome boy to carry my belongings and he agreed to do so with the cutest of grins.

Inspectors and detectives of inflated rank followed shadows of their own.

- Frank

Sunday December 2nd, 1888

Mr. Booth I was adept and quickly lost whatever pursuit there was. A cab carried me toward Tenth Avenue. The home was that of Mrs. McNamara, a kind woman, aged to a severe degree and a lover of all men. I had on occasion paid back rent by succumbing to her animal cravings.

The cab scurried at my suggested rate.

I knew they watched me but why didn't they question me?

Why didn't they ask the questions, which made them burn?

The hack discharged me not far from McNamara's. The driver was given instructions to take my belongings to the Cornish Hotel on West Street and leave them in care of the proprietor.

I stepped inside McNamara's and asked for a room; she remembered me. I was pleased. I asked for a cold drink. She left to retrieve it and I left her home from a rear door.

I was adept and for some weeks I was well protected by guise and name. It was New Years of 1889 and I was escaping into the arms of a young man who I had warmly welcomed to my twinkling hole on many occasions. I erred Mr. Booth and allowed him to know my location.

Having become comfortable that the British authorities had no evidence, and the American dullards had even less I told the New York World; "That an English detective, whose stupidity was noticeable even among a class not celebrated for their shrewdness had decided I was who I was."

Thanks to willing young men I left behind law enforcements curious glare.

- Frank

Wednesday March 13th, 1889

...Mr. Booth I was not poverty prone when I arrived in Rochester New York.

To whom would I turn for the final question?

I walked the banks of the Genesee out of total familiarity.

I was a boy again seeking minnows along the swollen rivers shoulders.

I poked their gills with sharpened cane.

I ate them without the touch of a flame.

I walked midnight hours seeking a long ago name.

Lawrence had died working hard at life's fanciful game.

His widow was gone. His children had grown.

To whom would I turn when the violets did bloom?

I often ate beneath the well-crafted bridge closest to Exchange Street. Nightly I'd rest behind the mill walls adjacent to the rivers promenade.

The winter had been mild.

The waters were fierce in their mission.

In cleansed attire and well-mannered tones, through municipal records it was Lawrence's daughter Alice that I found.

Mr. Booth she lived on Sophia Street not far from my old boyhood barn. In high step demeanor I bound over trestle and rail, past home and cottage to the front door of 569.

A woman, no longer a girl was on the porch sweeping what she saw as filth. I watched from the walk till she caught my stare. She looked up once and down just as sharply to continue her sweep.

My stare was continued.

She looked up once more for more than a brief pause.

Her sweeping stopped as she mumbled "In the Holy name of Christ..."

"I am your Uncle; may I come in?" I asked.

"You are not welcome, go without sin," Alice said.

My stare would not wane.

"I am hungry and I walk with great pain."

She paused and then with Christian love said, "I'll feed you here but outside you'll remain."

- Frank

Thursday April 11th, 1889

...The wind of April had a temper so we ate in the homes front room. Alice sat in the hall as I ate. "Your brother, my father died only months ago. He spoke of you once all these years."

..."Was he kind in his words?" I asked.

Her words said yes but her eyes said no. I smiled between bites of ham and sips of her tea.

"I see," said I.

"He was good to me when I was a boy. He fed and clothed me when I was used as a laboring toy."

Her charitable heart soon showed through.

"You are ill, we have one small room and we will charge you no bill," she said.

"I will pay. I am a doctor of reputable note and when the work is plentiful I will pay you more than similar worth."

...She sat silent.

"A doctor?"

I nodded.

...She sat silent.

..."Your mother..." she said.

...I sat silent.

..."My mother?" I asked through darkening eyes.

"Your mother...she is alive," she said.

...I sat silent.

"She is housed by the state there on South near Elmwood."

I pushed my plate.

"It is for the best," I said.

"What is?" Alice asked.

"Dear niece... I will seek work beginning now...may I call this home?"

"You may," she said through Christian eyes.

- Frank

Wednesday April 17th, 1889

I returned to the Genesee's edge and lapped its water for my throat was burnt. Spittle me this and mumble me that I sprayed as I stood and shit as I sat.

"Scenes of my childhood arose before my gaze bringing recollections of by-gone happy days."

Mr. Booth I owe, as you have said, mankind a service in exchange for nothing but a well shook hand. John, all I knew was that it was

April 17th. I walked with casual care, crafted cane and well cropped hair down Elmwood and this states cared for home.

I saw the trees first, and then setting back from the avenues daily travelers was the complex, multi-leveled, built by the state to house the insane. Mother was here and I was her boy.

I walked without pause. I heard my heartbeat followed by its echo. I approached the main double door. I passed odd looking faces all with scattered tempers, lives and self proclaimed duties.

I am a doctor and have much to offer and always free from pay. That Wednesday afternoon, I stood in the hall hearing screams of the tormented and the laughs of the lamented.

"You must be licensed to give us your work." I was told.

"You may work in our kitchen for there we always have a need."

"A galley aid?" I asked not believing my ears.

I took their offer for the violets would soon bloom.

"See Mrs. Tweed she'll show you your wares."

Mr. Booth for weeks to come I'd learn the halls, names and meals seeking dear Mother and the gown she may wear.

- Frank

Thursday May 9th, 1889

They'd confirm no name when I did finally ask; when so many come and go, learning their names is to big a task.

I worked when scheduled.

I worked when not.

Walking the halls and listening to doubled locked slots.

I sought mother's face while basking in the glow of a hard to find itch.

Mrs. Tweed was an ample breasted bitch. She governed the galley with nary a prolonged hitch.

She was difficult to please accept on her knees.

"Clean this shit and wash those pots," was her blunt morning reprise. Then one day I asked a nub headed cook have we a woman, Tumblety in states care.

His name was Merton, his last was O' Clare.

"Have we such a woman in this states care?" I asked again.

A laundress from nearby in giggled interruption said; "You must remember, Mary her name, Twomblety her last."

Merton puckered his brows as a smile emerged.

"I do, I do, and for years she was there on old number two."

The laundress's smile became a hint of Cheshire.

"She fucked everyone here, year after year!" Merton laughed.

"New ones twice and doctors thrice!"

"A baby or two was born to the forlorn," Mrs. Tweed did add.

My eyes grew dark and became but a slot.

I swayed to unheard rhythms while banging a pot.

"Why do you ask 'bout such a silly fucking sot?" Merton asked.

I pulled a knife I looked at their eyes.

"She is my mother believe it or not!"

I walked toward them circling the blade.

"Where is she now, I do need to know!"

One stood tall Mrs. Tweed with pointed elbow.

They believed my actions as I approached.

"She left long ago, to soft country ground. To Genesee County, you must be Bethany bound."

- Frank

Wednesday May 15th, 1889

John, true love of mine, it was May 15th of the year 1880 and 9. Springtime was here and the violets were due. By "Peanut Line" rail I walked through Batavia with a diddy on my tongue. I'd not share it but henceforth the time would come.

From hand drawn maps and kindness of priests I was in Attica an open field with few homes to show. "It'd be a walk, several miles by road, less by field," a hansom young man did say.

He nodded as he left.

I watched him walk away.

What seemed like hours caused me to rest, not for long for I best not tarry. I lay down to nap in the Brainerd Cemetery. To my left was Wanton Burlingham and to my right one Amos Muzzy, dead for some twenty-five years, though his stone was fuzzy.

My hands were palsied and my head shook without rest as from across the fields ready for corn came a whisper seeking my name. I rolled to Muzzy and sought his advice; the voices were blurred and his was asunder.

Come what may and come what will
Plant the corn in the soil you till
Finish the chapter for it is God's will.

As the sun crested from its work
I took to the walk
That would lead me from here
And to a creek I lapped the trickle
Eyeing a dying mother deer.

I lapped the water
Kneeling upon its crest
I took a rock and crushed the mother deer
I supped its teat
And the last of its milk
Was this hungry man's treat.

I wiped my chin and crossed the rising field and upon its peak I saw a church like spire. My throat throbbed. I could taste my heartbeats. The home of Bethany was being seen by all of me.

My spirit fully engulfed its frame.

I hovered above Bethany like a falcon to a mouse.

Tormented shrieks danced across Skates Hill Road.
Slow yet eager steps led me to within vision of milk white faces.
They laughed and pointed as if I was to be mocked.
I kneeled to scoop some springtime flowers.
In open spaces and without care the milk white faces with titles
they declared leapt towards me and gave me no air.
The staff posed with two dogs watching my approach.

East Bethany County Home.

I handed out flowers as a noble man would.
I gave one my hat.
I guided my frame to where an old tree stood.
They danced around till a chime did cry.

"It's dinner time, chicken, beef or beans you'll try!"

I walked up a guiding ramp and asked have you a Mary or Margaret with Tumblety the last.

"Have you a need to know?" a wide one asked.

I am that mother's son, a builder by trade.

With no doubting looks they led me away to several rooms within a room.

"At the end you will find her."

No looks were given no light my guide.

The smell was evil, as only evil would know.

Tormented shrieks and lamented laughs followed me.

It was her room at last I was home.

From the inside mother sniffed the air.

"It is my heir! My heir!" She declared.

I listened to an old time summons.

"I am forty generations deep, the seventh daughter of the seventh son of the seventh daughter of the seventh son am I."

I too sniffed the air.

My throat throbbed.

I could taste my heartbeat.

I slowly opened the door.

She was naked, standing before me as this son's mother.

I said I'd pay tribute no more and reaching for my cock I shut the door.

From Hell-The Final Days of Jack The Ripper is fiction but Francis Tumblety was a very real person. He was born in 1830 and died May 28th 1903. He is buried in Section 13 of the Holy Sepulcher Cemetery in Rochester New York.

LaVergne, TN USA
17 June 2010
186477LV00004B/87/P